The Golden Frog

by

Michael Mamas

1st WORLD LIBRARY Publishing Exchange

The Golden Frog
Michael Mamas

© 1st World Publishing, 2004
1100 North 4th St. Suite 131, Fairfield, Iowa 52556
TEL: 641-209-5000 • FAX: 641-209-3001
WEB: www.1stworldpublishing.com

LCCN: 2004112831

ISBN: 1-59540-901-7

The characters in this book are not representations of real life individuals. More accurately, they express the author's experiences of the one humanity we all share.

Readers are invited to contact 1st World Publishing at
www.1stworldpublishing.com

Dedicated to you

on

your journey...

beyond

conditioning.

Table of Contents

Acknowledgements

I'd like to thank all of the people who assisted me in the writing of this book. In particular, I'd like to thank Barbara Weisshaar for her endless hours of dedication to the project. I'd also like to thank Tony Ellis, Elizabeth Smith, Robin Bennett, and my wife, Tanja Mamas. They seem to have no idea how much I learned from even their most casual comments.

Part 1
The Nature of Memory

Chapter 1
Memory's First Images

I remember knowing he was there, my best friend Mathew's little brother Nathaniel, tagging along with the neighborhood gang. I was nine. He was three years younger, shy, quiet, and just a little odd. For most of that hot summer in Columbus, Ohio, Nathaniel was only a small detail.

But that changed the day our gang wandered onto the Scioto Country Club golf course. We knew we were not allowed, but that didn't matter. It was too alluring—a calculated risk—and we took it. Bewitched by the sweet-smelling lawns, we ran up a fairway and onto the green where we whirled about to the rhythm of the cascading creek behind us. Then we made our way over the arched stone bridge that spanned one end of a pond encircled by weeping willows, and threw stones at a bobbing turtle, testing our ability to drive him back into the water.

We spotted blackberry bushes along the banks of the creek that fed the pond. We moved closer. Despite my warnings we might be discovered, everyone descended like locusts on the fruit. Vying with each other for the most berries, laughing, we wore juicy stains on our clothes, hands, and faces as badges of conquest. It was another summer adventure. Lost to the frenzy, none of us noticed Nathaniel was missing.

I looked away from the other kids to the creek at the far end of the pond. Between the creek and pond, supported by a miniature dam, was a small wooden footbridge. The sun, as it set over the creek, was calling us home. About thirty yards past the footbridge—our favorite place to catch crawdads—I spotted Nathaniel gracefully stepping from rock to rock across the creek.

The sun glistening off the water silhouetted his small body. Despite the noise of the gushing creek, a stillness filled the air around him, as if his steps were in slow motion, deliberate and purposeful. The image I remember is of all nature in frantic motion around him, while he stood in perfect stillness. Everything stopped for me too, as if I somehow shared the source of his deep reflection. It felt as if we stayed that way a long time, together in the quiet.

Yet, the next instant, I knew he was in danger. This little boy had no business being out on those slippery, wet rocks. What if he fell? I imagined the water pulling him under. I panicked and ran to his rescue. Did I call out to his brother, or the others? I can't remember. I only recall the sensation of slipping and sliding on the slick grassy slopes of the creek, and falling knee deep into the turbulent water. Wading through the creek, sidestepping an area of unknown depth, I climbed onto some rocks. There, determining a bridge of stepping stones, I made my way to Nathaniel as quickly as I could.

His head turned towards me as I struggled to reach him. I grabbed him with both arms only to slip again, as we both plunged into a silent abyss beneath the rushing water. Stillness. There was a calm, weightless feel to his body. My lanky torso felt all elbows and knees around him as we sank deeper. Yet his body remained light—almost buoyant.

We found our way to the edge of the creek, crawled out, and stood there dripping. I was shaking—and furious. I wanted to yell at him, "What did you think you were doing out there? You almost got us killed!" But I just stood there, gasping and trembling.

He looked back at me silently. Nothing inside him moved. He was as still and undisturbed as I'd seen him on the rocks. His eyes were as soft as lamb's eyes, but his look turned me inside out. Nothing inside of me remained hidden. No corner or crevice within was left untouched. The look in his eyes extended all limits of my being out and into infinity. I stumbled back to get my balance.

Suddenly, we were surrounded by all the other neighborhood kids. Mathew took charge of Nathaniel, and I quickly faded into the group as we all rushed to make it home before dark. My thoughts turned to how I might hide my drenched clothes and delinquent golf course exploits from my parents. The evidence was against me, and I knew I'd be punished. So what sense did it make that the look in Nathaniel's eyes and the image of his silhouetted little body would carry me so effortlessly through the evening? I had no logical explanation for what that was about. I could only feel how deeply it touched me. That's what I remember.

Out of all the gang, I was the one who always needed to know what made things work: the how, why, and what-if that lay beneath life. I asked the questions, calculated the courses of action, observed the consequences, and noticed when things didn't make sense. That hot summer was when I first realized Nathaniel made the strangest sort of sense. Even though I couldn't understand why, I knew figuring out Nathaniel was the key to figuring out everything. This truth echoed through my soul. Hardly a scientific approach to the knowledge of existence, yet the one that caught me, kept cropping up, and finally led me to understanding.

But trying to remember how I came to be who I am is perplexing. The channels of consciousness and the order of events dissolve and melt one thing into another, until I am lost in a quandary of chronologies. I've learned that memory is elusive. It slips and slides and shifts with the seasons of our lives, according to our mental and emotional states. Worst of all, it's unscientific: it can't be measured or counted. So all I can do is my best to reflect upon my life through the gateway of my memory's images and their impressions upon me. Of course, Nathaniel would say it doesn't matter.

Chapter 2

The Golden Frog

That summer was one of those magical childhood summers that seemed to never end. The weather was perfect every day with morning dew disappearing early from the ground. Days were accented with sweet-smelling grass and flowers. Blue skies were softened with puffy white clouds, and warm evenings were filled with lightning bugs.

Every morning I would get out of bed and put on my favorite pair of tennis shoes, black with soft-white rubber trim. Every scuff mark was an old friend and I could proudly recall the source of many of them. I would ceremoniously don my long tube socks, pulling them all the way up snuggly over my calves, nearly to my knees. Then came my shoes, which I completed with double knots that mysteriously came apart throughout the day. Except for when it came time to take the shoes off. Then the knots were nearly invincible. I would often need a ballpoint pen, screwdriver, or other pointed appliance to wedge the knots free.

Each day between early and midmorning, I made my way over to Mathew's house in pursuit of that day's escapades. We rarely had plans for what the day would bring, yet every day was packed with adventure.

One morning, I pulled into Mathew's driveway on my trusty red bike, my best Christmas present last year, which I had named Scorpion. As was my custom, I tossed Scorpion down to the grass in his backyard and sprang toward the back door of his house.

It was then I saw Nathaniel on his hands and knees feverishly rustling through the hedge that lined the lawn.

"Bruce, come quick!" he called. "A golden frog! I see a golden frog!"

I leaped off the stone steps and over to him to see what was going on. He hopped over to the next bush, intent on his search. Caught up in his excitement, I found myself on all fours scurrying through the hedges in pursuit of his golden frog.

"There it is!" Nathaniel shouted as he popped over another two feet. "It's *gold!*"

I crawled beside him, but it was gone. We both fell silent and held our breath, hoping to catch a glimpse of the magical golden frog. The morning sunlight created a soft pattern as it highlighted the branches and ground beneath the row of hedges, still moist from the morning dew. We simultaneously moved along the hedges in the direction of the last sighting of the golden frog.

Again we stopped and stayed motionless, watching for the frog. Nothing. It had disappeared.

I stood up and brushed off my knees. "How big was it?"

Nathaniel, still looking intently between the branches, held up his hand, and putting thumb to forefinger, made a circle the size of a half dollar. "About that big," he said.

"Are you sure it was gold?"

"Yes," he answered. He got up and we walked along the hedges, our eyes scanning the base of the bushes.

"I think the sun lit up a normal frog and made it look gold," I told him.

My words passed right through his little body with no effect. I turned and walked toward the house, leaving him to continue his hunt for the elusive golden frog.

In the house Mathew was upstairs getting ready, so I went into the den to wait for him. Toys were spread all over the floor and furniture. I walked up to the couch, pushed some toys aside to clear a spot, and sat down to wait. The messy room felt good to me. I was comfortable there.

As I thought of the golden frog, I looked over to the morning light shining through the window across the room. All the little dust particles glowed as they moved in the sun's ray. I felt peaceful and reflective, my eyes transfixed on the sunbeam and the iridescent dust. I pulled my knees up to my chest. Somehow my double-knotted shoe-strings had come undone, and my sneakers fell from my feet as I curled up into a contented, transfixed little ball on the couch. Maybe it didn't matter if the sunlight just made the frog look golden.

Little Nathaniel quietly walked in and sat on the floor, leaning up against the armchair by the window. He cast his silent gaze on the dust sparkles as they moved in the sunlight. I wondered if he saw something there I didn't.

Chapter 3

The Slave House

It became our summer tradition to start each morning at Mathew's house. Every week or so, Mathew and I, along with the neighborhood gang, would hike up Cambridge Boulevard, the main street that led to our neighborhood, all the way to the local strip mall. Though we all lived in comfortable middle class homes, some of the houses we passed as we made the journey were real mansions. It was fun to traverse the huge front yards and peer up the hills where the large estates were surrounded by immaculate landscaping and lavish swimming pools.

On hot summer days when we finally made it all the way up to our destination, the first stop was the drugstore. Sweaty and tired but exhilarated, we would get a soda pop at the fountain and slurp it down. We were so excited when they began to offer vanilla and cherry flavorings. The storeowner didn't allow us to get up from the fountain until we finished our drink, unless we took it outside. So we usually drank it in front of the store, and rushed back in to the real gold: the candy bar section.

In those days, you could buy a huge candy bar for five cents. My favorite was Baby Ruth, but Peanut Butter Cups ran a respectable second. We had fun with the edible, wax, miniature soda bottles filled with brightly colored sugar water—grape, orange, and cherry. After sucking down the liquid, the wax served as a bizarre temporary sort of chewing gum. The paper straws filled with a sweet powdery substance and sealed at both ends were super cool. The powder tasted good enough, but the packaging made them really fun to eat.

One day, after finishing off our soda pop and candy, we decided to take a different path home. Instead of going back down Cambridge Boulevard, we took Waltham Road, the other main route down the hill, to enter our neighborhood through the back way. We had all made that trip innumerable times in cars with our moms, but walking it seemed to add miles.

At the bottom of Waltham Road and to the right was Mulvern Street, our old familiar tromping ground. To the left was a thicket of trees and bushes that lined the road, the edge of our neighborhood, the limit of our childhood world. Beyond that thicket lay an ominous presence—a huge and mysterious field. As we made our way to the bottom of Waltham Road and walked along the thicket, we could feel with every step, a resistance or repelling force radiating from that field. As our sense of the repelling force grew, so did our trepidation. The field seemed to be protected by an invisible space-time barrier, as if by entering it we would enter another world, and maybe even cease to exist in the one we knew.

We had heard of an old Civil War mansion that rested on a hill at the far end of the field. According to the story, a slave house could be found next to that mansion. Supposedly the basement of that house was an old hiding place for the Underground Railroad. One of the kids thought he had heard there were still chains on the basement walls. The decision was unanimous—we would set out in search of that old mansion and slave house.

We were hot and depleted, but excited by the unknown terrain on the other side of the thicket. Shadowy images of wandering hobos and wild packs of dogs haunted my mind as I contemplated what we might encounter. Intrigued and already half-spooked, we cautiously entered the thick brush. The barrier seemed impenetrable. We searched for a way through it, until the blackberries that covered the bushes distracted us.

We decided a snack was the answer, perhaps not so much to fill our bellies as to postpone our appointment with the ominous unknown. After polishing off our fill of the berries, we looked again to the row of trees and bushes for a way through the green barrier to the field beyond. Finally, we forced our way into the center of the thicket and discovered it enclosed a creek of rustling water—one of the many creeks in the area that led to the nearby Scioto River. We all knew "scioto" meant "hairy," and the Indians named it the Hairy River because all the animals that bathed in it filled the river with their fur. We found a natural rock stepping-stone bridge that led us across the creek, broke through the bushes, and came out the other side.

Before us lay the huge grass-covered field. One of the kids said Civil War battles had been fought there. It felt like we had moved into another land—a time and place far removed from our old familiar neighborhood. We had broken through the forbidden space-time barrier, yet we were still alive. For an instant, I wondered if we could ever get back to home and safety, but I pushed that fear aside.

Looking off in the distance to our left, the field sloped upward as trees began to populate the grassy terrain. Through the trees we could barely make out a very old, beautiful white mansion.

The mansion was a classic from the Civil War era—two stories, white pillars, black shutters, flat roof—right out of the picture books. In Ohio, the mansion appeared misplaced. It somehow belonged in Alabama or Georgia. Or perhaps, as we passed through the thicket and creek barrier, we also went through a warp not only in time, but also in space. I felt, at any moment, I might see a Civil War soldier ride his horse across the field. We all looked for Civil War artifacts on the ground as we cautiously made our way across the field and toward the mansion. Just beyond the mansion, through more trees, and darkly hidden in the shadows, we saw the old slave house. It was a dark, dirty, red-brick, two-story building with an attic. None of us talked unless it was a whisper. As we got near, I could tell the buildings were well cared for, but empty.

It was then I noticed Nathaniel. I was surprised the little guy had actually made it all that way. He stood off from the rest of us, staring at the old red-brick house. He was fixed in his spot, unwilling to move forward.

I walked over to Nathaniel. "Come on," I urged.

He didn't move or even take his gaze off the house. There was an eerie look on his face.

I leaned forward to bring my head to the same level as his. I squinted and peered into his eyes, trying to see what was going on inside him. Solid stillness. Silence. I whispered in his ear, "Come on, Nathaniel, let's get going."

Not moving a muscle or taking his gaze off the house, he murmured in a monotone, "No, there is too much fear in those walls."

A shiver moved through my body as I glimpsed back over my shoulder at the slave house. Though I didn't really know what he was talking about, I felt how something wasn't right.

In so many ways Nathaniel was just a typical little kid. But once again, I realized something remarkable was going on inside of him. He was like a mirror, reflecting back the hidden truth within the moment.

We were all afraid to get close to the slave house. It was too spooky. But without Nathaniel, I wouldn't have felt it so fully. I left Nathaniel and hooked up with the gang to investigate the area. I was glad when we got out of there and headed back.

That night, snuggled up in the safety of my own bed, exhausted, I drifted into a sound sleep.

Chapter 4

A Child's Wisdom

For this magical summer, we had an endless stream of adventures—tree forts, bike rides, poison ivy, picnics, and wondrous explorations. But finally the time did come to return to school. And before we knew it, we were back into the routine. Each morning was a frantic rush to get behind our desks before the bell rang, followed by endless hours of waiting for the bell to ring again, signaling the time to go home. After class one day, we were sitting around talking in the den at Mathew's house. I noticed a little handmade book on the coffee table. It was made out of regular-lined notebook paper, cut into quarters, and fastened together with three staples on one side. The hand-printed title on the cover read:

"Words of Wisdom"

I was intrigued, and immediately picked it up and started to read.

"That's Nathaniel's," said Mathew. "He's always doing weird stuff."

Mathew's comment bothered me. All the kids in the neighborhood thought Nathaniel was strange. But I thought he was neat. Shrugging off Mathew's comment, I began to read.

The first page said:

"Great people are where you find them."

I turned the page.

> *"Just because someone says wise things,
> it doesn't mean they have to be wise."*

Next page:

> *"Seeing how other people are wrong is easy.
> Seeing how you are wrong is hard."*

"Where did he get this stuff?" I asked.

"He thinks it up."

As I flipped back through the pages, I became more and more frustrated. I didn't know what he was trying to say. What was his point? Where did he think you found great men? In Washington, D.C.? Of course great men were where you found them. Where else would they be?

And how could people say wise things if they weren't wise? Maybe they were only quoting wise things. But why would they bother doing that if they weren't wise?

The one about being wrong made more sense. If you saw how you were wrong, you wouldn't be wrong. But was that what he meant? He must've meant something else. But what?

Mathew's mom called us for an after-school snack. I left the book on the table, but continued to wonder even more about Nathaniel.

The Golden Frog

Chapter 5
The Toy Giraffe

Gradually the evenings grew cooler and leaves began to fall from the trees. At last, it was my favorite night of the whole year— Halloween. It was getting dark outside and that meant it was time to go over to Mathew's house. We were getting a little too old for trick-or-treat, but I didn't want to admit to myself that my favorite holiday festivity was slipping through my fingers, soon to be gone forever. I sat on the floor in my bedroom and put on my trusty sneakers, still with double knots.

I leaped over the two steps from our house to the driveway and made my way across the yard in the direction of Mathew's house. The leaves on the ground were thick and crackly. I dragged my feet through them to enhance their feel up against my sneakers. I pulled my stocking hat down, my collar up to my ears, and bunched my shoulders together to ward off the chill in the air.

I walked along Mulvern Street toward Mathew's, noticing the nearly full moon. Its light shone through the sparsely leaved trees, their branches shifting gently with the wind. It seemed like I was the only person in the world. My feet shuffled through the leaves and the sweet smell of autumn overtook my senses. Something in the feel of the night made my thoughts move inward and I remembered Nathaniel's little book. I was intrigued and disturbed at the same time. It just didn't seem normal that a little kid would be thinking about wisdom. I felt a little resentment. After all, I was a whole three years older than he was. Who did he think he was? Maybe he was a little know-it-all, despite his gentle demeanor.

The clouds moved across the moonlit sky. The breeze shifted the leaves around my feet as I walked on. Suddenly I felt as if someone was following me. Whoever or whatever it was lurked behind cars parked in driveways as I passed. As I approached my favorite buckeye tree, I heard the crack of a branch no more than fifteen yards behind me—a shiver ran right up my spine. Without breaking stride, I bent over and swept a few buckeyes off the ground, thinking I could fling them at my pursuer if need be.

I glanced back briefly and then charged forward even faster. Mathew's home was at the end of the street, only a few more houses down. Fortunately, the bridge on Mulvern Street traversing the creek was just ahead. No one could cross that bridge without me seeing who was there. I nervously peeled the spiky casings off the buckeyes and began to roll them together in my hand. Even though nobody followed me over the bridge, my fear stayed with me. I walked faster. Finally, I could see the lights shining in Mathew's house. Safety was straight ahead.

I got to his back door, shoved the buckeyes into my pocket, and knocked. Then I knocked a little louder, a bit more rapidly, and several more times than usual. I quickly looked behind me, to one side and then the other, and then peered through the door window for signs of movement. Someone was coming.

Hurry up!

It was Mathew. I pushed past him as he opened the door and made a beeline to the den, leaving him to follow behind. I was safe.

Mathew's mom, nicely dressed as always, was running the vacuum cleaner. Though warm and friendly, his parents were always prim and proper, which at times made them seem distant. I spotted little Nathaniel all curled up in a ball on the couch and covered in a blanket. I pulled the buckeyes out of my pocket, sat in the armchair by the window, and peered outside into the darkness. Fiddling with buckeyes always calmed me down. Buckeyes were miraculous that way. One moment they served as ammo and the next, a great pacifier.

As I gazed out the window, I had no sense of anyone lurking in the shadows. In fact, quite to the contrary, the setting was serene and inviting—an ideal Halloween night. It no longer appeared to be devoid of neighbors, either. A few kids were scurrying from door to door as their parents stood along the curbs of Mulvern Street, flashlights in hand, awaiting their children's return with growing bags of treasure. Strange how that same scene could appear frightening *or* serene. Which was it really? I guess it was both. Kind of like buckeyes. Pacifiers, but at the same time, ammo. I wondered if everything worked that way.

Nathaniel was still curled up on the couch. He didn't appear to notice me. He was in another world. As the vacuum cleaner ran, he seemed to be entranced with the sound. Though he didn't move, he seemed to be active inside of himself, like the purr of a kitten or the idle of a finely tuned car. It felt strange to me. Finally his mom shut off the vacuum and left the room. It was suddenly very quiet. Mathew was playing with a little toy puzzle he had picked up off the coffee table. Slowly, Nathaniel sat up. His eyes were fixed on several African, hand-carved, wooden animals on the coffee table. His Mom used them as decoration, but Nathaniel often used them as toys.

Nathaniel was completely absorbed. His eyes were even deeper than usual. His whole body was one, little, alive, still unit.

I wondered what was wrong with him. Was he okay? I watched him for the longest time until he finally began to whisper to himself or to me. I wasn't really sure.

"I *am* that giraffe. I *am* that tiger," he whispered.

This was too creepy for me. But at the same time, curiously, he seemed right. It made sense, but I couldn't explain how. His behavior mystified me, like that day on the golf course.

"I *am* that elephant," he continued in a soft voice.

He wasn't playing a game. He appeared to be dealing with an actual experience. What a puzzling scene. I guess Nathaniel was like buckeyes too. One moment a little kid curled up on the couch, the next a magical key to the unknown. What was going on?

His mom called, "Nathaniel, time to get ready for trick-or-treat."

His attention slowly shifted as he made his way out of the den to the front of the house.

I was relieved.

Mathew and I went to man the front door as some trick-or-treaters began to knock. The foyer was quite large, with steps leading down into it from the bedroom level of the house. Bags of candy sat on the telephone table adjacent to the door. His mother was dressing up little Nathaniel as a hobo. She had burned one end of a wine cork to give it a charcoal-like surface and was applying the black chalk to Nathaniel's face to make a mock mustache and shadowy beard. His little head was cocked back as he stood still for the application. He was so childlike at that moment, innocent, pure—just a normal little kid. It was all so disconnected from the scene in the den only a few moments before. Yet unknown to me at the time, he had already begun to alter my world.

Chapter 6
Inner Solace

As the years passed, Nathaniel remained a mystery. Mathew and I stayed friends, although we each became increasingly caught up in our own lives—mostly sports, college, and girls. I didn't see very much of Nathaniel during that time, but he never left my radar completely. I do recollect he went through some awkward years. His hair and clothes were messy. He was always getting grass stains on his knees, and was painfully shy, especially around girls. He usually went directly home after school to hang out in his basement, doing who-knows-what.

While I was going to college at Ohio State, he met Susan. I knew her from my high school years. She was cute, 5'2", strawberry blonde, and well liked by students and teachers. I thought Nathaniel had done pretty well for himself. He was about 5'10", brown hair and brown eyes, with a moderately muscular frame. I guessed girls found him attractive.

Nathaniel and Susan dated for a couple of years. They were both deep thinkers, and Mathew told me they spent hours talking about all sorts of things. Nathaniel apparently became very close with her family, especially her Mom and two younger brothers. When they graduated from high school, Susan and Nathaniel went to different colleges. Susan went to her parents' alma mater and Nathaniel came to Ohio State.

One beautiful Saturday afternoon during spring quarter, I went for a walk on the Oval—a huge park in the center of campus, criss-crossed with sidewalks and adorned with a grassy lawn, benches, and many large trees. Typical of warm weekend afternoons, the Oval was packed with students studying, talking, playing guitars, and throwing Frisbees. As I walked, I came upon Susan and Nathaniel sitting on a blanket under one of the many huge maple trees. Susan had come home to Columbus for the weekend. It was good to see each of them again and it rekindled my curiosity about this mysterious young man.

He told me he was majoring in physics and mathematics. At Susan's prompting, he admitted to being in the honors program. This surprised me. He'd had such an easygoing attitude toward academics in junior and senior high school.

"Why physics?" I asked.

"I'm trying to figure out how the universe works, and physicists are the people asking that same question."

How cerebral, I thought. I mean, really. How many people decide they're going to figure out how the universe works? So Nathaniel was an "Einstein" type. At least that accounted for his strange behavior. But for some reason, his academic prowess threatened me. I needed to claim some status for myself.

Looking Nathaniel right in the eyes, I challenged him. "I'm a psychology major. I want to know what makes people tick." I hoped he was intimidated by the thought I could figure him out. Had I gained the upper hand?

"Bruce, that's great," he said, carelessly avoiding my challenge.

I flinched. Darn. It hadn't worked. I decided to try it again. Maybe this would impress him. "I am particularly interested in transpersonal psychology." That was impressive, wasn't it?

"What's that?" Nathaniel asked innocently.

Great, I had him. He was intrigued. "It is the integration of spirituality with psychology," I crowed. I bet that had impressed him. I felt stronger. Plus I knew something he didn't.

"Cool!" he replied easily.

Rats! This guy wouldn't bite. He didn't *really* seem impressed. I suspected he was simply being polite.

"You know," Nathaniel said, "we should stay in touch and try to get together sometime."

I was miffed, but tried to appear neutral. "That sounds good. Why don't you give me your phone number and I'll give you a call? You can have mine, too."

We exchanged phone numbers, but there was no way I was calling him. I was too afraid that he wasn't genuinely interested. So much for the smooth psychology major! I still had this fascination with Nathaniel that I didn't want to acknowledge to anyone, including myself, and especially him. Secretly, though, I did hope he would call me.

As I was leaving, I noticed a copy of *The Prophet* by Kahlil Gibran on their blanket and asked about it. Susan said sometimes they would take a break from studying and read it out loud. Oh, brother! That was too much. It didn't surprise me though. They were both like that.

Though they were obviously very happy together, as I walked away I got an eerie feeling I would never see them together again.

Nathaniel's parents didn't approve of their relationship. They liked Susan, but felt Nathaniel was too young to be so serious. Susan felt the relentless pressure and finally broke up with Nathaniel. Soon after, she was in a relationship with a young man from the university she was attending.

A year later, we were all home for spring break. I happened to be visiting Mathew and we were in the kitchen talking when the phone rang for Nathaniel. It was obviously bad news. He became very still as he listened to the person on the other end. A distressed feeling overtook the room. After the call was over, Nathaniel took the receiver from his ear and stared at it for a moment. He slowly hung up the phone, and looking at no one, quietly walked out of the kitchen. The silence he left behind was tangible.

The call was from Susan's mother saying Susan had died in an automobile accident the day before. I had no idea what to say or do. I felt so bad for him. He obviously still loved her and I suspected she had felt the same. Somehow, I don't believe he ever cried over Susan's death. I think Nathaniel retreated…into that inner place I had seen him go to as a child, staring at those wooden animals. I know his pain was great. I'm sure he grieved—but he did it alone, in his own private inner place.

Nathaniel and I did not speak of Susan again. Yet, for some time when we saw each other or spoke, I felt she was there in his thoughts. There was a quiet sadness to his presence. The depth of Nathaniel's soul, always so present in his eyes, was palpable as he softly mourned the loss of Susan.

Chapter 7

The Witnessing Game

After Susan's death, Nathaniel became unavailable. Over the next couple of years when I saw him, he had very little to say. I told myself he was preoccupied with his studies. But the silent shift in his demeanor left me wondering what was really going on inside this mysterious fellow.

Then, while studying one chilly fall evening, the ring of my telephone jilted the silence. It was Nathaniel. His voice sounded surreal, like an ancient hollow echo from out of nowhere. He said that this Friday evening he was attending a lecture explaining modern physics in laymen's terms. He asked if I would like to attend it with him and suggested we meet on the Oval. I was confused. Why did he call *me*? We had spoken so rarely, he almost felt like a stranger.

I had no idea at the time, but that lecture would be the first of a series we would attend together on different subjects.

On the way to the lecture, Nathaniel and I were discussing where to go for pizza afterwards when he suddenly changed the subject. "Bruce, you won't believe this. All of a sudden, everything is different. It's as if I'm watching everything from a distance, like a movie camera is running in my head monitoring everything. My legs are walking, my body is moving forward, and everything is going on as normal. But it's somehow going on by itself, outside of me."

"Did you take a recreational herb or something for the lecture?" I asked.

"No. It's nothing like that. I don't touch that stuff. I'm normal, except something is different."

It was typical Nathaniel, completely out of left field. For years, we had hardly seen each other and presto, he completely skips the small talk and dives right into the bizarre.

"It's like I'm not really here. Or, no, that's not quite it. It's like I am here but nothing really touches me, at least not all the way into me. A part of me, the deepest part of me, my awareness...is simply there—beyond all of this, watching silently—witnessing whatever happens without any emotion or opinion. In one sense everything is completely the same as always, but in another, it's completely different. I'm perceiving things in a completely new way, yet at the same time, nothing has changed."

"You've always seen things differently," I joked.

"But this is *really* different," he replied emphatically.

"Well, I hope you can sit through the lecture without freaking out. I've got to tell you, it's already a little too weird for me."

As we walked on, we didn't talk. Nathaniel was completely absorbed in his new experience. I felt left out. Did he perceive *me* differently? Did he still want me around? Though I was feeling uncomfortable with all of this, there was still something I liked about Nathaniel. I wanted to share his experience with him, but I couldn't. I couldn't understand it. I felt sorry for saying it was weird.

Throughout the lecture, I couldn't stop thinking about him. What was this grip he had on me? Something about him kept gnawing at me. But what was it?

The next day, Nathaniel and I agreed to meet on the Oval. He wanted to introduce me to his new girlfriend, Carol.

Carol was cute. She had long, straight, brown hair, big brown eyes, and was smart as a whip. I was surprised when shortly after he introduced us, Nathaniel tried to get Carol involved in this witnessing thing. But maybe Nathaniel didn't know about people, just about science.

"It feels like a game, Carol," he said. "Something fun—you know—something cool to do. Pretend there are movie cameras in your head instead of eyes. You are not walking. Everything is happening, but you are just watching, undisturbed, untouched in any way. It's as if you are a silent witness to your own body—your own thoughts and emotions. It's like everything that exists," he said waving his arm across the path, "the trees, the sky, all the cars—the whole world—is merely a mirage projected on the screen of your own awareness, your own being. It's all a movie and the movie screen is you! Isn't that cool?"

No, it was bizarre, I thought.

"You're crazy!" she snorted. "That's kooky!"

"Come on, give it a try. It's fun," Nathaniel urged.

This was good, I thought, settling in for some fine entertainment. How many times did you get to watch a couple arguing about something like this? Too bad I couldn't drag them to psychology class.

Nathaniel continued to press Carol as they went back and forth.

"Why won't you play the witnessing game? It wouldn't hurt to try," he urged.

But she clearly didn't want anything to do with it. I sided with Carol. It did seem kooky. Why would anyone want to do something that bizarre?

A few weeks later, Nathaniel told me he had discovered he couldn't turn his new game on and off. His physiology shifted in and out of it without his control. I said nothing, but wondered if he ever admitted that to Carol.

Several months passed. One afternoon, while Nathaniel and I were walking through the Oval, he suddenly stopped and stared straight ahead.

"Bruce, this is strange," he said quietly with his eyes fixed on a tree. His voice took on a new intensity. "I *am* that tree. I don't just feel like I am that tree. It's my direct perception."

"Really?" I couldn't hide the sarcastic tone in my voice. "Is this like the witnessing game? Am I supposed to pretend something?"

"No. This is not make-believe. This is an undeniable experience. I *am* the tree!" His voice grew more insistent.

Suddenly I remembered. "You mean like that Halloween night with the wooden giraffe?"

"Yes, but this time, it's…"

"What?"

"Overwhelming."

He *looked* overwhelmed—flushed and breathless. Feeling self-conscious, I looked around to see if anyone was listening to our strange conversation.

"I feel like that tree is a messenger from God." Nathaniel's voice was shaky. "No, that's not quite it. Somehow, that tree is *God*! I know that sounds outrageous. I can't really explain it, but what can I tell you? That is what I see."

Was Nathaniel going insane? I struggled for something to say. "I thought you didn't believe in God."

"Well, I don't. At least not like most people do," Nathaniel's voice trembled. "But that tree…that tree *is* God! It almost looks like it's transparent. I don't know how to describe it. It's like the tree is the source of everything in the universe—it's the center of the universe!" Nathaniel began to collect himself. "Bruce, I can see the entire universe in that tree. It knows everything. It *is* everything! It's beyond space and time!"

What on earth was he talking about? That tree is God? That tree is everything? Beyond space and time? I was having a hard time dealing with this. It was too incredible for words. I walked along beside Nathaniel as he staggered over to a bench and sat down.

"I don't know if what I am saying makes any sense. What can I tell you? If I wasn't experiencing it myself, my *own words* wouldn't make any sense to me. But it's the best I can do. I am directly experiencing *that tree as God*."

I got nervous. Was Nathaniel totally losing it or was he having an epiphany?

"But the strange thing is, Bruce, I can't even begin to say what God is." His bewildered voice became softer. "For me, this experience of God *is* God. I don't have words to describe it. It's not a mood. It's not an emotion. It's not an idea. It just *is*."

Nathaniel paused to catch his breath. Still agitated, he continued. "It's going to take me some time to sort all of this out, Bruce. It redefines my entire relationship with everything I have ever known. It's turning my whole world upside down...and inside out. But, I know I'm not going crazy."

"Well, I'm real glad to hear that." I knew my comment was stupid, but what do you say to someone who's telling you a tree is God?

Chapter 8

Life's Illusions

Nathaniel and I didn't see each other for awhile after that day on the Oval. When I would phone him, he acted a little standoffish, so I left him alone. But later that month I decided to stop off at his place to ask if he wanted to go for a walk.

At first he seemed reluctant, as if caught up in his own thoughts, but then he agreed. "Let me run upstairs to get my coat, and I'll be right out."

I waited for him outside. When he came out, we started walking along the sidewalk, quietly at first. It felt awkward, like I had intruded on his privacy.

Finally, he began to speak. "Bruce, I'm looking for answers. What in the world is going on? I mean *really*…. What is life? And what is existence?… Do you know what I mean?"

Looking away and feeling a bit uncomfortable, I mumbled, "I think so, Nathaniel." But really at this point, I wasn't sure I understood anything Nathaniel said.

"Physics describes how existence works," he went on, "but never asks what existence actually *is*. I've thought about these things my whole life. I've read philosophy books and majored in physics trying to find the answers. But now that all this is happening to me, I can't stand it anymore. These questions are burning me up inside. I'm feeling desperate and depressed. I've been walking the streets around campus at night, wondering, 'What do I really know? Do I really know anything? What is life? What is existence? What is all of this?'"

I couldn't think of anything to say. I felt sorry for Nathaniel and was worried about him. He seemed so lost and confused. We walked on silently. For a moment he stopped, sighed deeply, and looked up at the sky. Then he began to walk again.

When we got back to his apartment, he reached into his coat and pulled out an envelope. Handing it to me he said, "Bruce, I'd like you to read this. I've begun journaling and thought I'd share part of it with you."

A physics major journaling? That sounded serious. Was he reaching out for help? But how could I help? His questions were way beyond anything I knew.

Later that evening when I got home, I sat down in the armchair next to the front window, opened the envelope, and began to read:

◆◆◆ ◈ ◆◆◆

Life's Illusions

Everything parallels
maps onto everything else
...is everything else
holographic
multifaceted
echoes

A maze
a labyrinth
the web

Quicksand
the tar baby
confusing
seductive

The unfathomable mirage called existence
illusion
ignorance masquerading as knowledge

An echo of that which lies deeper
  mistaken for the depth
  mistaken for truth
  merely another clarity trip
  just another reality
  once more around the hamster wheel
    a dog chasing his tail

Lost

  searching
  grasping at echoes of truth as truth
    to feel

      safe
      smart
      wise

Life's nature

  elusive

• • • ◈ • • •

I leaned back in the armchair and stared out the window. Nathaniel was clearly depressed and I began to wonder if he needed therapy.

Chapter 9
Touchstone

From that point forward, I became Nathaniel's confidant. When I reflect upon his stories, I remember the feelings and mental images he created within me, more so than any facts or details. Memory works that way. To recount those stories is to recall them as my own memories as if they were my personal experiences.

Nathaniel shared with me detailed accounts, sometimes verbally and sometimes in writing. He described everything precisely. It was as if I was there with him. Deep within *my* awareness, I could see the images he related. Nathaniel's feelings became mine. What he touched, I touched. It was as if, for awhile, I merged with Nathaniel. There was something about Nathaniel—his presence—like that day so many years ago at the slave house.... He deepened my experience of everything. My memories, as a result, became something different. No longer external impressions, but more an internal awakening.

I'm not sure why Nathaniel accepted me into his world. Perhaps he needed a sounding board, a touchstone, someone with whom he could share. Maybe it was because I merely happened to be there at his critical moments. All I know is that when Nathaniel shared, my entire being attuned to something extraordinary.

Chapter 10

Goose

After our walk that Saturday afternoon, I didn't see Nathaniel again for several days. I talked to some of my psychology profs about his condition, but none of their responses satisfied me. I thought about calling Nathaniel, but didn't feel it was appropriate to intrude. Then one day, in his typical spontaneous fashion, he unexpectedly showed up at the psychology library where I always hung out to study.

I was sitting at my usual desk when Nathaniel approached. He didn't say much. He hardly even looked at me.

Tugging an envelope out of his coat pocket, he mumbled, "I guess I've been into writing lately. Here's a story from my journal describing some experiences I've been having. Would you mind taking a look at it?" He set the envelope on my desk.

I looked down at the envelope and back up at him. He was looking out the window. No eye contact. I was relieved to see him, but something still wasn't right. I hoped his journaling would explain it. I decided to play it cool. "Sure," I said as casually as I could, "I'll be glad to look."

Nathaniel still didn't make eye contact. He just looked at the clock on the wall and said, "Well, I've got to get going or I'll be late for class," and disappeared.

That evening I turned on my small bedside lamp, got under the covers, opened the envelope, and began to read:

••• ◇ •••

I recently rented a room in an off-campus house on Northwood Street. It's a beautiful neighborhood. The branches of the trees along the sidewalks form a canopy over the street. The houses are the classic three-story type. I'm living in an attic bedroom with slanted walls and pop-out windows.

I was studying in my room when I decided to go downstairs to get something to eat. It's quite a journey to the kitchen. The house is cold and we rely on space heaters in our rooms. So, I put on my jacket, climbed down two flights of rickety steps, swung around the old wooden banister, and followed the hallway to the kitchen in back. The kitchen was freezing and the linoleum floor uneven.

Someone was standing at the counter when I walked in. I introduced myself, picked up an apple, and rinsed it off in the old, white-enameled, double-basin sink. The pipes rattled as water flowed over the apple and down the drain. He told me his name was Bill, but everyone called him Goose, and he lived on the second floor.

I grabbed a plate and knife, and sat down at the fifties-style, aluminum-legged, Formica-topped table to eat. Goose went to the sink to wash his dishes. For some reason, I started telling him about my conclusions regarding life and existence.

I said Einstein had to be right. There must be one field unifying everything. Otherwise, how could mathematics possibly apply to music? How could principles in business so perfectly correlate to principles in biology? The only way everything could be that interconnected is if it all came out of the same one thing. That one thing must be the basis of everything and everyone.

I wanted to give Goose time to think, so I quietly cut my apple into quarters, removed the core from one quarter, and began to slowly peel it with my knife. I told him Descartes said, "I think, therefore I am." But I say, "I think, therefore I think I am." How can we know for sure this world is not just a big illu-

sion, like something out of 'Star Trek'? Really, we don't. Even the "I" could be part of the illusion. I paused and watched Goose's face, confirming he was with me.

Then I told him that the only thing we really <u>can</u> say is, "I think, therefore consciousness is." Though the "I" could be an illusion, consciousness <u>can</u> <u>not</u> be. Even if what we are conscious of is an illusion, the consciousness is irrefutable. I was glad when Goose asked me to give him a second. It told me he was really thinking about what I just said.

I told him that because this is truth, somewhere there had to be a group of people who knew it and that I was going to find them—abstract logic, but to me, it made perfect sense.

Goose simply stood there calmly drying his plate. He said if I liked that kind of stuff, I should study with Indian gurus. There were even people on campus already doing that.

I was so excited! I jumped up, knocking over the chair. "I can't believe it! I thought it would take me years to find them!"

I had no idea about gurus. The word "guru" brought images of "Indian rubber men" twisting their bodies into all sorts of outrageous positions. But when Goose said that, something immediately clicked.

That was it. I decided to get some books on Eastern philosophy and learn to meditate.

The next day I went to the Student Union and checked the bulletin board for a meditation group on campus. I was amazed to see how many there were—kundalini meditation, Zen meditation, a hatha yoga group, and more. One poster even had a picture of some guy in a loin cloth lying on a bed of nails. And another picture of the same guy, with a needle through his tongue. I passed on that one right away. But one poster, offering the Surya Meditation, appealed to me. Particularly a line that read, "Like the unfolding of a rosebud into a blossom, human evolution is a natural process." I took down the phone number, called, and set up an appointment to learn the Surya Meditation on Saturday.

Following their instructions, I went to bed early Friday

night and got a good night's sleep. Saturday morning I took a shower, had a very light breakfast, and went to an off-campus house where the meditation was taught. The girl who answered the door was named Michelle. I liked her.

We sat down in her living room and she explained how to meditate. Then she asked me to close my eyes and try it for a few minutes as she meditated along with me. I found the experience immediately restful. I became absorbed in my own consciousness with almost no sense of my physical environment. After a little while, she instructed me to take a minute or two to open my eyes. When I did, it appeared as if a very soft fog filled the room. I felt very light and floaty. We spoke for awhile before I left. I knew something very significant had happened, but couldn't quite explain it.

Over the next few days, my life took on a cleaner, more crystalline quality. My awareness became more awake and fresh. It seems to me you only have to meditate once to know it's something you want to do the rest of your life.

I called Michelle the following weekend to ask if she knew of a guru I might be able to go see. Her response was mysterious. She said several years ago, while still in high school, she took a course with an Indian man who was touring the United States. She learned from him how to teach the Surya Meditation, but after he resumed his tour, she lost track of him. Michelle told me she believed his teacher was a real guru, but the guru's location was a secret. She said real gurus, real masters, were very rare, and she didn't know of any who were accessible. She quoted an ancient proverb: "Spending a long time looking for the right teacher is much better than spending any time with the wrong one."

••• ◈ •••

I was intrigued. I was also relieved to learn Nathaniel was having a positive experience with something. I took his communication as an invitation to talk. So the next evening, I called him. I could tell from his voice he was happy to hear from me.

"Bru-u-uce." he greeted me, sounding much more like his old self.

"Hey, Nathaniel, how've you been doing? The last few times we talked, you were a little off. And that poem you wrote awhile back was pretty negative."

"Oh, yeah, that. Well, you know, it was a little rough there for awhile. I'm sorry I exposed you to it. When I saw you yesterday, all of a sudden I got really embarrassed about the whole thing."

"Oh, so that's what was going on. I could tell *something* was wrong."

"Yeah, well I'm fine now. Did you read the journal entry I gave you?"

"Yeah, I did."

"What did you think?"

"It was good. I also liked the way you wrote it," I added. "It made me feel like I was there."

Nathaniel's tone became thoughtful. "Life is all about feeling. I tried to convey what I felt."

Nathaniel paused, but I said nothing, hoping he would continue.

Nathaniel shifted into his philosophical mode. "*Feelings* are what touch us.… They are what move us.… *Feelings* are what really count. Thoughts matter little. How you feel about those thoughts makes all the difference."

"Yeah, I can understand that. I wanted to find out more about meditation because of how your journaling made me feel about it."

Nathaniel's voice became louder and he started to talk faster. "Bruce, that's great. You know, meditation is the biggest engine you have available to propel your growth. It feeds your whole life by awakening your essence."

It felt like the dam broke. Nathaniel was all excited and went on and on about his new discovery. "Some people meditate to have flashy or meaningful experiences in meditation. That's all wrong. It's like sleep. You don't sleep for the experience of sleep. You sleep to refresh yourself so your day will go better. You meditate to enrich yourself so your life will *be* better."

Oh, oh. It sounded like Nathaniel had found a crutch to help him through his hard time. But maybe that was a good thing, at least for now. "So Nathaniel, why don't you tell me how to meditate?"

"The key to proper meditation is that it's natural and effortless. Many meditation techniques try to force the mind to be still. That's all wrong. Proper meditation allows the mind and body to unravel naturally."

I wasn't convinced, but wanted the bottom line. So I asked again, "Nathaniel, would you teach me how to meditate?"

His response surprised me. "No, I think you would do better with someone who has experience teaching it." He gave me Michelle's phone number. "Give this girl a call. She can teach you how to meditate."

When I called Michelle, she was very friendly and down-to-earth on the phone. Some people are spontaneously that way. They can strike up a conversation with a perfect stranger and go on and on, like they are talking to an old friend. Her naturalness somehow reassured me Nathaniel hadn't gotten into some kind of cult. So, I made an appointment to learn that weekend.

Michelle lived a few blocks away from Nathaniel. From the outside, her house appeared very similar to the one in which Nathaniel lived. But when I walked in, I immediately noticed the atmosphere was distinctively light and crisp, and carried a subtle hint of what I thought must have been incense.

Michelle was medium height and build, with curly reddish-brown hair, and an effervescent personality. Though Michelle's personality was very light and cheery, there was a sense of somber wisdom at its base. Her dress was very neat and clean, an upscale take-off on the fashionable college trend of the time. All of this created an aura of mystery around her that was most intriguing, yet somehow unapproachable.

As she walked me into the living room, I noticed the cream-colored carpeting was new, as was the furniture. She sat in one of two beige-colored armchairs and I sat in the other. The quality of the furnishings was not at all typical of off-campus housing. From my years in college, I had become accustomed to beanbag chairs, orange-crate coffee tables, and close-out-sale sofas. The interior décor of Michelle's house was distinctively high class. I wanted to ask her about that, but didn't feel it was appropriate. So I pretended I didn't notice.

Michelle explained to me how to meditate in a very friendly and straightforward manner. We meditated together for a few minutes. Then she talked a little more and answered any questions I had. Though my experience wasn't as dramatic as Nathaniel's, I found the technique very relaxing and enjoyable.

When I left Michelle's house, I noticed the feeling and subtle scents of the house stayed with me as I walked home. It was a most unusual experience. For a moment I thought maybe a supernatural event was occurring and wondered if Nathaniel was caught up in something weird. But quickly I decided the smell of the incense had simply permeated my clothes and shrugged off the thought. However, the feeling of mystery stayed with me.

Chapter 11
The Face of Being

Several months passed. One evening, Nathaniel stopped by my place to look over my old notes from a class he was now taking. I was engrossed in my studies when he knocked at the door. Without even taking my eyes off the book, I stood up and walked over to open it. I let him in muttering, "Hi, Nathaniel," and quickly started back to my chair.

But then, freezing in my tracks, I slowly turned back around. "Nathaniel, what happened to you?" I asked, shocked at his appearance. "You're so *clean* looking." I couldn't find words to describe the sudden change in him. He looked lighter. Brighter. I couldn't imagine what had happened to him.

Nathaniel said nothing as he walked in. He looked for a moment, and then without even sitting down, turned around, mumbled that he had to go, and walked out.

Dumbfounded by his strange behavior and remarkable appearance, I watched through the window as he strolled down the street and out of sight. In typical Nathaniel fashion, I didn't see him again for several weeks. I probably should have phoned, but didn't want to seem nosey.

A few days later, Nathaniel stopped by the psychology library right before closing. He gave me another excerpt from his journal, said he was running late, and rushed off. Hoping he hadn't taken another turn for the worse, I quickly closed my books and hurried home, anxious to read what he had written. I got ready for bed, turned on the lamp, crawled under the covers, and started to read:

••• ◇ •••

I came home after classes on, what was to that point, a typical day. I was enrolled in a class Bruce had taken a couple of quarters earlier, so was going to his apartment to look over his notes that evening...

This was it! This was what happened right before Nathaniel came over to study my notes!

...I decided to meditate before going to Bruce's. I sat down on my bed and closed my eyes. Suddenly, time ceased to exist. It was as if the flow of my life abruptly stopped. When time started again, I was lying on my side. I opened my eyes, astounded, not knowing if two minutes, two days, or two weeks had passed.

The witnessing experience was now in full force, unlike any of the previous glimpses I had of it. I was one with everything I saw. The entire room and everything in it had a soft, exquisite, golden glow coming from within. Gradually, I stood up and slowly made my way out of the house and over to Bruce's. Everything looked so lovely, but once I got outside, I was staggered still again. Plants, grass, sky, and trees were more beautiful than I could have ever imagined. Everything was so alive and glowing. The movie camera in my head was a silent witness to my every experience. The entire world appeared to be lightly etched on the face of my being—on the surface of my awareness. My own being was the basis of everything, including what I had formerly thought of as myself. My body, my personality, my thoughts, and my emotions were superficial in contrast to this deeper sense of self that had awoken within me.

During my walk over to Bruce's apartment, I could see

people's moods. It reminded me of comic strip illustrations. I could see the brightness around people who were happy. I saw dark heavy clouds around people who were disheveled or sad. I saw a girl radiate like a light bulb when she greeted her boyfriend as he arrived to visit her. I could actually see rays of light shooting off of her body as she lit up.

Eventually, I got to Bruce's place…

That was why he was acting so strangely! Ever since that evening, I had wanted to know what happened to Nathaniel *after* he left my place. In my hands was the writing that might tell me. I skimmed the next paragraph, and there it was:

…As soon as I got there, I realized there was no studying in the cards for me that night, so I turned around and left. I spent the rest of the evening walking around campus and marveling at my new experience of the world. Everything was so pristine. Even dirt in the gutters. It reminded me of when Dorothy landed in Oz. Prior to that, everything was in black and white. Now, suddenly, everything was in living color. At one point, I saw Elaine, a girl from one of my psychology classes, walking towards me down the sidewalk on the opposite side of the street. As we approached each other, she let out the strangest cackle, waving both hands in the air as she called to me. "Hey, Nathaniel, you look like a clean-cut all-American boy!"

I quietly waved back at her, smiled, and nodded as she went her way and I went mine.

Curiously, it reminded me of Bruce's comment: "You're so clean looking." Her comment somehow made sense. I felt pristine. Any clouds, cobwebs, or constraints that previously shrouded my awareness had, that evening, simply and suddenly disappeared.

I decided to take a stroll toward campus and down High Street. It was an outlandish experience. I could see the constrictions that ran people's lives. It was all around them. It permeated their bodies and their minds. How could they possibly not see it? I wondered. But even more, I could see the genius within them, the beauty, the elegance. Yet it was apparent they could not see that either. The world was caught up in a dichotomy of paradox. Inner greatness overshadowed by a veil of senseless confusion. And I wondered, How could anything as magnificent as the sun be overshadowed by the thinness of a flimsy veil? Yet there it was, before me. Blatantly obvious. My feelings were not of despair, sadness, or malevolence. What was, simply was. Paradoxical, yet exquisite. Everything for me was now, well, clean.

◆◆◆◇◆◆◆

I slid down further under the covers and stared at the ceiling for a bit, reflecting on the incredible account I had just read. How had Nathaniel put it? He saw their constrictions and their genius.

That reminded me of my childhood fascination with buckeyes. Maybe everything embodied contradictory qualities. Could the world be nothing but paradox? Perhaps Nathaniel had slipped into a state where that wasn't a philosophy—it simply *was*.

At that moment, I didn't know what to do with it all. I was too tired to think, and decided to just get some sleep.

Chapter 12

Within the Looking Glass

Several days later, Nathaniel and I met on the Oval for lunch. He talked about the shift that had occurred in his awareness.

"I'm having a hard time dealing with this, Bruce. I feel like I used to be experiencing life from inside out and didn't even know it. Then it got turned back to where it is supposed to be—inside in and outside out. I don't know how to describe it. It was like something out of *Alice in Wonderland*—like I was looking at the mirror and then somehow walked into it. Now it feels like I'm looking out at life from within that looking glass. What used to be real is now virtual. And what used to be merely a concept or a virtual notion suddenly became real. It's like waking up one morning and suddenly realizing you have three arms, when all along you thought it was normal to just have two."

"That must be strange," I smirked.

"Yeah, it's taking time to adjust." Nathaniel opened his eyes really wide. "It never goes away! And it's not only my perception that changed. The way I understand things is totally different, too!" Nathaniel tilted his head back, ran his hands through his hair, and looked to the sky.

I felt sad for Nathaniel. Obviously, he was having a hard time dealing with all of this. Then I felt guilty. Why did I have to smirk at him? He was having a hard enough time already. I didn't know what to do, but maybe I could help by listening. Trying unsuccessfully to make eye contact, I offered my support, "What do you mean that you understand things differently?"

"Words, for example. They have whole new meanings for me."

"New meanings?"

"Yeah, like the word 'karma.'"

We had both read a lot of Eastern philosophy. The definition of karma, I thought, was clear and straightforward. "It has to do with punishment for bad actions and reward for good actions," I said.

"Well, but it's so much more than that," he gushed. "I understand it so much better now. Karma is action. It is movement. Actually, *apparent* movement because really nothing is moving, nothing is happening. The laws of karma describe the rules governing that apparent movement. Don't you understand? It's more than mere words. I can actually perceive it now. Bruce, I experience it emerging from the depths of my being and extending out from me to all of creation. It's no longer a theoretical concept that makes a certain level of sense. Does that sound self-centered or grandiose?"

"No, not at all," I blurted out. But inwardly, I thought yes, completely.

He paused for a moment. "Maybe I would still define karma the same way as I did before, using the same words. But the meaning of those words is now very different for me. It's the difference between description and direct experience, and that difference is everything. And even more, it's not the meaning of a word here or there, but the meaning of everything and I mean *everything*!"

I was now even more lost than I had been before. "So are we even going to be able to communicate?" I asked, trying not to sound sarcastic.

"I'll tell you," he replied enthusiastically. "I'm not just dealing with words. I'm also dealing with a whole new phenomenon within me. It's a whole new experience of who I am, what I am, and what *essence* really means—it's the soul of everyone and everything in the entire universe. My body, thoughts, and emotions are superficial. In fact, all "things" are superficial. Objects and people are simply virtual projections of essence. This whole experience I'm having is like learning to walk all over again." He sat back, his face flushed, and his eyes glowing with excitement.

At this point, Nathaniel had me exhausted. "Nathaniel, you become more fascinating every day," I said flippantly. "Let me know if you're ever interested in being a case study." I shifted the conversation to more mundane things as we began to eat lunch.

Unfortunately, the whole thing became too much for Carol. She had dated Nathaniel throughout that entire strange time. On a Saturday afternoon, as Nathaniel, Carol, and I were sitting in a booth at Charbert's, a popular campus diner right off High Street, Nathaniel launched into his usual monologue.

"Carol," he said, "pretend like the world is one big television screen and all of this is merely a projection on its surface. All of this is a virtual image." He waved his arm out in front of him as if extending it to the universe. That had become a common gesture for him.

After putting up with such talk for weeks, Carol had finally had it with Nathaniel and blew up. "What's your problem? Nothing affects you anymore! All you think about are your stupid experiences!"

Nathaniel showed no reaction.

"You don't care about anything that really matters! I can't even relate to you! What's going on, Nathaniel?" She began to cry.

Nathaniel took hold of her hand from across the table. It was an awkward scene. I knew he and Carol loved one another. But it was obvious that Carol was unable to comprehend Nathaniel's new life and probably never would. I couldn't see much future for them. Though their relationship was off-and-on-again for some time, eventually they went their separate ways.

Chapter 13

Judging Discernment

Nothing was ever the same for Nathaniel. Although on the surface he appeared to return to normal, Nathaniel's experience of life was totally different. It simply required some time for him to get used to his new physiological state. Throughout the months that followed, he searched for someone who understood and shared his experience. Nathaniel read books and attended lectures on the subject, but they didn't satisfy him.

Together we attended a number of talks by spiritual teachers. Nathaniel was terribly judgmental. Indian gurus, Taoist masters, Buddhist lamas—none of them satisfied him. Some of them he called showmen, a few he called con artists, and others he felt were well read, but lacked direct experience of what they'd read about. He felt many didn't understand what spirituality really was. Much of what they said he called sheer dogma. He said many of them were merely getting people worked up emotionally, but accomplished nothing of any value. One by one, he rejected them all.

When a Buddhist lama offered fifteen spiritual laws to live by, Nathaniel called it "cookie-cutter spirituality with no *real* change in the person."

A shaman came to town, put on some lovely music, had everyone hold hands and sing. He told them to feel their love for one another, all humanity, and all living creatures throughout the whole world. Nathaniel called it a "self-indulgent waste of time."

When a spiritual healer came to town and straightened out people's energy systems, Nathaniel called it "energetic manipulation." He said it wasn't true healing at all. Just a Band-Aid approach—sweeping the real problem under the rug.

When a psychic demonstrated her ability to read auras, Nathaniel called it "cartoon consciousness." He said, "All you have to do is look at the funny papers. Cartoonists are drawing auras all the time—bright rays around the heads of happy people and dark dirty clouds around messy little kids. The reason people laugh is that they can totally relate to it. That's all there is to seeing auras. It's not a magical gift, it's simply a delightful perspective. The psychics may be well intended, but they're misguided and are misleading all the sincere seekers in the audience."

I felt Nathaniel needed to lighten up. Some of the spiritual healers and shamans were admittedly a little dingy, but I had fun at all the talks. Though I did understand his point, I wondered if he might actually be jealous. After all, they were the well-known experts in the field of spirituality. And let's face it, he was a spiritual nobody!

When Nathaniel phoned to invite me to go see yet another Indian saint, I called him on it. "Nathaniel, I'm tired of going to these talks just to hear you bash the speakers afterward. Who do you think you are and what makes *you* the authority? Why are you so judgmental?"

The telephone line went quiet.

For a moment, I thought he had hung up on me. "Nathaniel, are you there?"

"Yes, I'm here." His voice was controlled.

"What do you have to say, Nathaniel?" I demanded.

More silence and then a meek whisper. "Are you judging my judgmental-ness?"

Something in his voice, more than in what he said, made me feel guilty. "Are you okay?"

"Yeah, I'm okay...." Hesitating, he said, "Actually, no. I feel hurt. I thought you understood me better."

"Oh Nathaniel, I really didn't mean to hurt you. But I do think you've been awfully judgmental."

"Judgment is one thing, discernment is another. I'm really dedicated to finding someone who truly knows what spirituality is all about. In order to do that, I must be as discerning as possible."

I fell silent. Oh man. He'd done it again. He'd turned our conversation back around on me. But it was something to think about. Was I judging him for being judgmental when, in fact, he was being discerning? Was I the judgmental one? Perhaps judgment was bad, but discernment was good.

In that instant, I got it and grinned. "Nathaniel, I'm sorry I snapped at you. Let me think about this for awhile." Then I changed the subject, not wanting to acknowledge he'd won our debate. We agreed to see the saint that evening at a satsang—a spiritual get-together—being held right off campus.

The satsang was led by an Indian saint who was touring the United States. When we arrived, everyone was sitting on the floor in a semicircle around him. The group was being led in chants and devotional songs. People were entranced, swaying from side to side.

Nathaniel was critical as usual, whispering to me that the chanting and singing was "just a bunch of spiritual emotionalism." While I was swept along with the euphoric mood of the moment, Nathaniel sat motionless with a scowl on his face, standing out like a sore thumb. I became quite uncomfortable when I noticed an Indian man, sitting off to the side of the room, glaring at Nathaniel.

When the satsang was over, the man began to approach Nathaniel. I told Nathaniel he was on his own and that I needed to get back to my apartment to study. I didn't want to see the scolding I expected Nathaniel to receive.

But of course, I did want to know what happened and the next evening I stopped by Nathaniel's apartment to find out. We sat down on the black vinyl furniture in the living room of the old house. At first, he would not go into any detail about the conversation with the Indian man, but only said he had found the person he wanted to study with.

I was incredulous. "You can't mean the Indian man who approached you last night. He's not the one, is he?"

"No," Nathaniel murmured.

"Well then, who is it?" I demanded.

"It's someone the man told me about," he replied softly. "He asked me to keep the guru's location a secret. He said the guru does not want to be known by the public at large."

I was flabbergasted. Nathaniel had been so skeptical of everything. Now, with almost no information, he was jumping in with both feet. Incensed, I continued to challenge him. "That's it? That's all you know about the guru?"

"No," he replied. "The Indian man also had a picture of him in his wallet. I'm going to go to India to study with the guru."

I couldn't believe my ears. "What? Are you crazy?" I screamed. "You've been so critical of all these different saints we've seen. Now you pick one you've never even met, and are going to go halfway around the world to see him? Is this what you call discernment?"

"I guess that's about it." Nathaniel's voice was matter of fact.

He *was* crazy, I thought. How could he be making such a huge decision and be so casual? We both sat there without speaking for what felt like an eternity.

Then reflectively, almost in a monotone, Nathaniel explained. "I know he is the man I've been looking for. I don't even know his name, but I saw it in his face. It came right through his picture. I also saw it in the face of that man. Plus, when he spoke, he made sense. Finally, somebody made sense."

"So why not study with him? At least for awhile?" I pleaded.

"No, I need to see the guru in India who lit the flame in his soul. That man is still a student, like us. He even told me he's not capable of giving me what I long for, but that his guru is."

Exasperated, I closed my eyes, rubbed my forehead, and sighed. "What exactly *is* it you long for, Nathaniel?"

"I don't know exactly what 'it' is." Nathaniel's eyes were fixed and his jaw was firm. "I only know that I'm going to India."

Didn't know what he wanted, but was going halfway around the world to get it. That was awfully impulsive. I was worried.

"Many talk about it, and get emotional about it, but they do not know *it*," he continued. "They only think they have it because they know something about it and do their best to act it out. But, that's not *it*.

"Last night, I told the Indian man that he seemed to understand spirituality, but something confused me. Why was he there?

"I told him, 'This swaying around and getting enthralled in an emotional trance with this so-called saint won't help people grow spiritually. It will only sidetrack them from what spirituality is really all about. Your presence here may encourage them to believe this guy knows what spirituality really is.'

"He answered me by saying, 'I'm here because I am of this culture. This reminds me of my home and my childhood. It's a part of my tradition.

"'These people are here because this matches their particular level of understanding. It isn't wise to take toys away from children because *you* have outgrown toys. In time, the child himself will outgrow toys and then he will stop playing with them all by himself. Everything has its appropriate time.'

"Then I said, 'I have wondered why some saints allow their devotees to do this sort of thing. Sometimes, they teach them to do one thing, but allow them—almost encourage them—to do another. With your help, I'm beginning to understand why.'

"He said, 'People think what they think and do what they do. There's little we can do about it. Saints understand that. When the devotee is ready to hear, he or she will listen, not before. Your life will be different from many. You will inspire people to move beyond their current limitations. People can waste time getting stuck in old habits, just as water flowing down a river can get stuck in an eddy current when it wanders off to the side of the main flow. You will prod people on and encourage them to move forward, beyond their habitual behaviors and perspectives.'

"I asked him, 'How do you know that?'

"He answered, 'I don't know it. I feel it. But I can assure you, it will happen.'"

I wasn't sure why that story affected me so strongly. It seemed so pure and truthful. It made me ashamed of the rational way I approached my feelings and my life.

"Bruce, I have a big favor I need to ask of you." Nathaniel's tone only left room for the response he wanted. "I will need about $2,000 to go to India. Do you have any idea where I might be able to get it?"

Nathaniel was aware of the fact that I had recently inherited $20,000 when my grandmother died, not to mention the comfortable trust that would kick in when I turned thirty. It was clear he was asking for a loan.

I paused for a moment, only to hear the words come out of my mouth. "Nathaniel, I would like to loan it to you."

He looked at me with such a soft and loving smile that it almost seemed he was made out of gelatin or vapor. In that moment, he felt sweetly vulnerable, though at the same time powerful and completely in command of my fate.

"By the way, Nathaniel added, "the Indian man asked me if I meditated. When I told him I did the Surya Meditation, he smiled, nodded, and said, 'There are many forms of meditation. Very few are genuine and pure. You have chosen very wisely.'"

I was glad to hear that and felt reassured about the Surya Meditation, especially because I was practicing it too. But at that particular point in time, what was really on my mind was my $2,000. "That's great, Nathaniel," I blurted out. "But you have to be sure to pay me back."

He smiled tenderly and said, "I promise. I will pay you back."

Chapter 14

Curses and Gifts

Nathaniel was gone. He was somewhere in India. I thought about him a lot—worried really. It was early July before I heard from him. School was out for summer break, and I was staying at my parents' home on Mulvern Street. The day his letter arrived, I had wandered out from the kitchen, and was standing for a moment on the back steps under the hot Ohio noonday sun. I was wearing only a T-shirt and an old pair of cutoff shorts.

While looking down at the ground, I noticed my legs. They were pale white due to lack of sunlight and terribly skinny. I was hoping a good tan would improve their appearance. Then my psychology background kicked in and my thoughts drifted to how negative body image relates to self-image. I began to wonder about myself and to look more closely at my feelings and motivations. Did I have a self-image of weakness or frailty? Did I unconsciously become a psychology major to work that out, or compensate for it? Did that cause me to feel somehow inadequate around Nathaniel? Something about him was always so solid and strong. Even when he was awkward, confused, or upset, something within him was always unshaken.

Squinting in the brightness of the sun, I looked up to the tall branches of the maple tree in our backyard. No wind. The branches were still. I loved that old tree. No matter what time of year, even in fierce storms, the trunk was always solid even when the branches thrashed in the wind. Nathaniel was like that tree. On the surface—

change, sometimes even chaos, yet always a solidity to his soul.

These thoughts made me aware of how fragile my ego was. The slightest wind from any direction unsettled me to my core. Even something as mundane as my pale skinny legs. In an attempt to avoid my discomfort, I decided to check the mailbox in front of the house.

I leapt off the steps onto the driveway. "Ouch!" My bare feet hit the fire-hot asphalt. A hop, skip, and a jump, and I was on the grass, making my way to the mailbox. My feet hurt, but at least I was off the hook. No more psychological inner exploration, at least for the moment.

Amidst the mail was an envelope made of thin and tattered paper, affixed with exotic Indian postage. I immediately knew it was from Nathaniel. Cutting through the flower beds to avoid the asphalt, I rushed back into the house. I left the other mail on the kitchen table and took Nathaniel's letter out to the backyard, where I sat at the picnic table under the big maple tree.

I opened it and began to read. At first, I wondered if it was the standard obligatory letter because of the loan. But then it felt very different from that. A warm feeling overtook me as I realized I was still his close confidant.

Shade from the sprawling maple tree and the gentle breeze created a pleasant sanctuary from the hot sun as I read:

••• ◈ •••

Dear Bruce,

The journey to India was long and tiring. After flying from Columbus to Chicago, I had a several-hour layover. Then I went on to San Francisco and had another several-hour layover. Without sleep, I boarded a plane to Hawaii, then on to Hong Kong, and finally to Delhi. I had little success sleeping in flight. I arrived in India exhausted, but excited. The combination of fatigue and repeated cabin pressure and depressurization left me feeling like I was in an echo chamber. India didn't appear to be so strange, at least not until I got out of customs.

Suddenly, the airport was packed with hot and sweaty bodies clamoring about, as they all pushed against one another.

There are no lines in India. Everyone shoves their way to the front. It's perfectly acceptable to cut ahead of whoever is in front of you. For that reason, most everyone got their luggage before I did. It was only after the baggage claim area cleared that I was able to locate my luggage. All the while, taxi drivers assaulted me, demanding to take me to my place of destination. They were, at the same time, curiously polite. It was just their way. Things are different here.

Being forewarned of thieves, I carried my own luggage to the taxi. I pushed my way through the hoards of people out to the sidewalk. Many small children amongst the crowd held out a hand for money. Also forewarned, I did not respond. I was told that if you give money to one, you will be instantly attacked by many children, all pulling, tugging, and coercing you to hand them a rupee or two.

How odd it was, amidst all that congestion of humanity, to see an elephant nonchalantly stroll by. I'm not sure what we do in our country with the maimed and malformed people, but they are certainly plentiful here. Fortunately, I arrived in the morning because the taxi driver told me that it wasn't safe to drive to the ashram after dark due to the preponderance of nighttime robbers along the way.

The ride north to the ashram was very long. I must say that the countryside is beautiful, not only in its natural beauty, but also in its simplicity. There was, in essence, no gas-powered anything. Carts towed by water buffalo were the primary farm technology. There was an exquisite sway of timeless dignity to the motion of the women carrying large bundles of straw on top of their heads.

When I finally made it to Guru Surya's ashram, I was tired, hungry, and dirty. I was politely greeted and shown to a tiny room in an old masonry structure. I walked in, shut the door behind me, set down my suitcase, sat on the little cot, silently looked around, and thought, "What am I doing here?"

I have written you this letter, sitting on that cot, this, my first morning in the ashram. I guess I'm a little hesitant to leave my room, but I'm also really excited to see what happens next.

I'll write you again.
　Your friend,
　　Nathaniel

••• ◈ •••

The sudden ending of the letter surprised me and kicked off an unexpected surge of anger. What was it about Nathaniel that held so much power over me? Was I envious? Jealous? Resentful? Why did I care so much what he did? Sometimes he reminded me of my father, a self-righteous know-it-all. A psychologist would say I was in transference, projecting all of my father issues onto Nathaniel. My father always thought he knew better. He never respected my opinion. He always assured me that some day I would grow up and see things his way, but that day never came. And now I was feeling that same resentment towards Nathaniel.

My God, this was murder. But I couldn't stop. I had to face it. He had become my father—my despicable authority figure, the archetypical tyrant of my superego. A textbook love-hate relationship. A double-bind.

My psychology profs would probably say, "Excellent. Nathaniel has given you a real gift. He is helping you look within." That thought made me even madder.

That was it. I couldn't do any more. The whole situation tied me up in a knot. I sat under the maple tree, alone with myself, fuming and confounded.

Chapter 15

The Tiger of a Dream

For the next several weeks, I took some time each day to work with my father issues and how I transferred them onto Nathaniel. Evidently, something good was coming out of it. I resolved that the next time I heard from Nathaniel, I would take it easy and simply enjoy the friendship he offered.

Yet as I received his letters, I continued to question Nathaniel's motivation. Did he feel obligated to me because I loaned him money? Did he simply enjoy writing? Maybe I'd become his touchstone merely because I happened to be there during so many of his bizarre experiences. Or was there more to it?

••• ◊ •••

Dear Bruce,

I trust this letter finds you well. I'm not at all disappointed with my visit here. Surya is who I hoped he would be. After my first night's sleep, I was led to a room where Surya was speaking with a handful of disciples. I entered in the rear of the room. I was the only Westerner. As I sat down on the floor with the other devotees, Surya, without interrupting the flow of his talk, cast an expressionless gaze into my eyes. That glance was enough to assure me I was in the right place. There was wisdom, gentleness, and strength in his eyes.

Fortunately he, like most people here, speaks English. However, many of his talks are in Hindi. So for those, I require a translator. Sometimes when he sees me in the room, he switches from Hindi to English. Surya's teachings are like balm on a wound. Finally, someone who really makes sense. Yet much of what I've learned hasn't been through the spoken word. Instead, it has been through a simple gesture, a glance, and my observations of how Surya deals with diverse types of people. All of that intrigues me and satisfies my thirst for more and more understanding.

Surya is introducing me to a number of other great teachers. At the same time, he has cautioned me to avoid most teachers. (Bruce, from our days at Ohio State, you know I'm pretty good at doing that.) He directs me to specific teachers he feels I should visit.

Surya told me that, in any religion, there are only a very small handful of people who truly understand spirituality. Generally, he said they remain on the sidelines choosing not to be a part of the dogma permeating organized religion. He said that instead of philosophizing about their religion, people would do better to find a competent teacher who could show them the truth underlying all religions. It was such a relief to hear someone say what I've been feeling for so long.

I'm sure I've found a competent teacher in Surya. I immediately felt a deep connection with him and it's growing with every passing day. I can tell he likes me. He invites me to join him when he travels around India to lecture. Surya is becoming like a father to me. I love my new life and want only to stay in India and be with my newfound family.

Be well,

Nathaniel

$$\cdots \diamond \cdots$$

I was relieved to hear his guru had worked out. What a disaster it would have been to go all the way to India for nothing!

I was also relieved to get through a letter from Nathaniel without getting angry. My psychology training was paying off. It was becoming easier for me to feel my vulnerability regarding Nathaniel.

The next letter I received from Nathaniel was beautiful, but odd. Like his journal entry about Goose, it read like a short story. Everything about Nathaniel intrigued me, even the way he wrote:

••• ◈ •••

Dear Bruce,

The other day during lunch, I was told that Surya wanted to meet with me. I was instructed to go into the garden behind his house. There I would find Surya waiting. Obeying those instructions, I immediately rushed off.

I found Surya sitting on a stone bench in the shade of a large sprawling tree. Though it was hot in the sun that day, the slight breeze, combined with the shade from the trees, created an ideal setting. When I approached, Surya's gesture directed me to sit in the aluminum-framed, woven-plastic chair several feet in front of him. Surya and I were both dressed in the regular ashram attire—dhoti with sandals. My chair was curiously out of place in the surroundings that could've otherwise passed for ancient times. When Surya spoke, his tone was somehow strangely foreboding. I sensed he was trying to warn me about something.

"Nathaniel, do you know what business we are in?"

I thought that was a curious question. I paused for a moment. I didn't want to disappoint him with a foolish answer. Finally, I suggested we were in the business of enlightenment.

Surya smiled affectionately and nodded. He said that though I was right, it was sometimes better to think of it as the business of ignorance. He said the physician seeks disease and the spiritual teacher seeks ignorance. Without ignorance, we would have nothing to do. Surya chuckled lovingly, but I was puzzled. I was trying to understand where he was leading.

This, he said, is the time of Kali Yuga, the age of ignorance. He warned that as my passion to eradicate ignorance rose, I would need to remember that ignorance keeps the world spinning around. Without it, this universe would cease to exist.

Ignorance comes in the form of convictions. Our work, he said, is to free people of such ignorance, not reinforce it. Throughout the world, including India, people have limitless convictions about spirituality, but in actuality they have no idea. Very few people are willing to learn because it means moving beyond their current convictions.

The wise, he cautioned me, are condemned by the ignorant, as ignorant. Through the eyes of the ignorant, discernment of wisdom is often mistaken for negativity. This is the inevitable nature of things. People cannot be asked to comprehend that which is beyond their comprehension. Yet the role of the teacher is to help others in that process.

I wondered if Surya told me all this for my benefit, or simply because it was troubling him. Surya usually spoke so clearly and precisely. He was being so vague. It wasn't typical of him. His heart was heavy. I wondered what was bothering him.

Surya told me that being who I am will, in and of itself, be my greatest teaching. Acting the way your students expect the enlightened to act only reinforces their convictions about enlightenment. It postpones their enlightenment. It encourages them to reach for a mirage in the sky.

As humbly as I could, I asked if what he was saying was not also a conviction. He said that this is the world of convictions. The trick is to live in it without losing yourself to it. Then he asked me if I understood what he was saying.

I nodded yes, but wondered if I really understood all the implications. I'd never seen Surya so meek. He almost seemed sad.

We sat quietly for what felt like a long time. Then, he softly said, "You cannot kill the tiger of a dream with a real gun. You need the gun of a dream." After more silence he asked again if I understood.

I remained silent. I didn't want to say no. As I struggled to understand, I realized the befuddled look on my face gave me away.

Surya smiled and said that students must be met on their own level, within their current dream. Then, slowly, they can be moved forward out of the dream. He emphasized that the path of real teaching is subtle indeed.

I understood that he and the other teachers were meeting me within my own dream, on my own level, to help me move beyond it. It was a great lesson in how he worked with the consciousness of another person....

At this point in Nathaniel's letter, the type of paper and color of ink he was using changed. It seemed clear that he resumed writing at a later time. I set down the letter and wondered about the tiger of a dream. What was the nature of the dream I was dreaming? And what was Nathaniel's dream? As I reflected upon our lives, I recollected our early childhood adventures.

One steamy hot summer day, we decided to take a long hike to the end of Mulvern Street, up Waltham Road, through the adjoining neighborhood and back. To leave Mulvern Street was to leave behind what was familiar. Waltham Road always felt mysterious. The presence of the old Civil War mansion and slave house loomed over us as we trekked up the hill. As we turned in to the adjoining neighborhood, that presence was at our backs. What lay before us was unknown. Mansions resting upon hilltops. Immaculate and foreboding.

The long and laborious journey was strewn with many obstacles. When two large black dogs charged, we all froze as we had been taught. Wet and filthy from what was no doubt a recent dip in the nearby creek, they brushed against and sniffed our still bodies as we held our breath, hoping they wouldn't bite. After what felt like an eternity, they lost interest and quickly disappeared.

As we resumed our walk up the long steep hill, the muscles in our legs began to ache. The hot summer sun baked our tender little bodies, as perspiration saturated our clothes and dripped from our brows. Halfway up the hill, several of us modeled walking sticks out of branches from a roadside pile of trimmings.

We attempted to shorten the trip by cutting across the sprawling yard of a hilltop mansion. At just the wrong time, a shirtless man, most certainly the owner, stepped out of the garage, startling us. Like a line of ants, we immediately deviated from our path to move directly away from him. The march back down the hill, in the direction from which we came, only added more distance to our journey.

Finally we reached the top of the hill and continued to follow the winding street. By this point in our hike, we'd all become desperately thirsty, parched by the hot summer sun. The babbling waters of the creek that crossed under the road only heightened our desire for refreshment. But being fully forewarned of the potential contaminants, none of us dared drink the water.

Finally the street rejoined Waltham Road. Leaving that neighborhood was somehow a relief. Waltham Road now seemed like old familiar ground. We could sense our neighborhood far down the hill and to the right. With every step forward, that sense grew stronger, as did the presence of the slave house and mansion. When at last we reached Mulvern Street, a fresh wave of familiarity carried us home.

Picking up Nathaniel's letter, I had the thought that nothing ever really changes. As children, we were fascinated with new adventures, as if out there somewhere something would fulfill our dreams. Nathaniel was now in India doing the same thing—searching to fulfill his dreams. I had the sobering thought that perhaps everyone, in their own way, is doing that. It made me wonder what fulfillment was, and if, in fact, there was any such thing. I looked down at the letter and resumed reading:

> ...A few days later, Surya sent me to visit a saint, named Vasistha. He lived in a remote village. The directions I was given were typically obscure and convoluted: "Walk into the village on the main road from the east, turn left at the spice vender's cart, go down past the school house to the large banyan tree, continue to the hut beneath that tree, and knock on the door."
>
> When I finally arrived, a tiny Indian woman approached me before I could knock. Pointing to a small stone seat beneath the tree, she told me to wait. I obeyed. After a short time, the

lady returned and directed me to enter.

A little man with a Nehru hat sat on a cot within the hut. His head moved side to side in the characteristic Indian manner. "Come in, sit, sit."

I again obeyed. Without hesitation, he told me I was being very thoroughly trained. He told me I'd be leaving India to teach in America and that my teachings would spread all over the world. The rest of the conversation was a blur. All I can say is I left with a headache and was glad to get back to the ashram that evening.

Bruce, I don't want to leave India. This feels like where I belong. How could I ever leave all of these great teachers? I'm trying to forget about my encounter with the lovely little saint, named Vasistha.

Best wishes,

Nathaniel

••• ◈ •••

I did a double take. Could that be true? Nathaniel's teachings…spread all over the world? I wondered how accurate Vasistha could be. At first I was impressed. Then I felt jealous. I decided Nathaniel must be on an ego trip. He had found somebody to boost his ego and that was all there was to it.

Suddenly I caught myself. Time for more personal process. More issues. Right when I thought I had worked through all that stuff.

But then it hit me—if it were true, boy was I lucky. I had known Nathaniel practically his whole life. Wouldn't it be great if it actually did happen and I was there all along watching. When his next letter came, I was excited to find out more.

••• ◈ •••

Dear Bruce,

Over the past several months, I've talked frequently with Surya. He is a truly incredible being. Sometimes he takes me with him into the city. It amazes me that no one notices him and his greatness. It dawned on me as we were buying some fruit that this was one reason he took me with him. Now I truly understand that sainthood goes completely unnoticed in this world.

Surya has continued to direct me to a number of remarkable saints. I wanted to tell you about one of them named Gupta.

Over the past month or so, I have been meeting with Gupta every morning for a few hours. He's teaching me the art of pulse evaluation. It's an ancient art of India where one learns to evaluate the health and life of an individual through the pulse. Gupta's teachings make no linear sense. He'll talk about the planet Jupiter and the number five and somehow relate it to the pulse. This has been going on for weeks. I leave Gupta with my head spinning, day after day. The odd thing is that somehow, almost magically, I really am learning how to evaluate the pulse!

Gupta says that my Western education trained my brain to function unnaturally. He tells me he's freeing my brain from that unhealthy state so it can operate properly. He says that deep inside, everyone already knows everything. By freeing the mind so it can function naturally, we're able to tap into that place of wisdom and knowing that dwells within us. As a result, we learn to speak a language that's not of man, but is of Mother Nature. It's a more beautiful, efficient, and natural language than the one to which we are accustomed.

There's so much more to say, but I'm too tired to go on right now.

Take care,

Nathaniel

♦ ♦ ♦ ◈ ♦ ♦ ♦

The abrupt ending of the letter almost got me angry again. Exactly like conversations with my father, I was left hanging and feeling ignored. Enough! I'd had it. I wasn't going to let those old issues with Dad cloud my friendship with Nathaniel. But he sure did push the same buttons!

Nathaniel remained in India for several years. He continued to send me letters regularly, but I always sensed he would not, and could not, share some of his most powerful experiences. He would never tell me where his teachers were. He said few people care to be in the public eye, and that's so for saints as well. They gave him strict instructions not to share the information of their full names or whereabouts with anyone. He always obeyed those instructions.

Then one day, I received the following letter:

••• ◈ •••

Dear Bruce,

Surya has instructed me to go back to the United States and finish my college education. I'm making arrangements to return to Columbus.

I look forward to seeing you soon.

Nathaniel

••• ◈ •••

So, Nathaniel was coming home. My reaction surprised me. I was a little scared. What would he be like? After India, would he still want anything to do with me?

I was still divided in how I felt about Nathaniel. On one hand, he was a wise seer. I wanted to know more about him and wanted to hear all about his experiences in India. On the other hand, something about him bothered me. Sometimes he felt like a self-indulgent know-it-all. How could he be so sure he knew so many things better than everybody else? Sometimes I felt like he was crazy and I had to be crazy to listen to him. But I had to admit that when I really paid attention to what I felt, there was a longing for what Nathaniel had, without really knowing exactly what that was. And that is what bothered me about him the most. I just couldn't let that longing go.

Chapter 16

The Light of the Moon

When he arrived home, it was summer break. We met at his parents' house. Nathaniel had lost some weight, but looked healthy and bright. It was a warm night and we sat on lawn chairs in the backyard. The moon was a slight sliver in the dark clear sky. We could even make out the Milky Way. The air was sweet and clear.

"Bruce, remember that summer day when we were little kids and you rode your bike over in the morning and found me chasing that gold frog?"

We were sitting a short distance from where the frog was sighted. "I sure do. In fact, it's the oddest thing. To this day, I have a very clear picture of that frog in my head, even though I never actually saw it!"

"Those were wonderful days, weren't they?"

"Yes, they were," I fondly agreed. "Scorpion is still leaning against the back wall in my parents' garage. Short of needing air in the tires, he's still ready to go.

"By the way, Nathaniel, I thought you'd like to know that I tried to call Michelle while you were in India. I suspected the Surya Meditation she taught came from your guru, Surya. I wanted to ask her if she knew anything about that. But I couldn't find her anywhere. I guess she graduated and moved away."

"Yeah, I realized the same thing. It's exactly the same meditation they practice in the ashram, so I'm sure it came from Surya. But it would be interesting to talk with Michelle...." After remaining quiet for a bit, he changed the subject.

"Remember those experiences I was having a few years ago, around the time we started going to those free lectures?" Nathaniel asked.

I nodded. How could I forget? It was around that time our friendship really started to become closer.

"When I went to India, I really needed to ask Surya about my experiences. He was always so accessible, but whenever I wanted to ask him about it, I could never get to him. There was always a place he needed to run off to or a crowd of people assembled around him. I got really frustrated with this after a time, but vowed to keep trying until I had the opportunity to talk to him. Finally, the perfect chance came. He stood right there in front of me with nowhere to retreat, and I approached him.

"'Guruji,' I began. 'I had an experience not long ago that changed my life.'

"As I described it, he became restless and said, 'Yes, yes, yes, very good, doesn't matter, just continue,' and he walked briskly away.

"He had always been so open, except for that moment. At first I couldn't comprehend it, but now I've come to understand his behavior. You see, Bruce, it's not appropriate to label yourself as 'enlightened.' First of all, it's like trying to win a gold star that says you're the special one. Labeling it like that dishonors its purity. Secondly, speaking it out is a bit like walking around outside naked. It's simply not proper. It should remain something more personal and intimate. Trying to wear it like a medal has many tentacles that reach in unhealthy directions. A person's experiences create who that person is. That's all. As time passes, I more and more appreciate how wise Surya's response to me was."

We remained quiet for a time until I said, "Nathaniel, tell me how your trip to India changed you."

"It didn't." Nathaniel grinned and softly chuckled.

I silently waited for an explanation.

"One afternoon, I was sitting with Surya and a number of his disciples. The mood was light and playful. At one point, Surya said, 'Here I am a spiritual teacher with so many coming to me to evolve, but the truth is, people don't change at all!' And with that, Surya let out a laugh."

"What?!" I interrupted, "are you telling me that Surya is a phony?"

"No, no, no, not at all. I'm trying to say that evolution is not about changing your personality—the way you think, behave, or feel. It's more subtle than that. You don't change your personality. You change your relationship with your personality. What you are on the surface of life is of very little importance. True development of character lies deeper."

We sat quietly as I pondered what Nathaniel had said. His personality was somewhat reserved and at times even aloof. His parents were certainly that way. In fact, I remember thinking they reminded me of Ward and June Cleaver from the television show, *Leave It to Beaver*. But what about him was deeper than that?

After some silence, Nathaniel changed the subject. "What an incredibly beautiful night this is. Look at all the stars. When the moon is a sliver like that, I like to imagine it as a ball in a big dark room with a flashlight shining on it from an angle. It has such a different feeling than when I view it as a sliver in the sky."

I still had many questions regarding what he said about Surya, but I didn't want to push it any further. I was beginning to suspect he knew best about such things.

Nathaniel continued. "In India, they say it's good to stand in the moonlight. It creates soma in the body. The moonlight is pure soma."

"What's soma?" I asked.

"Soma," Nathaniel said, "nourishes the deepest level of your being. It's referred to as the nectar of immortality, the ambrosia of the gods. The moon is the mother, all about feelings and nourishment. She is the life-giver and the one who gives life meaning."

We remained quiet as we looked up to the sky.

Though hesitant to break the silence, I decided to mention something that had been on my mind. "Nathaniel, I really appreciated the letters I received from you. The conversational way you wrote them made me feel like I was right there with you."

Nathaniel was gazing at the moon as he spoke. "Writing can convey such beautiful and sublime feelings, but actually I think you're probably a better writer than I am."

"Really? How so?" My curiosity was aroused.

"I think you're more of a romantic than I am and probably more sentimental. In that sense, I'd say you're more like the moon and I'm more like the sun, intense."

Nathaniel's description of himself made me chuckle. "Yeah, I guess you are pretty intense. But you know, Nathaniel, I never really thought of myself as a romantic."

Nathaniel stood up and as he began to walk, casually said over his shoulder, "Time will tell."

Then we both strolled through the backyard and into the house. Mathew wasn't around, no doubt off with his girlfriend. Nathaniel and I visited with his parents. Though the conversation was heart-warming and sweet, what I really wanted to do was hear more about what Nathaniel learned in India. When I was getting ready to leave, Nathaniel handed me some of his writing, and simply said, "I'd like you to check this out and let me know what you think."

The cover page read, "Ancient Scripture Reinterpreted." It was like he'd read my mind. I protected my treasure carefully as I left their house and made my way home.

Chapter 17

Reflections from Within the Looking Glass

I hurried to get ready for bed. Turning on the small bedside lamp, I crawled under the covers. The sweet evening air poured in through my open bedroom window. The sound of crickets in the distance comforted me as I settled in and began to read.

The first line read, "To understand life, it must be viewed from within the looking glass."

I liked the feeling of those words, but wasn't sure what he meant.

What followed were well-known quotes with Nathaniel's comments. The first quote simply read, "...the kingdom of heaven dwells within. Luke 17:21."

I knew Nathaniel was not particularly into Christianity, so I was a little surprised by the first quote. I had expected them all to be Buddhist or Taoist, or at least some sort of Eastern philosophy. Interestingly, his commentary was in the form of a poem:

> An underlying basis to all existence
> The unified field of physics
> Where all things are one.
> The source of you
> me
> everything.

Its nature…infinite
    order
    harmony
    intelligence.
It created and sustains the universe.
Experience it: "the kingdom of heaven, within."

I was intrigued and wondered if he was leading up to something. The next quote read, "The sound of one hand clapping."

Anything…one with everything else
    abundant with the knowledge of all.
To name something
    to label it
      to think we understand it
        is to compromise it.
Its true nature…
    vast
    unfathomable
    ungraspable
    "the sound of one hand clapping."

I wasn't sure I knew exactly what he was talking about here, but I got the general idea. Actually, I guess that was the point. To define something exactly was to compromise it. I liked that. It was sort of a relief. Boy, it was different than what I'd been doing with my psychology work. There I'd been trying to name every thought and emotion I had. I pondered and then read on.

The next quote was from an ancient Indian text, called the Bhagavad Gita: "Be without the three gunas."

I knew very little about the three gunas, but did know they referred to what Hindus called the relative aspect of life, or worldly life, or some such thing.

"Be without the three gunas"
People believe that to be spiritual,
> *you must have no worldly possessions*
> *or live in a cave.*

This is not so. You can be spiritual and live in the world
> *yet not be lost to the world*
> *not be overwhelmed by the world.*

Your essence remains untouched.

The kingdom of heaven resides
beyond the three gunas.

I didn't know about that. There Nathaniel went again. What made him the authority?

I caught myself. There *I* went again. It was easy for me to perceive Nathaniel as arrogant. But there was something to what he was saying and I wanted to give it an honest chance. So I kept reading.

"And Jesus said unto them, I am the bread of life; He that cometh to me shall never hunger; and he that believeth in me shall never thirst. John 6:35."

Jesus knew he was one with The Source of all that is
> *the Unified Field*
> *"the bread of life"*

Jesus said "cometh to me"
> *the unified field*
> *"the kingdom of heaven within"*
> *the wellspring, the source of all.*

Fantastic that you can actually find
> *the kingdom of heaven within.*
They call it enlightenment.

That was quite beautiful. I felt a calm come over me. Imagine if it were really true—everyone could discover the kingdom of heaven within. I wondered if Nathaniel had discovered it within himself.

What Nathaniel was saying was actually beginning to make sense, though I had to twist my brain to grasp it. But as I allowed myself to do that, I became even more fascinated. I turned the page.

"Truly, I say to you, whoever does not receive the kingdom of God like a child shall not enter it. Mark 10:15."

Children
> *hearts open*
> *minds unconditioned*
> *free*
> *unprogrammed by*
>> *parents*
>> *teachers*
>> *friends*
>> *religions.*

Recognizing your conditioning is challenging
> *letting it go is even harder.*

To do so is to become like a child again
> *open*
> *unencumbered.*

Only then can you know your own true nature
> *rest into yourself*
> *enter "the kingdom of heaven"*
> *become enlightened.*

WHAM! That hit me right between the eyes. That was it! Wasn't that what we did in psychology? We looked at our issues, our programming, from our parents and all of our other life experiences. I wasn't sure what enlightenment really was, but whatever it was, I knew I wanted it.

"Then God said, 'Let us make man in our image, according to our likeness; let them have dominion over the fish of the sea, and over the birds of the air, and over the cattle, and over all the earth and over every creeping thing that creeps upon the earth.' Genesis 1:26."

Darwin said, "species evolve."
To evolve...
>*to gravitate back to Oneness*
>*to the likeness of God.*

Darwinism (biology), creationism (spirituality)
>*two views of the same one process*
>*evolution.*

You can become a beacon light
>*radiate harmony*
>>*bliss*
>>*intelligence*
>>*wisdom*
>>*"over the fish of the sea, and over the birds of*
>>*the air, and over the cattle, and over all the*
>>*earth and over every creeping thing that*
>>*creeps upon the earth."*

Now I was really feeling inspired. Remarkable! That was certainly a different take on humanity. What if it was actually true? Darwinism and Creationism, two sides of the same coin. That was major.

Humans
>*like cars with big engines*
>>*powerful.*
Drive carefully.

Now *that* I agreed with. I was starting to like the way Nathaniel thought. I was really getting tired, but forced myself to read on.

The next quote was also from Genesis: "...'We may eat of the fruit of the trees of the garden; but God said, 'You shall not eat of the fruit of the tree which is in the midst of the garden, neither shall you touch it, lest you die.' Genesis 3:2-3."

Be spiritual
> *<u>and</u> live in the world.*

But do not lose your Self
> *do not eat "of the fruit of the tree which is in*
> *the midst of the garden."*

To lose your Self is to "die."
As Ramakrishna said,
> *"the trick is to*
> > *have the boat in the water,*
> > *but no water in the boat."*

This is the secret to life.

"To lose your Self is to die" sounded a little strong. Was he trying to say that if you were not enlightened, you were dead? Well, maybe not. The Ramakrishna quote was cool, but was that all there was to the secret of life?

I was really sleepy. I flipped through the pages to get an overview of Nathaniel's work. There were quotes from many religions and even from some scientists and mathematicians. These quotes pointed to the idea that great people throughout history had all shared this understanding of life. Yet, they had expressed it in different ways and with varying degrees of clarity.

I went to the last page to check out the final quote:

"'The only true wisdom is knowing that you know nothing.' —Socrates."

I was wondering what he would finish with. Interesting choice.

For every perspective
> *a labyrinth*
> > *of equally valid*
> > *yet contradictory perspectives.*

The wise
> *see this absurdity*
> *even as they state their perspectives.*

Using perspectives
    free yourself
        from the labyrinth of perspectives.

However, to do so
    you must listen carefully
        think carefully
        reflect and ponder.

Use perspectives
    to free yourself
        from the clutches of your perspective.

Thereby, attain wisdom.

I rolled over and pulled up the covers. Man, I hoped he wasn't saying my psychology training was just another perspective. That would really make me mad. But forget it. I was too tired to deal with it.

The night air, the sound of the crickets, and the soft pillow began to overtake me. It was all I could do to reach up and shut out the light before I drifted off to sleep.

Chapter 18

The Essential Search

After undergraduate school, I had begun to assist in personal growth workshops while taking master's degree courses part time. In the spring, I took a class on human behavior. I liked my professor, Dr. Winters. She encouraged us to do our own thinking and to express our personal opinions of the classical perspectives in modern psychology. Our grade for her entire course was based upon one assignment—to write a paper on what determines human behavior. I decided to use it as an opportunity to develop my thoughts on the matter.

That evening, I walked out on the Oval. It was a beautiful spring day, particularly warm for that time of year. I sat on a bench underneath a cluster of tall oak trees and looked out over the fresh cut grass, illuminated by the rays of light from the setting sun. At the far end of the Oval, an elderly couple sat on their lawn chairs sharing a newspaper. I imagined they lived just off campus and frequented the Oval on evenings as beautiful as this.

Looking out over the Oval, I pondered over the subject and form my paper would take. The laboratory for my study, I decided, would be my own awareness. I would examine how I experienced and processed my thoughts and emotions. I would try to determine what contributed to the formation of my mind. What structured it? How did one person's mind function differently from another's? What, in those terms, defined the nature of human behavior and psychological health?

I concluded that the nature of memory and how it factored into the equation of life was of particular importance. It had an odd way of coloring things. When viewed through the eyes of memory, seemingly insignificant events turned out to be crucial. Then again, some seemingly important events turned out to be irrelevant. I realized that memory was a vital part of the equation, and yet it was so abstract and intangible. That image of the golden frog from my childhood. It still floated in the depths of my memory. But why? What did it mean?

I started writing. "What leaves impressions upon the hidden facets of my mind and heart, what molds the textures and contours of my soul, what cultures my consciousness and determines the nature of my behavior is accessible only abstractly through the portal of my memory." Pretty poetic. It sounded more like something for an English class than a psychology class, but I had to start somewhere.

I sat on that bench for over an hour. In time it became a bit chilly, so I went into the library and continued to write down my thoughts. Over the next weeks, I worked hard on that paper, relieved when I finally turned it in. Eventually, the day came when our papers had been graded and were to be returned to us. I apprehensively sat in my seat as Dr. Winters passed them out one at a time. She walked by my desk, giving me a brief glance and subtle nod as she set my paper in front of me, face down. I nervously turned it over and saw an "A" at the top. Proud, I relaxed in my seat.

Funny how that paper created more confusion than clarity. It marked a major shift in my life. Prior to that time, I searched the world for answers to my questions. After that time, I realized the essential search had to take place within me. Yet I didn't know how to proceed. And I had no idea where it would lead me.

Chapter 19
What Matters?

The next few years sped by in a blur. I became engrossed in my life as did Nathaniel, so we didn't see much of each other. From time to time, I thought about him and I wondered if our friendship was dwindling. One moment, I was his touchstone, and the next, our paths barely crossed. However, I did talk to Mathew on the phone with some regularity. I was quite surprised when Mathew told me Nathaniel had switched his major and decided to become a veterinarian. I was offended and hurt that Nathaniel didn't even tell me. Had we really grown *that* far apart? I wondered if I'd ever be his confidant again.

Not wanting to dump that on Mathew, I simply asked him why Nathaniel changed his major.

"I don't know," he said. "I've given up trying to figure Nathaniel out. When I asked him about it, he said something about physics only describing how existence works instead of asking what existence actually *is*. He said the same thing about *life*. He said that M.D.'s only study one small point on the spectrum of life. He said he wanted to study the full spectrum of life, from amoebas to humans. He went on and on, saying, 'Science only describes how life *works*. It does not understand what life actually *is*.'

"If you ask me, my brother has gone off the deep end. He said understanding and working with living beings is 'his path'! Can you believe that? I guess he went into veterinary medicine to try to understand life. He wanted to help all living creatures. I don't know. I give up. My brother is weird."

Nathaniel did become a veterinarian and opened what quickly became a thriving practice near Clearwater, Florida. He had a great deal of good fortune in real estate during the boom days of the seventies and lived in a huge beautiful home nestled in the tall Florida pines. He "had it made" and was well known and respected in the community.

Several years later, I took a vacation to visit Mathew who had relocated to Miami, Florida. On the way back home, I stopped in Tampa to see Nathaniel. He was busy with his practice, so we only met for lunch. He invited me to meet him at the four-star restaurant Bon Appetite, his favorite place to dine. It was on the water in Dunedin. He told me we'd be required to wear a coat and tie.

I watched the pelicans along the boat docks until Nathaniel arrived. I could tell he was busy, even rushed. Though he was excited to see me, he was obviously preoccupied with his practice. He led the way into the restaurant, where all the waiters wore tuxedos. His usual waiter, Sergio, greeted us and showed the way to Nathaniel's favorite table. It was near a window overlooking the water. The table was set with a very fine tablecloth, beautiful cut crystal glassware, and delicate porcelain plates. The place was completely first class.

I asked Nathaniel if he ate there often.

"Yeah, several times a week. The food here is great."

Nathaniel reminded me of a busy business executive. His mind functioned quickly. He appeared to be juggling ten thoughts at once. His motions were jerky. At the same time, I could tell he was doing very well. His lifestyle didn't seem to be unhealthy, just very active.

After lunch, Sergio brought over the pastry cart. Nathaniel insisted I sample a couple of his favorites. Sergio happily divided each of the two desserts into equal parts so we could both try them. He then refilled our cups with coffee and left us.

Partway through dessert, Nathaniel reached into the pocket of his sports jacket, pulled out a thick envelope, and set it on the table in front of me. "Bruce, I'm sorry it took me so long to get this back to you."

I lifted the envelope and looked inside to find a stack of one hundred dollar bills.

"This is to pay back, with interest, the loan you gave me so I could go to India. I'll never be able to thank you enough."

I looked up from the money and into Nathaniel's eyes. It was then I knew for sure that my old friend, Nathaniel, was still there inside that busy businessman body with all the same depth, love, and wisdom. I understood in that moment that for Nathaniel, our friendship transcended time. It didn't matter to him at all that we had spoken quite infrequently over the past several years. The look in his eyes told me I was still his confidant, still as dear to him as I ever was. Feeling into the timelessness of our friendship was for me an unusual sensation. We picked up exactly where we left off. That timeless feeling reassured me Nathaniel would always be my friend and I would always be his confidant.

"Nathaniel," I said, "you've already paid me back many times over. I can't possibly accept this money." I smiled and pushed the envelope back towards him.

The love in Nathaniel's eyes overwhelmed me. In that moment, I learned that true spirituality has little to do with a mellow or peaceful demeanor. It has everything to do with what dwells within a person's heart and soul. Every time I was around Nathaniel, I learned one more spiritual lesson.

After we finished our dessert, Nathaniel hurried back to work and I rushed off to the airport to catch my flight.

During the flight home, I reflected on my visit with Nathaniel. On the surface, his life was intense and chaotic. But when I looked into his eyes, I sensed what resided deep within him. In that moment, I more fully understood that looking at the surface of a person's life means little. The depth is what really matters.

Chapter 20
Paupers and Kings

Over the next couple of years, Nathaniel called me from Florida with some regularity. Because he was so busy, I always waited for him to phone. But after a number of months without communication, I called him. He immediately started to tell me about a beautiful, hot Sunday afternoon in June when he and his current girlfriend, Kathy, had entertained some friends.

"We all grilled a fantastic lunch beside the screened-in pool," Nathaniel said. "Everyone enjoyed swimming and sitting in the Jacuzzi. Around mid-afternoon, I quietly broke away from the group and began to wander from room to room in my huge palatial home. I ended up in the master bedroom, sitting alone on the corner of my king-size bed.

"It was very strange. An odd feeling came over me. It was like I was connected to something. The connection was beyond space and time. But it was very real. I could feel it."

Nathaniel was quiet for a moment. I said nothing. I could tell he was going somewhere with this, and didn't want to interrupt.

"I could feel something inside me. It was calling to me. The words, 'It's time to go back to India,' popped into my mind and tugged at my soul."

I still didn't say anything to Nathaniel. There was silence on the phone. It was a strange feeling. It seemed as if he was engrossed in thought.

Finally, he began to speak again. "Everything shifted in that instant. My life in Florida was over—just like that. It was done."

Dazed, I murmured, "Nathaniel, are you crazy? What are you doing?"

Nathaniel responded in a monotone. "Well Bruce, everybody's having that same response. Kathy is really upset. But what can I say? I have to do this. When my attorney found out, he went ballistic, but my mind was made up."

"Nathaniel, why don't you calm down and give it some time," I urged. "You don't want to do something you'll end up regretting."

But Nathaniel cut me off. "Bruce, all this happened a few months ago. I've already sold my house, my practice, all my real estate holdings, my cars, and all my material possessions except for what I can carry in two suitcases. My bags are packed and I'm leaving in the morning."

I was stunned. It was so abrupt. For a moment, I sat in silent suspension. Why hadn't he told me earlier? Nathaniel left no room for discussion. I just wished him a good trip and got off the phone as soon as I could. When I hung up the phone, I leaned forward in my chair, put my elbows on my knees, closed my eyes, and hung my head in confusion. What would happen to Nathaniel now...now that he had thrown everything away?

Nathaniel disappeared to India. The months turned into years. Whenever I thought of him, an eerie hollow feeling overtook me. It was as if the place he once occupied in the world had become an empty mystical void. His letters, which eventually came with regularity, carried a strange, dreamlike quality.

•••◊•••

Dear Bruce,

The ashram is austere. My room is plain: stucco walls, cement floor, a cot, and one small three-legged stool. I eat a simple lunch of rice, dahl (lentils), and veggies, which is my only large meal of the day.

My routine is intense. I start at 1:30 a.m. with a quick bath, a cup of tea, and herbal supplements. Then I meditate alone in my room until noon. After lunch, I visit with one or more of my teachers and return to my meditation until bedtime. This routine is only interrupted occasionally when one of my teachers sends me on a journey to visit a saint or guru. They're always careful about where they send me. So many teachers are merely spiritual actors who think they understand spirituality, but really don't.

My teachers do not wish to be critical of others. The topic of spiritual actors actually saddens them. Surya once spoke of it this way: If a pauper puts on the clothes of a king, he may believe that he is truly a king. He may convince many others he is a king. Yet in truth, he is still a pauper. Surya emphasized, "It is important to always protect your mind. Never forget that."

I'll write you again soon,

Nathaniel

••• ◈ •••

At least Nathaniel seemed happy about returning to India. What mattered to him was deep thought—not a nice house, prestige, or money. Even as a small child, he had been that way. Like when I visited Mathew one day. Little Nathaniel was walking thoughtfully outside their house with his arms behind his back, totally absorbed. I wondered if, at his age, he was even allowed to be outside alone. It was a strange scene. He walked as if he was very old, even ancient. That demeanor caused me to approach him with reservation.

"Nathaniel, what are you up to?" I asked.

"Oh, I'm just taking a walk and thinking," he replied. The heaviness in his heart didn't match his young age.

"Is something the matter?"

"I'm worried about the world. It isn't fitting together right."

Saying nothing, I backed off and walked away. When I was his age, I didn't even know there was something called "the world."

Surya, like Nathaniel, was obviously a deep thinker. I liked his expression "protect your mind." It made me think. Psychological health requires that you protect your mind. An accumulation of negative memories affects the psyche adversely. And an accumulation of positive memories affects the psyche in a positive manner. Memory is a barometer of psychological health.

However, two people having the same experience remember it differently. Psyche affects memory. And, memory affects psyche. It works both ways. Fascinating.

Nathaniel's letters seemed to manifest out of the ether. He was like a ghost in a dream, as if he no longer existed in physical reality. When his next letter appeared, it carried with it that same mystical feeling.

◆ ◆ ◆ ◆ ◆ ◆ ◆

Dear Bruce,

One morning, my meditation was interrupted by a knock at the door. I was told to get ready to leave. I was being sent to see Vasistha again. The news made me happy. I remembered my visit to this little fellow with the Nehru hat the last time I was in India. Though I didn't quite recall our conversation, I did recall the sweet, wise presence of Vasistha.

During my journey to Vasistha's hut, I became absorbed with the love I felt for my life in India. The delicacy of the knowledge enthralls me. But then Bruce, my thoughts turned to the teachers we experienced together in America. It saddened me. I feel people are ready for a much deeper level of understanding and I long to give it. So right then, I made a decision. I'm coming back to the United States to teach.

I was excited to share this with Vasistha. Upon my arrival, the same old Indian woman escorted me to his hut. And there he was in his Nehru hat, sitting on a cot with his little head tilting from side to side.

When I gave him the news, Vasistha looked at me with a perplexed and painful look on his face. "Why do you want to go out in all of that mud?"

Staggered, I took two steps back. Exactly like last time, the rest of the conversation was a blur.

During my journey back to the ashram, I was confused. Vasistha responded as if I had gone crazy. But the last time I saw him, he told me I was destined to spend my life teaching in the United States! Somehow I found that funny and I suspect he did too.

Back in the ashram, I tried to ask Surya about my decision, but he suddenly became unavailable. I felt like he was avoiding me, like he did years ago when I wanted to ask him about my enlightenment experiences.

Finally, I realized what was happening. If I had to ask whether I was ready to take on the role of a teacher, then I was not ready. If I had to ask, I was still a student. I reflected for some time until I arrived at what was, I am sure, the right decision: It is time for me to leave.

Your friend,
Nathaniel

••• ◊ •••

I laughed out loud. There you go Nathaniel, now people are turning the table and throwing *you* a curve for a change! How does *that* feel?

Four weeks later, I learned that Nathaniel was back in the United States, living among the redwoods in northern California.

Chapter 21
Lake Hope

After receiving my master's degree in psychology, I went into private practice for several years. You'd think after all of this psychology training, I could've found a good relationship. But things didn't work out that way. I was currently dating Leslie, whom I met through one of my psychology associates. She was a newscaster for Channel 6, a local TV station. Leslie was short and slim with brown hair, brown eyes, and always immaculately dressed. Her hobby was fashion. She had a huge closet filled with beautiful clothes. Shopping malls, beauty salons, and high-end designer stores were her passion. She was always prompting me to attend concerts, fine restaurants, art exhibits, and the like.

One afternoon when Leslie was over at my house, she saw the large stack of letters and journal entries from Nathaniel that I'd been accumulating over the years.

"What's this?" she asked.

"Oh, these are letters from a friend I've known since childhood."

As she flipped through the envelopes, she pointed out an exotic postage stamp. "Where does he live, Tibet?"

"Oh, he lived in India for a time, but he's back in the States now. He's quite a character."

"Oh yeah?" she said. "Tell me about it."

"Gee, I don't know where to begin. How do you explain

Nathaniel to somebody? Let me just tell you some stories, okay?"

"Works for me," she replied.

"Well, his older brother, Mathew, and I were best friends growing up. Once Mathew invited me to go with them on their family vacation to Lake Hope."

"Oh yeah, I know Lake Hope. It's a few hours south of here, isn't it?"

"Yeah, something like that. Anyway, it was a summer while we were in high school. We took boats out on the lake almost every day. Nathaniel liked the canoes, but we preferred the more spacious rowboats. One steamy hot day, while we sat under a tree on the banks of the lake, I asked Nathaniel why he liked canoes.

"He said they made him feel like he wasn't really here. The way they cut through the water made him feel like he was cutting through time and space. That answer was typically Nathaniel, mysterious and odd.

"When I asked him why he didn't want to be here, he said, 'Well, think about it. If your body was really healthy, there would be no friction. If there was no friction, there'd be no interaction with anything. So you'd disappear. Wouldn't you?'

"I looked out over the water in silence, then finally told him, 'Well, Nathaniel, I'd have to take your word for it.'

"He stared off into space like he commonly did. After awhile he said, 'I'm wondering if anything *really* exists. Do you know what I mean?'

"I said no and asked him to explain.

"He sighed and said he didn't really know. 'It was only a feeling.'"

Anticipating a negative reaction, I looked at Leslie and said, "What do you think?"

"I don't know what to say. Tell me more." She maintained a perfect poker face.

Leaning back on the couch, my thoughts returned to Lake Hope. "Well, the next evening, Mathew, Nathaniel, and I sat outside the mountain-top lodge, our feet resting on the stone wall that encircled the patio. We looked out at the lake below and the sun as it set over the distant mountains. Mathew soon got restless and decided to take a walk. Nathaniel was content to sit and talk. I was feeling that same way.

"Pointing in the direction of the sun, Nathaniel said, 'That's me.'

"I asked him what that was supposed to mean.

"'Oh,' he said, 'there's a picture in my mind that I doodle sometimes. Two arches that look like those two mountains with another tiny arch, the sun, peeking out between them. Usually it's the sun. Other times it's the moon. I'll put a few lines below the mountains. They represent a field, maybe a pasture, or water, like a lake.'

"I liked the image. By that time, I knew Nathaniel's moods pretty well, so I remained quiet, expecting him to say more.

"He did. 'Everybody has a picture they draw or at least imagine. It's a symbol of what makes them tick. It's who they are.'

"I tried to think of mine, but I couldn't."

"I can't think of mine either," Leslie volunteered. From the sound of her voice, I could tell she wasn't into it, but at this point, I didn't care. I just wanted to tell Nathaniel stories.

"I asked Nathaniel what his picture symbolized.

"'On the other side of those mountains, you don't find the sun,' he said, 'just two more mountains with the sun beyond them. It goes on and on like that forever.'

"As often happened with Nathaniel, I didn't know what he meant. So, I just sat with it. I told him that his comment was similar to what he'd said about canoes.

"He agreed, saying it had the same intangible feeling."

Leslie interrupted me. "What does that mean?"

"To tell you the truth, I'm not even sure. I wondered if he even knew, but I didn't say anything. We sat there for a bit, enjoying the view."

Leslie had a blank look on her face, but I ignored it and came up with more Nathaniel stories. I was starting to have fun.

"Oh, here's a good one," I told her. "On Saturdays when we were kids, our parents would drop us off at The Boulevard Theater, where we'd meet my cousins, Cliff and James. We'd first run into the White Castle on the corner of Fifth Avenue and Northwest Boulevard for an eleven-cent square hamburger and a frosty. Then we'd run next door to the theater where, for fifty cents, we'd see a double feature. The first stop in the theater was always the snack stand. We'd stock up for the day with popcorn, sodas, Jujubes, and M&M's. Everybody else liked Jujubes, but I thought they were obnoxious. I would sit in my chair trying to pick them out of my teeth as I watched the movie. Of course, that never stopped me from eating my share of those disgusting little nuggets!"

Leslie laughed as I continued my story.

"Previews of coming attractions always included aliens attacking the earth, a mummy or a zombie cornering some girl, and a war film. We would reliably call out, 'Real! Fake! Fake! Real! Real!' with each war scene. Whoever called out correctly first, won a point.

"One day the main feature was about the lost continent of Atlantis. Crystal power and magic elixirs ruled. When they showed an Atlantean sorcerer pouring a magic elixir down someone's throat, I could sense Nathaniel tensing up.

"I leaned over and asked him what was wrong.

"'I remember making those elixirs,' his frightened little voice whispered.

"I wondered what in the world he was talking about. Nathaniel was always giving me the creeps."

Then I remembered: "Years ago, I was at their house and Mathew was looking at a science book. It had drawings of people from other races including a blue race. Mathew asked his mom if there was such a race. She couldn't say for sure, but Nathaniel insisted that there was. I wondered how he could possibly have known that."

"You're not thinking of reincarnation, are you?" Leslie smirked.

"Well, listen to this." I was getting excited. "When I was in junior high, Mathew, Nathaniel, and I went to a bookstore. Nathaniel was still in elementary school at the time. When I noticed Nathaniel strolling off to the religion section, I followed him. He pulled a book off the shelf and quickly flipped through the pages, until his whole body suddenly recoiled.

"Looking over his shoulder, I asked what was wrong.

"'Oh nothing,' he said.

"I grabbed the book out of his hand and looked at the page he had turned to as Nathaniel scurried away. Now here's the weird thing. It was a picture of a Dali Lama from the nineteenth century. Nathaniel didn't have time to read the next page, but I did. And guess what?"

"What?" she asked.

I hoped she was really interested.

"The Dali Lama's life story was identical to a story Nathaniel had told me earlier. Though he didn't understand how or why, he had experienced the Dali Lama's life. He remembered it."

"Are you telling me you believe that he was the Dali Lama in a past life?" Leslie rolled her eyes.

Her reaction annoyed me. "I'm just telling you what happened. Make your own decision."

She shook her head as I thought of another Nathaniel story.

"A few years ago when I was in Florida, I had lunch with Nathaniel."

"I thought he was living in India," Leslie said.

"Well, yeah, but he's a veterinarian and had a practice in Florida until he sold it to join the ashram."

"The ashram? What's an ashram?"

"It's sort of like a monastery, a place where people devote their lives to spiritual growth."

"Are you saying he left his practice to be in an ashram?"

Chuckling, I nodded and continued. "Listen to this. While we were at lunch, an elderly lady came by our table and gushed over Nathaniel.

"'Oh, Dr. Harrison, I can't thank you enough. Suzie is doing so great now!' She went on and on.

"'Well, Mrs. Skocher, I must say, I'm delighted,' Nathaniel warmly responded.

"When she left the table I asked Nathaniel about her.

"'She's a sweet little lady who brings her dog to me. That dog is everything to her.' Nathaniel looked away in a manner that said there was more to it, so I pressed him.

"'Come on, Nathaniel, I know that look. What gives?'

"'Oh, you know,' he shrugged his shoulders and looked down.

"'No I don't,' I prodded. 'Come on, what is it?' I was enjoying his shyness.

"He was embarrassed to tell me that Mrs. Skocher's friend said he had healing powers. She insisted that when he held her dog, all its warts went away. So, when Mrs. Skocher's dog got inoperable cancer, she brought it to Nathaniel and the dog spontaneously got better. Evidently, this created quite a ruckus in the community. People were bringing their pets to Nathaniel just so he'd hold them. And they got better! It all embarrassed Nathaniel. He said he simply wanted to have a traditional practice."

"Are you trying to tell me he has magical healing powers?" Leslie blurted out.

"I don't know," I shook my head. "But I can tell you a lot of people were absolutely convinced of it."

"Well, do you think Nathaniel believes he has healing powers?"

"If you understood Nathaniel like I do, you'd realize he'd never acknowledge such powers even if he knew he had them. But if you want, I've got a million more Nathaniel stories."

Leslie responded with a smug, "Yeah, well, I don't know. I'm not really into that kind of stuff. To be honest, your friend Nathaniel sounds like a real nut case."

Zap. That cut right to my quick. It was okay if I knocked Nathaniel, but I really didn't like other people doing it. Especially Leslie, when she hadn't even met him.

Leslie sarcastically continued. "I'm not into that hocus-pocus sci-fi stuff. I like movies, dinner parties, and having fun. I'm not interested in getting caught up in any of this craziness. I just want to live a normal life."

"Normal? You call a life of movies and parties normal?" I felt my anger flaring up. "I call *that* ordinary."

Leslie again rolled her eyes and condescendingly mumbled, "Oh brother."

Feeling she was treating me like dirt, I lost my temper. "No wait a minute. I call it superficial, mundane, *and* ordinary."

Clearly insulted, Leslie stood up, grabbed her designer jacket and made it for the door. "Look it, I really don't need this. And besides, I've got to go home and get ready. I'm going to a party tonight."

I was shocked. It all happened so abruptly. I came to my senses and tried to apologize. "Gosh, I'm sorry. I didn't mean it. I was only trying to make a point."

"Yeah, whatever," she said. "That's fine. Don't worry about it."

I could tell she wasn't being sincere. But then again, neither was I. In that moment, I realized she actually was superficial, mundane, and ordinary. Not to mention boring. Alas, one more relationship bit the dust.

Chapter 22
Realities and the Persian Rug

While I was continuing to pursue a healthy relationship, Nathaniel again disappeared from the face of the earth. Strangely, he felt closer when he was in India. At least then he communicated with some regularity. Finally, a brief note arrived:

••• ◈ •••

Dear Bruce,

I rented a small cabin in the mountains of Northern California. My life is simple. I enjoy it day by day.

Hope you are doing well.

Your friend,

Nathaniel

••• ◈ •••

The next correspondence was a remarkable entry from his journal:

••• ◈ •••

Before I fall asleep at night, I lie in bed and in my awareness float over the nearby mountains and lake. I particularly enjoy floating over the lake on full moon nights. On windy evenings, I soar like a leaf in the wind, skimming just above the water. I can smell the mist as it rises from the choppy waters and feel the refreshing dew against my face and brow. Then I twist up with the draft, curving back around and about in whatever direction I'm carried.

Over time, I ventured off beyond the mountains, coming to small farms and towns, even floating over large cities. One day I was looking over a map. To my astonishment, all of the roads, towns, and cities were on that map, exactly as I saw them! I thought those travels were just imaginary fun. But now I know they were real!

My understanding of the word "imagination" has changed as a result. It's far beyond fantasy. Now I realize imagination, in its deepest form, is awareness functioning from the level of your being where you already know everything.

One afternoon last week, I decided to lie down for a nap. Before I dozed off, I found myself up against the ceiling, looking down at my body on the bed! I instantly realized I could go anywhere.

I had the thought, "Mars" and immediately found myself shooting out of the room and through the blackness of space towards Mars!

Then I thought, "other galaxies," and straight away, I zoomed past planets and stars, accelerating through the universe.

I was astonished, thrilled, and fascinated, but then I suddenly became terrified. What if I couldn't get back?! Suddenly, I felt a powerful jolt as I slammed back into my body. The jolt was physically painful. I realized it was unhealthy to travel around without my body! So, I stopped the practice.

Sometimes when I lie in bed at night and wrap my head in a pillow, if I'm extremely quiet and listen carefully, I can hear music, very beautiful music. Often it's a chorus of angels. Other times, a panpiper surrounded by the forest darkness, sitting *beside a gentle stream. I don't just picture him, I see him. He's real. A faint glow around the piper illuminates the night.*

His music is composed of faint, yet crisp, clear single notes. One enchanting note rolls over into the next. The piper knows full well his purpose—to bring peace to the valley and serenity to all its creatures.

One quiet summer morning, I noticed if I held my breath, I could hear a symphony of celestial musicians accompanying the singing of angels. Impossible to reproduce, it dwarfed in beauty any Mozart mass or chorus I could even imagine.

Then I realized something that, at first, undermined the moment. The sound I was hearing was water running through pipes to the toilet with a faulty valve. I had to smile. How elegant. I realized then angels are the subtlest of vibrations, dancing through the ether of the entire universe. They exist everywhere, even in something as mundane as water running through pipes.

◆

That journal entry reminded me of a time during high school when I visited Mathew at his house. His mom said he was in the basement. When I went down the steps, Nathaniel was lying on a big Persian rug and wearing headphones. I stopped to say hello. He showed me an album cover. It was a recording of Indian music. On the cover was a drawing of musicians in a courtyard performing for a king and queen on their balcony.

"Look closer," Nathaniel prompted. "See how the picture is triple stamped? At first I wondered if that was a mistake, but now I'm convinced it's not. See, look. Only the picture is triple stamped. The words and everything else on the cover aren't!"

"Yeah, so what's your point?"

"Don't you see? It's a message!" he insisted. "It's the same image, but a little different each time! That means something. It's about reality!"

"What about it?" I scrunched my eyes and scratched my head.

"There are a bunch of them," he said breathlessly.

"A bunch of what?" I asked.

"Realities!" With that, he put his headphones back on, laid his head down on the rug, and drifted off into who-knows-where.

I wondered if that's what was happening to Nathaniel in California—he was entering other realities.

Several months later, I received a cryptic note from him:

••• ◈ •••

Dear Bruce,

It's important you use time wisely. The potential is so enormous. The world is not as we were led to believe.

Sincerely,

Nathaniel

••• ◈ •••

The paranoid tone of that letter worried me, so I sent him a brief note:

••• ◈ •••

Nathaniel,

You haven't gone nuts, have you? I think you should come home for awhile. We could talk.

Hope to see you soon,

Bruce

••• ◈ •••

Chapter 23

The Golden Glow of Knowledge

Nathaniel didn't respond to my note. If it was anyone else, I'd have been sure they were angry. But with Nathaniel...you never knew. I heard nothing from him until another journal entry arrived:

• • • ◈ • • •

The morning started out routine enough. I meditated, had a light breakfast, and went for a walk.

As soon as I stepped outside, I saw that everything radiated with a beautiful golden glimmer from within. The entire world emitted a very subtle, varnish-like glow. It was breathtaking—a new reality. Everything was transformed. Flowers were tiny tunnels leading to other universes. Their petals appeared transparent. I was afraid to shift my gaze, fearing I wouldn't be able to bear the beauty of whatever I saw next.

Intelligence permeated everything. Answers to all possible questions existed right in front of me—so completely self-evident, yet so profound.

The sun's rays imbued everything they touched with the sublime persona of the sun. A small babbling stream, trickling down the hillside, glistening like diamonds in the sun's rays, told the story of the sun. My legs buckled beneath me as I fell to my knees at the edge of the stream. The way the sunlight danced on the water revealed the sun's soul. The sun was alive. He was a god.

I wobbled as I rose to my feet and continued my walk. As I looked around, I could see that everything had a soul. Even a tiny clearing, tucked away in the brush, was alive and filled with celestial beings—gods, devas, earth spirits. I saw what fairies and leprechauns were—the souls of flowers and plants.

There was a vast hierarchy of celestial inhabitants. Some, for example like the soul of a tiny wildflower, were simple and innocent like a small child. Others, like a huge string of mountains, were majestic, grandfatherly, and wise.

Surya once told me that celestial perception is different from hallucinations, channeling, or psychic visions. It's actually quite subtle, not a blatant display of colored lights or voices. Yet when you first awaken to that level of consciousness and actually see celestial beings, it is overwhelming. But in time it goes practically unnoticed and is fully integrated with ordinary life. I'm only beginning to have that level of comfort with it.

When I went into town for groceries, I experienced people in this new way. I could see right into them and feel their motivations, psyche, heart, and soul. I could see that the depth of their being was one with the source of the universe. It radiated from within them. Any psychological, emotional, or physical flaws were merely superficial dust.

Interestingly enough, this created within me a certain sort of naivete. Though I saw people's flaws, I was paradoxically shocked when they acted from those flaws instead of their divinity.

••• ◈ •••

I wanted to write Nathaniel back, but how do you respond to such a letter? No words seemed appropriate. I sat back and pondered. My mind drifted back to a time when we were kids and we came upon a cluster of morning glories in a field.

"Oh look," Nathaniel said, "these flowers are the same shape as the universe!"

At the time, I thought he was goofy, but now it made me wonder. Could the universe really be shaped like a morning glory?

Part 2
The Phenomenon of Inner Conflict

Chapter 24
Sweet and Sour

In the spring, I attended a psychology conference in Atlanta. When I came home late one Sunday night, a letter from Nathaniel was waiting for me in the mailbox with a San Francisco postmark. I kicked off my shoes, sat down in my armchair and read:

••• ◊ •••

Dear Bruce,

I decided it's time to share what I have gained with other people, so I moved to San Francisco to teach.

I met a lady, named Nancy, who teaches spirituality and energy healing. She has a very large national following and asked me to join her in teaching the classes. I happily agreed. Almost overnight, I've become quite popular with Nancy's students. I'm having a wonderful time!

Your friend,

Nathaniel

••• ◊ •••

I was delighted to hear Nathaniel was doing well. But I was surprised he was into energy healing. Back at Ohio State, the energetic healers we heard speak were silly. Nathaniel had even called them "spiritually immature." This could be interesting.

The next several months turned out to be pivotal in Nathaniel's life story. It was during this period he developed his unique manner of teaching. It was important for him to be alone at that time. His teachers wanted it that way. Only then could he learn to express the eternal knowledge of life and existence in his own words and in his own way. His teachers saw him as a bridge between ancient wisdom and modern mentality. Nathaniel was to be their voice, explaining eternal truth in a manner comprehensible in today's world. Yet they intentionally didn't tell him this—he needed to discover it from within himself.

Nathaniel explained all of this to me years later. I've often wished I could've been there in those days—following him step-by-step, day-by-day, seeing what he saw, sharing the experience. But it was not to be.

While Nathaniel was relocating to San Francisco, I was busy with my practice. I spent most of my waking hours at the office. One afternoon, I became distracted by noise in the hallway. I suspected someone was moving into the vacant office on my floor. During my afternoon break, I peeked out my door to see what was going on. Startled, I ducked back inside and quickly shut the door. I'd just caught a glimpse of a girl I had a crush on in grad school.

Her name was Ashley. I never found the courage to say more than a passing hello. She was beautiful, warm, and vibrant. She had a nice slim figure, wavy brown hair, and an effervescent personality. Surely, she could date whomever she wanted and wouldn't have any interest in me. After all, I was a homebody. She would, no doubt, find me a real bore.

Ashamed of my cowardly behavior, but unable to shake it, I spent the rest of the day hiding inside my office until I quietly slipped out of the building and drove home. I obsessed all the way. She was so beautiful. Why didn't I at least say hello? How can I hope to be in a good relationship when I have such a poor self-image? Still feeling down on myself, I arrived home to find another letter from Nathaniel.

So there I was, throughout the years, receiving journal entries from someone with whom I rarely spoke. Typically Nathaniel, but the eccentricity of it made me feel even more displaced and inadequate. Our odd friendship, in conjunction with my shyness regarding Ashley, left me feeling depressed. I slumped in my chair and opened Nathaniel's letter, but its disheartened tone only made me feel worse.

◆

Dear Bruce,

I'm still working with Nancy, the energy healer I told you about. But I'm very disappointed with her. At first, when I noticed her saying something that was not quite accurate or doing something in a healing session that was not really correct, I let it slip by. But time has made things worse. She is teaching her mis-understanding of spirituality and healing.

The other day Nancy asked me what people's energy systems looked like to me. In all innocence, I enthusiastically told her about my subtle sight.

Nancy got quiet. She looked away and said she didn't actually see those things. She only pictured them in her mind's eye. Her embarrassment was obvious. It was an awkward scene.

I felt badly for her, but real trouble started at class. On stage, Nancy gave a talk, using my words, to describe her subtle sight! She was lying to all of those people!

A few days later, I told Nancy about a healing I did on someone's brain. "Twenty years of chronic pain gone in one session!" I said, delighted with the miraculous results.

Nancy couldn't get over it. She was absolutely amazed. Then, unbelievably, she did it again. At class, Nancy gave a detailed description of the healing, telling the students she had done it! I was shocked. It's not that my ego wanted the credit, but she was blatantly lying!

I don't know what I'm going to do.

◆

I felt terrible for Nathaniel, but even worse for myself. I needed to do something about Ashley. If she wasn't dating someone or married, I was going to ask her out. I remembered she and I had shared a common friend, Martha. As I recalled, they were close. Later that evening, I flipped through my Rolodex and called Martha at her home in Cincinnati.

We talked a bit before I found a tactful way to bring up Ashley. "Oh Martha, incidentally, remember Ashley from grad school? I think she moved into my office building today."

"Really? You've got to be kidding!"

I couldn't understand why she sounded so surprised. "Well, yeah, I mean, I didn't talk to her or anything. I just saw her in the distance. But I'm sure it was her." I tried to act nonchalant. "And Martha, I was kind of wondering—if you knew what she was up to."

After a brief pause, Martha said, "Well, what do you mean?"

"Umm, to be honest, I was wondering if she was seeing anyone. I mean, I was thinking maybe of asking her out. The thing is, I don't really think I'm her type. Maybe I should just forget it."

"Oh my God," Martha laughed. "Don't you know that Ashley has had it bad over you for years?"

"What? No way! I don't believe that for a second."

"Bruce, listen to me. I'm telling you. How could you not have known it? I think everybody in grad school knew it but you."

"Well," I stammered. "Why didn't she tell me?"

"Yeah. Sure, Bruce." Martha was laughing affectionately. "Do you have any other ridiculous questions?"

Over the next two weeks, I looked for Ashley every day, but never saw her. The anticipation was driving me crazy. I began to think she didn't even rent the office. When I finally caught up with her, I asked if she wanted to get together for coffee. She said yes! We really hit it off and began seeing each other.

But the time soon came when Ashley told me she had plans to attend an advanced course for therapists in New York. She was also visiting a girlfriend there, so I wouldn't be seeing her for three weeks.

The way I was feeling about her, that sounded like an eternity!

The day after Ashley left for New York, I arrived home from work to find a brief letter from Nathaniel:

••• ◈ •••

Bruce,

I had signed a one-year contract with Nancy. So, I've decided to quietly finish out my contract and next fall, start my own school.

The words of my teachers in India have taken on more significance than ever before: "It is best to avoid teachers who may know about spirituality, but do not truly embody it."

Your friend,

Nathaniel

••• ◈ •••

Chapter 25
The Death of Death

The experiences Nathaniel was having with Nancy started me wondering again. Nathaniel claimed to easily see people's flaws. But if he saw Nancy's flaws so easily, how had he, at first, been so oblivious to them? How could he be so perceptive and yet still so blind? Nathaniel was just one big paradox.

I hoped his next communication would help solve the mystery. Finally, a letter arrived:

◆◆◆ ◇ ◆◆◆

Dear Bruce,

I need to say more about my experience with Nancy. Hope you don't mind. She goes back and forth between intentionally lying and being in denial. D-E-N-I-A-L means Don't-Even-Know-I-Am-Lying.

She thinks people grow spiritually by agonizing over their pain, swelling in the intoxication of love, and becoming entranced by her dogma. That just isn't so.

She suckers people with drama and flashy glitz. Nancy gets up, waves her hands around, flutters her eyelashes, acts like she's in some sort of trance state, talks with an exotic inflection, and thinks she's being spiritual. It's barbaric!

Then she manipulates people with spiritual half-truths and psychobabble. If students disagree with her, they have "unresolved issues." If they don't obey her, they are "passive-aggressive." If they won't roll around on the ground, cry, moan, and howl, they are "emotionally inhibited." If they point out where she is wrong, she says they are being "too heady." Any noncompliance she calls negative and nonspiritual.

I'm sorry to bother you with all this Bruce, but I had to get it off my chest.

Thanks for being there.

Your friend,

    Nathaniel

••• ◈ •••

That night I dreamt about a dark, deep jungle. There were numerous, narrow hidden paths of wet black mud, haphazardly burrowing through the thick foliage, and on occasion, intersecting with one another. I was trying to find my way through the jungle, shifting from one path to another, in search of the most promising route. Finally, I turned down a path strewn with dead and withering human bodies. As I peered far, far down the path, I could make out a hint of daylight. The light flickered, as a distant human form jaggedly moved in front of it, away from me, side to side, further and further down the path. It was Nathaniel!

Startled, I awoke from the dream. Still half asleep, I tried to understand and interpret the dream. Was Nathaniel there to lead people out of the jungle of life? If so, why the dead bodies? Was he responsible for their deaths? Was he trying to prevent other people from dying?

I remembered something about the death of death.... Did it mean the birth of immortality?... Or was it the death of ignorance? Or both? I couldn't exactly recall. Like a typical psychotherapist, I jotted down some notes about my dream. I wondered what Ashley would say about it.

Chapter 26

101 Concepts

It had only been a few days since that memorable dream. Ashley had been gone for two weeks and my insecurities were beginning to surface. I hadn't heard a word and didn't know how to reach her. I imagined she had lost interest and met someone else in New York.

That afternoon, I resumed therapy, a requirement for further psychology training. Aware of my problem with anger, I had chosen a therapist known to focus on emotions. He was completely committed to the idea of feeling your emotions fully and deeply in your body. In the very first session, we role-played. He mimicked everything I hated about my father and encouraged me to yell, scream, stomp my feet, and tell him off for doing it. When I finally became uncontrollably enraged and was pushed completely past my limit, he threw a cushion on the floor, said it was my father, and handed me a baseball bat. He had me beat the cushion with the bat, while all along he fed my rage by repeating my father's insults and condescending remarks. By the end of the ordeal, I was emotionally and physically exhausted. When I got home from the session, I was an infuriated, trembling wreck.

Before I walked into the house, I checked the mail. I was again disappointed to see there was nothing from Ashley. But I did find a thick package stuffed in the mailbox. As I struggled to pull it out, my frustration turned to anger. "What is this stupid thing?" I seethed. It was from Nathaniel. I stomped inside, opened it, and found a 100-

page, bound, typewritten manuscript with a typically short note on the cover. "Does he really expect me to read this whole thing?" I growled. His cheery note rubbed me the wrong way.

••• ◈ •••

Bruce,

How are you doing? I'm keeping busy here and things are really starting to move forward with my teachings. I've been invited to give a talk in New York City and will be stopping by Columbus for several days to visit and give a lecture. I get into Columbus on April 21st. I hope you can free up your schedule so we'll have plenty of time to talk. I'm looking forward to seeing you.

Your pal,

Nathaniel

••• ◈ •••

In the state I was in, almost anything would have set me off, but for some reason that note really did it. I felt like Nathaniel was taking me for granted—expecting *me* to adjust to *his* schedule. And that was so much like my dad. It was always about him. I wasn't important at all.

With all of this churning inside me, I tore off the note and read the manuscript:

••• ◈ •••

101 Concepts to Change your Life
by Nathaniel Harrison

Concept 1: Identity

As human beings evolved out of more primitive forms, they began to create notions. How they felt about everything, from politics to God, was determined by their notions. They became conditioned, or programmed, to identify with their notions and could not see beyond them. If something aligned with their notion-based identities, it was good. If not, it was bad.

Humans still function that way. Scientists identify with their logic and religious leaders identify with their chosen doctrines. Psychotherapists have an identity regarding how people should think and behave. Clients are called healthy when they align with that identity.

Humanity has become deadlocked in a torrent of conflicting identities. Moving beyond identity is the next huge step in human evolution...

In my bad mood, his words came across as pompous and arrogant. Did he think everybody was screwed up except him? And how dare he knock my profession like that!

Concept 2: The Self-Correcting Mechanism

Everyone knows an inner intelligence guides the healing of a cut finger. It's called the self-correcting mechanism. Psychotherapists must learn that the self-correcting mechanism is what heals the psyche. Their job is to assist it...

I'd been studying psychology for a long time and never heard anyone talk about the "self-correcting mechanism." He had to be mistaken.

Concept 3: Infinite Realities

There are an infinite number of simultaneously valid yet contradictory realities. Ignorance is identity with one reality. Wisdom is embracing whichever reality best serves the moment. The wise can freely move from reality to reality.

For example, modern physics (and many spiritual teachings) tells us we are all one. Classical physics (and common sense) says I am me and you are you and we are separate. They are simultaneously valid yet contradictory realities.

Couples often harm their relationship when each partner fervently adheres to his or her own reality. To be ignorant means to ignore. When we identify with one reality, be it religion, physics, psychology, or anything else, we are ignoring an infinite number of other realities...

He might as well have sent me a letter that read, "Dear Bruce, you're ignorant!" And suddenly he was an expert on couple's therapy too!

Concept 4: Idealized Notions

Identities carry with them idealized notions. Idealized notions tell us who and what we should be in life. For example, our spiritual ideals may dictate we never get angry and always remain peaceful. If we succeed in doing that, we decide we are a spiritual person. Or, we may think our body should look like a Barbie or Ken doll. The problem is our idealized notions may not be consistent with our true nature.

Buddhists talk about the Wheel of Karma as moving from lifetime to lifetime until a person finally becomes enlightened. I view the Wheel of Karma as moving from identity to identity until you become free of the shackles of identity.

We don't know what we'll be like when we evolve spiritually, just as a gardener doesn't know what a bud will be like when it blossoms...

I shook my head. Nathaniel was preaching in senseless riddles. Didn't he understand how important identity was? I spent hours every day in therapy helping people find their identity. Having a solid identity gets us through life!

Concept 5: Knowing About vs. Embodying

There is a big difference between <u>knowing about</u> and actually <u>embodying</u> spirituality. Spiritual growth isn't about adhering to an attitude, behavior, emotional state, or philosophy. It's a physiological transformation that naturally refines not only the psyche, but the whole person...

My anger boiled over. Unable to take it anymore, I threw the manuscript against the wall. I was the transpersonal psychotherapist, *not* him! I had helped many people by *supporting* their identity. What did he think an identity crisis *was* anyway?!

Vowing to set Nathaniel straight when he came to Columbus, I walked over and gave his manuscript a good kick.

I'd had it. Grabbing a magazine off the coffee table, I plunked down on the couch and tried to get my mind off Nathaniel's journal. The stupid magazine pages crunched all up as I flipped through to a picture of Gandhi staring right at me. I glared back at him. Not another self-righteous know-it-all, I thought.

Right then, my inner voice kicked in. "Take a look at your behavior." Oh man, why had I ever gone into psychology? Now I felt guilty. So I picked up the manuscript again and flipped through to the last page:

Concept 101:
"*The only true wisdom is knowing that you know nothing*"
—*Socrates*

••• ◊ •••

"I already knew that," I sizzled.

Chapter 27
The Subtle Art

For a long time, my anger issues had plagued me. But the morning after I read Nathaniel's manuscript, I felt particularly guilty about it. All my work with emotions and I was still behaving like that! At least it was happening less frequently. I resolved to keep my anger in check when Nathaniel came to visit.

By the time Ashley was due to arrive in town, I was an angst-ridden mess. My imagination had gone wild. I had convinced myself she had forgotten all about me and was in a brand new relationship, possibly even engaged to someone else.

Finally the time came for me to pick Ashley up at the airport. I hoped she was still interested in me. She walked out of the gate and gave me a kiss and a hug. Immediately I knew she was delighted to see me again. My fears were totally unfounded! We resumed our relationship as if her time away had never even happened.

The day Nathaniel was to arrive in Columbus rapidly approached. I made arrangements to pick him up at the airport, and asked his parents not to tell him. I wanted it to be a surprise. When I arrived at the airport, there was plenty of time to spare, so I parked the car and walked around the terminal for a time. I decided as soon as Nathaniel got off the plane, I'd set him straight.

I hadn't wanted to admit it to myself, but I was a little nervous to see him. Walking around the airport, I tried to figure out why that was. I knew I transferred my father issues onto him, but Nathaniel was also responsible for how I felt. After all, he wasn't perfect. Maybe I could help him with *his* issues. With that thought, I became more comfortable. I decided to think about the whole thing later. After all, it was time for me to get to the gate and greet my guest.

Nathaniel's plane from San Francisco was arriving. After a short time, people began to deplane. My heart started to beat a little faster in anticipation. Then I saw Nathaniel. His eyes met mine and a big warm smile came over his face. That same look was still there in his eyes—the one I first saw on the golf course and again during our lunch in Florida. He looked good. More rested and less frantic than in Florida. But still, he was curiously ordinary in appearance. Somehow, I expected a really spiritual person to look more majestic or dramatic. He looked too normal.

"Bru-u-uce." Nathaniel greeted me in his traditional manner, affectionately drawing out the "u." He gently tilted his head back as if he was savoring every moment of the occasion. "It's great to see you again."

I smiled, but also felt my resentment about his manuscript. Shifting into automatic, I extended my hand and said, "Nathaniel, it's great to see you too."

"Bruce, I'd like you to meet my friends, Tara and Joseph."

We smiled at each other and I shook hands with Tara. She was slender with long blonde hair and beautiful blue eyes. I tried not to let on that I noticed her exceptional beauty. Her teeth were pearly white and her skin was porcelain.

"Welcome to Ohio," I said.

"Hi, Bruce, how are ya doin'?" Joseph asked as he gave me a hearty handshake and big smile. Joseph's large size and earthy appearance put me off. He was about 15 years older then Nathaniel, overweight, and had a gray beard with partially balding gray hair. I thought he would be more appropriately placed behind the wheel of a semitruck than around a spiritual teacher.

"Joseph, welcome to Ohio."

"Joseph travels the country with me when I give my talks," Nathaniel said. "He runs the audio equipment."

Joseph let out a big belly laugh. "Yeah, I do all the work and Nathaniel gets all the glory." He laughed again.

Nathaniel smiled and looked down at the ground.

"Tara, how long have you and Nathaniel known each other?" I asked.

"Oh, about a year." Tara was soft-spoken and angelic in demeanor.

"Are you dating anyone, Bruce?" Nathaniel asked.

"Yes, I am. Her name is Ashley. She's fantastic. You'll get to meet her while you are here." I purposely hadn't brought Ashley along in hopes of having a chance to talk privately with Nathaniel. But now Tara and Joseph were there. I was really disappointed. I looked at Nathaniel and his eyes quickly shifted away.

"That's great," he said. "I'm looking forward to meeting her."

I escorted my guests to the baggage claim, picked up the car, and met them curbside. Noticing that Joseph was doing most of the work, I offered to help him load the baggage into the car.

"That's my job, ma-a-an," Joseph said, refusing my help and letting out another belly laugh.

I started to wonder about Joseph. It seemed like he was trying to hide his insecurity with laughter.

"Nathaniel, I have a few books that I thought might interest you."

Joseph let out his biggest belly laugh yet. I was starting to dislike him.

Nathaniel came to my defense. "Oh, okay, I'll take a look."

Tara was trying to hide a smile too. There seemed to be an inside joke going on that I didn't get.

Nathaniel changed the subject. "Bruce, tonight I'll be catching up with my parents. Why don't you come over tomorrow night so we can spend some time together?"

I tried not to show too much or too little enthusiasm. "That sounds great."

I dropped the trio off at Nathaniel's parents' house and drove home disappointed and upset. Bad enough that I didn't speak with Nathaniel privately, but on top of it, I was just a limousine driver, left out of the inside joke.

The next evening, Tara retired early and Joseph borrowed a car to go check out Columbus. I stopped by the house to see Nathaniel right after supper. I intentionally forgot to bring my suggested reading books along. I suspected the inside joke was that it's disrespectful to go to a teacher bearing books for him to read. Instead of going to him for learning, I'd be telling him what he needed to learn.

It was good to sit in the den of his parents' old house again. Since Mathew had moved away, my visits to the house had all but stopped. Though the furniture was new, the feeling in the den had not changed. Nathaniel had the TV on. I was glad. It allowed me to relax, not having to fill the silence with inane conversation. I thought I would bide my time and wait for the right opportunity to confront him about his manuscript.

"Nathaniel, I really liked reading all your letters about the saints in India. But I always felt you had more to say. I was hoping you could tell me about it." I leaned back against the sofa and adjusted the pillow. "I guess you remember that I was a psychology major and that my specialty is transpersonal psychology."

"Yes, I do." Nathaniel got up, changed the channel to *Star Trek*, and sat back down. "I think it's great. Psychology is a field of great importance. Oh look, I've already seen this *Star Trek*. It's the one where Spock takes his former captain to a world where aliens are masters of illusion. Pretty good philosophical overtones. It's a lot like the people of our world, isn't it?" Nathaniel chuckled.

I wasn't sure I got his joke, but not wanting to admit that, forced myself to chuckle along with him for a moment before I said, "Nathaniel, as a psychology major, I've spent a lot of time looking at my issues, you know, my quirks and childhood woundings. Have you done much of that kind of work?"

"Oh," Nathaniel sighed, "you have quirks and I have quirks,

everyone has quirks. The difference is that you seem to be tormented by yours and I don't really care about mine." With that, Nathaniel began to softly chuckle.

His response upset me. "That's terrible! Don't you care whether or not you're a good person? Don't you care if you're psychologically healthy or not?"

"Of course I do," Nathaniel nodded, "but being healthy and being good are by-products of simply resting into your own true nature, whatever that may be."

"Well, Nathaniel, that would be a really convenient rationalization for a criminal. They could just say they're resting into their own true nature, which is to commit crimes."

Still looking at the television, Nathaniel said, "Any knowledge can be used or misused. That would be a gross misuse and misunderstanding of what I'm saying. Exploring your issues can be good, but trying to correct them is a mistake."

Nathaniel leaned forward, picked up a magazine, and began flipping through the pages. For a moment I felt angry, like he was rudely shutting me off. I wanted to ask him to explain what he meant, but instead I just sat with it. Somehow, I was sensing that there was a purpose to his way that I simply couldn't understand.

I decided to change the subject. "What do you think of Buddhist philosophy?"

"Well, it's okay, but philosophy is philosophy." His eyes shifted to the television screen.

"What do you mean?"

"'Philosophizing about…' can only take you so far. Trying to figure things out is of only so much value."

"Oh, right, I agree!" I sat up and faced Nathaniel. "You need to feel it in your heart, not just philosophize about it in your head."

"Well, yes, feelings are good." A commercial had come on and Nathaniel got up and started changing channels.

"But…?" I crossed my arms.

"It's not only thoughts that are superficial. So are emotions." He flipped the channel back to *Star Trek*.

I was perplexed. "What else is there?"

Nathaniel turned to me and looked right into my eyes. "You have been thinking about 'it' and getting emotional over 'it' for years, but that 'it' you've been longing for cannot be attained through thoughts or emotions."

"Oh-h-h, like the sound of one hand clapping."

"That is what I call the 'I get it syndrome,' Bruce." Nathaniel's eyes were bright and intense as he returned to his chair. "We decide that we understand something simply because we *intellectually* understand it. For example, 'one hand clapping'."

I started to say, "Right" again, but caught myself. That would be the "I get it syndrome" all over again. I felt frustrated, boxed into a corner, and a bit angry. I snapped back, "How do *you* know what 'it' is?"

Nathaniel leaned back in his chair and again looked at the TV. "It doesn't matter *how* I know. It only matters that I do know." Nathaniel took a sip of water. "It doesn't really even matter that I *do* know it. What really matters is that I can help you to know it. Better said, I can help you to *become* it." Setting the glass back down, he added, "Even more accurately, I can help you to awaken to the place within where you have always *been* it."

I started rearranging the little African hand-carved animals that still decorated the coffee table. "Wait a minute, what are you talking about here when you say 'it'?"

"It has many names. It is called oneness, the transcendent, consciousness, the Tao, and the unified field, to name but a few. But to name it, is to label it. And when we label it, it loses its meaning. It lies beyond thing-ness and all 'isms.' It cannot be grabbed onto. It cannot be comprehended. It can only be lived."

I shoved the tiger. It bumped the giraffe and they both tipped over. "And how do you do that, Nathaniel? You know, I keep getting the feeling that you're mocking me, bashing my profession, and not taking me seriously. I'm getting a little tired of it." Luckily, I caught myself. I had resolved not to get angry. I decided to let it go and show some humility by simply asking a question. "Nathaniel, can you show me how to live it?"

Nathaniel turned his head away from the television and back in my direction. The look in his eyes was suddenly very soft and loving. In spite of my challenges, Nathaniel had remained peaceful. His body was relaxed; his voice, calm and compassionate.

"I do that by working with your consciousness. Giving you spiritual thoughts to think or notions of spiritual ways to behave is of little value. Using those thoughts or notions to work with your consciousness is a very different thing. And that, my friend, is a very subtle art. Yes, at times it can be an uncomfortable process, but birthing is an uncomfortable process, isn't it?"

Bewildered, I stared back at Nathaniel. How could spiritual thoughts and ways to behave be of little value? Weren't these the moral and ethical framework for society? What was wrong with that? I knew I'd helped clients open up to their spiritual side by replacing their beliefs and giving them new behavioral patterns. I'd opened up to my spiritual side with the help of those also.

I sat back and stared at the little wooden animals. What did it really mean to work with someone's consciousness? Wow, that was beyond me. I looked at Nathaniel and reflected. I could tell from the look in his eyes and the tone of his voice that he was completely sincere. I felt my resentment easing. I started to consider that much of the anger I felt towards him had more to do with my ego than with Nathaniel. I'd always felt that Nathaniel had something to offer me. I decided to give him a chance. "Nathaniel, I would like you to work with my consciousness. When can we start?"

Nathaniel turned his head back to the TV and mumbled, "What do you think we've been doing?"

I was stunned. Had Nathaniel started working with my consciousness just tonight? Maybe he started when he got off the plane yesterday. Maybe he decided to start when he wrote me the letter saying he was coming to Columbus. No, probably it was when he gave me his writing "Ancient Scripture Reinterpreted." Then again, maybe it started the day Nathaniel chased the golden frog. Or that day on the golf course when we fell into the water together.

I sat back and gazed blankly at the TV. After pondering for some time, I began to wonder if Nathaniel was working with my consciousness right then.

It seemed rude for him to watch television while we were having a conversation. Or was he actually using the television to give me space for my thoughts? Perhaps I'd underestimated the depth of his wisdom and the gentleness of his style. I started to see that Nathaniel was further beyond my comprehension than I'd ever previously imagined. He was playing by a whole different set of rules, if he was playing by any rules at all.

We sat quietly in front of the television for the rest of the evening. At one point, I realized I never got around to confronting Nathaniel. But it didn't matter. I was absorbed in my thoughts about our conversation. I hoped that Nathaniel was too. We had talked enough for the time being.

Chapter 28

The Best Medicine

My relationship with Nathaniel had made a real shift the night before. It was as if my ego let go and I opened to allowing him to be my teacher. Not that it was a total metamorphosis or anything, but something inside me had definitely shifted.

Yet, I was feeling conflicted. On the one hand, I was open to him being my teacher, but on the other, it still felt like he was taking potshots at everything I based my life on. So I was skeptical, but open. There was a tug-of-war within me. It was all very awkward and confusing.

That afternoon, I called Nathaniel to see if he wanted to get together. After telling me he already had plans to take Tara and his parents out to dinner, he relayed Joseph's invitation for me to visit while they were away. Ashley was going to be at her cousin's bridal shower and I had nothing else to do. So I got stuck with Joseph, and couldn't find a polite way out of it.

That evening, when I went over to the house, Joseph and I sat in the den. He took the more desirable seat, the armchair by the window, and left me with the couch. He had a great time telling me all about the lectures Nathaniel had been giving at bookstores in the Bay area for the past several months. He threw in the most mundane details, including the standard, almost ritualistic attire Nathaniel donned for those lectures.

"Nathaniel wears a short-sleeve, white T-shirt, with a dark pin-striped vest," Joseph said. He always wears khaki pants with dark socks and sandals. If you ask me, he dresses kind of like a nerd. When it's cold outside, he brings along a corduroy sports jacket. When he wears it, he reminds me of an eccentric Berkeley professor. Nathaniel never wears shoes, just sandals. After living in India, he says shoes are too uncomfortable. He likes to kick his sandals off so he can sit cross-legged. I haven't been able to sit like that since I was ten years old."

I tried to speak a couple of times, but couldn't get a word in edgewise. Joseph bragged about how Nathaniel never planned his lectures, but he could speak endlessly on any subject. He said that remarkably, Nathaniel, who was usually quiet and shy, became dynamic and passionate when he got up on stage. In the face of Joseph's incessant gabbing, I was forced into a passive role and said nothing.

Joseph gave me the whole history. He explained that he and a number of other people were regulars at Nathaniel's talks during that time. Many of them, including Joseph, discovered Nathaniel while he was teaching with Nancy. He was obviously having a great time assisting Nathaniel driving him to all the lectures, running the audio, and doing whatever else was needed.

"A few months ago, I bought a camera and started filming some of Nathaniel's lectures. I thought I'd show one to you. It's Nathaniel's famous San Rafael lecture—I guess I should say infamous." Joseph let out a huge, bellowing roar of laughter.

Obviously, Joseph was thoroughly overjoyed at any opportunity to show somebody that film. I felt trapped, but there was nothing I could say, nothing I could do, and nowhere I could go. So, I sat back and prepared myself for a long and laborious evening. Howling with laughter, Joseph provided me with prolific, unending commentary as the film ran.

The film began with Joseph picking up Nathaniel to go to San Rafael. Joseph was showing Nathaniel the movie camera he'd installed in the rear of his van. "This should be good," Joseph told Nathaniel, "I'll make an off-the-wall documentary about your lecture."

"You're a real character," Nathaniel laughed. "You do love your gadgets, don't you?"

"Yep," Joseph smiled, "the fun meter's on high now!"

"Yeah, we're pinning the needle!" Nathaniel grinned.

Joking and giggling, they settled into their seats to begin the journey. As they drove along, the camera recorded mostly the back of their heads, but occasionally it caught their profiles when they looked at each other or out the side windows. I must say, viewing them from the rear as they drove along did somehow give the scene a comical feel. The film continued as they silently made their way through downtown traffic and over the Golden Gate Bridge. (Joseph used those initial ten or fifteen minutes of silent footage to set the stage for the ensuing escapade and proudly told me how he mounted microphones to record their conversation.)

Right after they got off the Golden Gate Bridge, Nathaniel glanced at Joseph and then at the camera, calmly saying, "You know, this isn't a normal thing to do."

They both chuckled as Nathaniel coolly turned his head to look back out the side window. (At that point during the viewing, Joseph, who was sitting in the armchair by the window, began laughing uncontrollably. I was beginning to appreciate Joseph's unorthodox sense of humor).

The film continued as they drove along in silence until Nathaniel looked at the camera, smiled, and teased, "So this is your latest contraption, huh?"

They both chuckled together as Nathaniel again looked out the window. For the remainder of the trip, they talked back and forth as if the camera wasn't there. I could see each of them occasionally let out a little giggle, no doubt because the camera was on. It was difficult for me to hear their dialogue in the face of Joseph's annoying armchair commentary. The film seemed a little weird, but the more I got into it, the funnier it became.

When they parked the car in San Rafael, Joseph switched to the built-in microphone and removed the still-running camera from the tripod. (Joseph wheezed with delight as he pointed out to me how, during that process, we the viewers were being thrown about in a haphazard manner.) The film continued with Joseph recording Nathaniel as he walked to the bookstore where the lecture was to be given. Characteristic of Joseph, he struck up several conversations with complete strangers along the way. Their chats were totally audible. Characteristic of Nathaniel, he walked along in silence. You could see on film how he was awkwardly entertained by Joseph's extroverted behavior. I found it interesting that Nathaniel, whose sense of humor was clearly very different from Joseph's, could so easily go along with Joseph's goofy movie production. When they arrived at the bookstore, Joseph walked right in with the camera and filmed the whole place.

There was a big glass display window in front filled with statues, books, and spiritual paraphernalia. Within, beyond the rows of books, were two rooms. One had an assortment of statues for sale, ranging from tiny to extremely large. It was set up like a temple, complete with burning incense and Buddhist chants playing quietly in the background.

As the camera panned the room, I could hear Joseph being his usual talkative self. The moment he noticed a large statue of Buddha, he shouted out loud, "Man, this is beautiful!" His thunderous bellow shook the sacred silence of the room. The shocked look on the faces of several people caught on film was really quite a funny sight. While still operating the camera, he walked into the other room, a combined café and lecture hall. At the far end of that room was a handmade, wooden twelve-by-fifteen-foot stage that stood about one foot off the floor. It was partially covered by a Persian rug with a wooden armchair, small table, and microphone stand.

Once again, the viewer was thrown about as Joseph set the camera on a tripod. As he worked, he spoke loudly to the camera. "Now I have to set up the audio equipment and rig up the lapel mike." His large form appeared on screen cutting between chairs in the audience, as he continued to explain his actions in a loud and intentionally obnoxious tone. "Nathaniel can't use a stationery mike because he likes to move around on the stage when he talks." Joseph fumbled around with what appeared to be the lapel mike, then finally spoke again. "It looks like there are about eighty people here, so I need to hook up an extra speaker in the back."

The film revealed that at first, the people in the audience were disturbed by Joseph's antics. But after awhile, some of them began to relate and joked with him a bit.

This all stopped when Joseph loudly and obnoxiously cleared his throat to silence the crowd. (Laughing inside, I found myself overtaken by Joseph's wacky comedic sense.) When things quieted down, Nathaniel walked onto the stage. He kicked off his sandals, clipped on the lapel mike, sat down, and addressed the audience. (At this point, Joseph, who had been talking incessantly, got up from the armchair, held his index finger to his lips, and had the audacity to shush me while all along I had been sitting quietly on the couch watching the film!)

Nathaniel began to speak. "Hi, my name is Nathaniel Harrison. What would you like to talk about?"

The crowd was a diverse one, from business suits to tie-dye. Some people appeared confused, others distressed. Murmurs could be heard as the audience rustled. If you listened very carefully to the film, you could hear someone ask, "Doesn't he have anything planned?"

Then a thin, balding, smartly dressed man demanded, "Who are you?"

Nathaniel humbly, but confidently, shrugged his shoulders and raised an eyebrow. "My name is Nathaniel and I'm here to talk with you, if you would like. We can talk about anything. The subject really doesn't matter. Everything is connected to everything else. The context from which we speak is what really makes all the difference."

"So, tell us. What is *your* passion?" asked a well-dressed woman with a shawl over her shoulders.

Nathaniel openly responded. "My passion is everyone's passion. We all long to live a life of fulfillment. But, fulfillment comes from living in unity. And you can't just decide to live in unity. Unity isn't an attitude or philosophy. It's a state of human physiology that can be attained."

"We know all about unity. What else can you talk about?" the man called out.

"You can know all about unity. You can behave the way you think a person in unity would behave. But in the final analysis, those things have *nothing* to do with being truly unified. To live it naturally, the physiology must be cultivated and refined."

The man tried to interject something, but Nathaniel just continued.

"True spirituality is a natural state of human function. It's not a philosophy or behavioral conformity." Nathaniel waved his arm, gesturing to the rows of spiritual books that filled the store. "All those books out there, giving ten steps to a more spiritual life, are misleading you. They're promoting a programming to adhere to. That's not what spirituality is about."

The restlessness increased as someone walked in front of the camera and apparently out the door. Based on Nathaniel's nervous gestures and rapid eye movement, he appeared to notice their distress, but what could he do?

"So what form of spirituality do *you* condone? What do *you* teach?" another man asked in a patronizing tone. He looked intensely intellectual.

Nathaniel stood up, passionately gesturing as he paced the stage. "True spirituality is the final frontier of human endeavor. It's not possible for me, in a one-hour talk, to explain what I teach in a manner you would really understand."

"Why not?" The man snarled.

"If a physicist was here to give a talk on quantum mechanics, no one would hope for more than a glimmer of understanding from his short one-hour talk." The tone of Nathaniel's voice conveyed his sincere effort to carefully elucidate. "This is true of almost any field of life: biology, economics, mathematics, you name it. It seems the only exception to that is spirituality. We tend to believe we can understand any spiritual perspective with ease. The truth is the opposite. Spirituality is the last and most challenging field to understand, not the easiest."

"You don't know who you're talking to." The man was almost shouting. "I've been studying spirituality for over thirty years. I take a little piece from one teacher and little piece from another, and put it together for myself."

Nathaniel stopped pacing, and with a pensive look on his face, slowly turned to the man. In a sincere and sorrowful tone, he said, "How unfortunate that you've been looking for so long, and in all those years never found a competent teacher."

The man bristled and started to speak again, but if you watched the film carefully, you could see his female companion reach over and grab his arm to stop him.

Nathaniel continued. "The state of unity isn't readily attainable. Comprehending it intellectually counts for very little. It's a state of consciousness that's cultivated over time. The path of that cultivation is very delicate and easily misunderstood. That's why it's referred to as 'the razor's edge' or 'moving through the eye of the needle.'"

The audience was quieting down.

"I like to say that the flip side of wisdom is humility. As you cultivate unity, you are cultivating wisdom. So at the same time, you are cultivating humility. Thinking you can pick up a book by a great enlightened master and understand it, just like that, is a grave error. It's very important to find a competent teacher to help you."

A lady close to the camera asked, "Nathaniel, I heard about you through a friend who thinks you are a great enlightened being with all sorts of supernatural talents. Would you perform a miracle for us?"

Nathaniel responded, "When you see a magic trick, you understand the magician is using simple laws or principles of nature you're just not aware of, like a trap door or secret compartment. Miracles are the same. They're not supernatural events. They don't defy nature. The performer is simply using principles the viewer isn't aware of. But in the case of what people call miracles, the viewer starts believing the performer is beyond nature, supernatural, and begins to worship the performer of the miracles. That's all wrong. It leads the viewer down a blind alley."

"Well," the lady asked, "can you perform miracles?"

("Good grief," I rolled my eyes. "Poor Nathaniel. They either treat him like he's nothing or want to see a miracle.")

"If you think about what I just said," Nathaniel explained, "you'll see that I already answered that question. But if you'd like, I'll answer it another way by saying that I *can* perform miracles, but I *won't*. Or I could say there's no such thing as a miracle."

"Why don't you just answer the lady's question!?" a hostile man called out.

Nathaniel was taken aback. With a bewildered look on his face, he answered, "I thought I just did."

The crowd rustled as another lady called out more questions. "Nathaniel, tell us about your life. What were your parents like? What was your childhood like? I'd like to get a better feel for who you are."

Nathaniel responded in a sincere tone. "In India, the tradition is for spiritual teachers to not discuss their life history. Who a person is lies far deeper than what the story of that person's life can possibly reveal. If by knowing my story, you felt you knew me, you would be mistaken. And that mistake often interferes with a person's ability to look deeper. My purpose is to help you look deeper, not only when you look at me, but even more importantly, when you look within yourself."

A man in the audience threw up his hands and shouted, "You are sidestepping every question!"

("Gads," I said, "if these people would just listen for a second, maybe they'd learn something."

Joseph giggled under his breath. His glance reminded me that I often reacted to Nathaniel the same way.)

"But Nathaniel, from what I've heard, you encourage your students to talk all about *their* life stories," the lady said.

"Yes, that's true, but the purpose is very different. Students explore their life history to become free of it. That's very different from believing their history defines them or somehow puts them in a box. I want you to know *me*, not by putting me in a box or looking at the surface of my life, but by discovering the place within *you* that lies much deeper than your story or your personality. I'd like you to know me through my teachings. Of course, knowing a person's story is of value, but my purpose here is to assist you in moving deeper within yourself, so I think we'll do well not to reinforce the superficial."

(When the lecture ended, Joseph hopped up from the armchair to pause the film and boisterously broke his silence with another stream of commentary.) Joseph eagerly told me that by the time Nathaniel's lecture was over, everybody either loved or hated him. There was no middle ground. He went on to talk about all the people who thanked Nathaniel after the lecture, saying things like "The world needs to hear this," "You are ahead of your time," etc. He thought it was absolutely hilarious that Nathaniel couldn't take in their compliments. He wailed with delight when he told me that instead, Nathaniel's eyes were on the people who walked out in angry silence.

Then he started the film again, and set the scene. "Okay, the film switches here to Nathaniel and me driving back home after the lecture. This is great. Nathaniel was really upset."

The film resumed in the van with Nathaniel sitting quietly while Joseph roared with glee, "Man, that was great! For awhile there, you reminded me of a Baptist evangelist. You really kicked some spiritual butt!"

(I couldn't help but laugh out loud.) Nathaniel smirked. He too was enjoying Joseph's humor.

Joseph's huge laughs and outrageous comments continued throughout the trip home not only on film, but also in the den as we viewed the film. Two Josephs uncontrollably laughing at the same time was almost more than I could take.

On screen, Nathaniel would occasionally chuckle, but his speech would then return to a pensive tone. "I can't compromise what I want to teach. I can't water it down. There must be a way I can share this knowledge with more people. But can I do that without upsetting so many?" Joseph prodded Nathaniel with howls of delight at every reflective comment Nathaniel made. It seemed that by goofing on Nathaniel's perspective, Joseph was helping him move past it. Sometimes humor really is the best medicine.

As they drove along, Joseph ceaselessly teased Nathaniel. "Unlike some of us, Nathaniel, this experience is new for *you*," he mocked. "All *your* life people have just naturally taken to *you*. Time to sort things out, eh, Nathaniel?" Joseph howled and jiggled with laughter.

Nathaniel, with a reluctant grin, shook his head, and glancing at the camera said, "Joseph, do you think we can shut that thing off now?"

With that, Joseph roared with laughter and bounced up and down as the screen went blank.

Chapter 29

Spring Peepers

The next day was warm and gorgeous. That evening was Nathaniel's talk and I was looking forward to attending one in person. I wondered if it would be anything like the fiasco I experienced with Joseph the evening before. Around mid-afternoon, I opened all the windows throughout the house. Ohio winters can be so cold and long that when the first warm day of spring finally arrives, it's a tremendous explosion of celebration. The buds on the trees and bushes appeared to have grown overnight. My parakeet, Fred, was chirping with joy. The smell of springtime filled the air.

The lecture was on Summit Street by Ohio State University. Since Ashley and I had both graduated from there, we thought it would be fun to have dinner near campus before the talk. We decided to go to Mike's Pizza on High Street—right in the middle of our old stomping ground.

We took my car to campus and found a parking place on High Street. It was fun to walk down those old hallowed sidewalks again. We looked in the windows of the long row of storefronts, remembering what shops had been there before, and recounting adventures we each had enjoyed there. Across the street was campus. It hadn't changed a bit. I felt I was looking back into time.

The Ohio State University area had the most diverse range of outstanding pizza joints I had experienced anywhere. Venetian pizzas were in many ways the best pie—loaded with thick, stringy, piping hot mozzarella cheese. You would take a bite of pizza with one hand and use the other hand to contend with the long strands of cheese. When I was a little kid, my mom occasionally took us to Mike's Pizza. There was always something special about it. I think my parents may have known the owner, Mike. At any rate, for some reason I felt that we had a personal connection with Mike's Pizza. I think I liked it more for the nostalgia than for the pizza. Mike's pizza had a thin crisp crust with cornmeal on the bottom. There wasn't a lot of cheese, but it was delicious. The tomato sauce had a unique tangy flavor that will always say to me, "Mike's Pizza."

After a leisurely stroll, Ashley and I arrived at Mike's. We walked up the concrete steps that led to the entryway and opened the metal-framed glass door. The noise of High Street was dampened as the door swung shut behind us. The same thin-framed, bald-headed old man was still there behind the counter. His friendly smile led me to believe that he still remembered us, but of course that wasn't possible. We enjoyed ordering our pizza and sodas in the traditional manner before sitting down. Taking a table by the big glass window overlooking High Street, we watched the perpetual show of people walking by.

Ashley was always full of life. It made me feel alive to be around her. Though I had always found the idea of marriage scary, I felt she was the one for me.

After what I experienced with Leslie, I decided not to say much to Ashley about Nathaniel. I did that not only for the benefit of our relationship, but also to help me get a clearer perspective on Nathaniel. I found her sixth sense about people to be exceptional and she was an insightful psychotherapist.

Ashley had been into metaphysics for awhile, but had cooled off on it in the past couple of years. She said it was too flaky for her. I hoped she wouldn't consider Nathaniel to be in that same category. She and I stared out Mike's storefront window until the pizza came.

"So tell me about Nathaniel," Ashley said.

"Gee, I don't really know where to start. He's the little brother of Mathew, who was my best friend growing up all the way through high school. Mathew moved to Florida, but we still stay in touch. When he comes back to Columbus, we always get together. It's like we never missed a beat. Our friendship is really solid that way. Nathaniel was a quiet little kid. He has always sort of intrigued me, I guess. Do you know what spring peepers are?"

Ashley shook her head. "No. I've never heard of them. What are they?"

"They're tiny little frogs that no one ever sees but everyone hears every spring. A lot of people think they're hearing crickets when they're really hearing spring peepers."

She leaned forward in her seat. "Really?"

"Yeah. One spring night when I was a kid, we went spring peeper hunting. Past the golf course, there was a pond surrounded by a huge undeveloped field. Mathew and I took Nathaniel with us. We walked down a long path and then cut through the thicket and reeds to get to the pond. It was so dark, we needed flashlights to see where we were going."

"A real adventure, huh?"

"Yeah. Once we got to the edge of the pond, we took out a little board with a string tied to one end, put a candle on it, lit the candle, and pushed the board and candle out on the pond. Then we hid behind the reeds a few feet away, and waited quietly with our eyes fixed on the flame. After a little while, a spring peeper would hop onto the board and be hypnotized by the candlelight. We would then slowly pull in the board, grab the peeper, and put it in a little jar with holes punched in the lid. Then we'd do it again."

"That's really cool. You guys were so clever!"

"It was great fun. I can still recall peering through the thicket until suddenly, a peeper would appear on the board."

"Were they cute?"

I didn't know how to answer that. I stopped to eat a bite of pizza. Ashley was already on her second slice.

"Anyway, we caught several peepers, and put them into the jar one at a time. But when we were ready to go home, we couldn't trace our steps back through the thicket."

"Oh, no. I bet you were scared."

"Well, you know, kids. We wouldn't show it if we *were* scared. So anyway, we decided that we had to blaze a new trail. We headed in the direction we thought our homes must be. When we finally got out of the thick brush, we found ourselves in a very small old grave-yard from the pre-Civil War days."

"Wow!" Her eyes grew big. "I bet *that* scared you!"

"Well it was spooky, but it was also a great adventure. There was a large tombstone that stood out among all the rest with an inscription on it. We read the inscription, and that's when we got really scared! Lighting it with our flashlights, we read:

> 'Look and see as you pass by.
> As you are now, so once was I.
> As I am now, so you shall be.
> Prepare for death and follow me.'"

"I can't believe it! You still remember it word for word!"

"Yeah, I don't know why. My mind just works funny like that, I guess. Anyway, at first Mathew and I were both terrified, but then we became captivated. We decided to memorize it."

"I can just picture that." She giggled.

"Well, eventually the tombstone released us. At least that's how it felt. Then we decided to go, but we couldn't find the jar of spring peepers. When we finally did find it, the jar was open and the peep-ers were gone."

"Oh, no. What happened?"

"We were sure that Nathaniel let them go, but we could never get him to say either way. I guess that sums up my experience of Nathaniel."

"What do you mean by that?"

I stared off through the window, while still monitoring Ashley's reflection on the glass. "I guess I really don't know. Maybe I was hoping you could tell me."

Ashley flicked her head and raised an eyebrow. "O-O-Okay. Sounds like there is more than one story behind that one. Want to split this last piece of pizza?"

I was glad when she changed the subject. I didn't want to influence her impression of Nathaniel. That way, she could better help me figure him out.

Chapter 30
Weaving the Web of Wisdom

Ashley and I finished our pizza, went to the car, and drove the short distance to Summit Street where Nathaniel would be giving his talk. Summit was a major street off campus that ran parallel to High Street. It was lined with the three-story brick homes typical of off-campus Ohio State, except that in this particular area, they were larger and more nicely maintained. We were lucky to find parking directly across the street from the house where Nathaniel was to speak.

It was a lovely home. The yard was filled with beautifully manicured vegetation. The hedge, lining the sidewalk in front of the house, was interrupted only by a gate. We followed the walkway and ascended the freshly painted wooden steps to the covered front porch. It was adorned with potted plants, and an inviting porch swing hung from the ceiling.

A handwritten sign on the front screen door read: "Welcome, please come in." The beautiful, newly refinished, oak-wood floor was covered with an Oriental rug that reached all the way to the back of the home. I detected a slight hint of incense that delicately commingled with the fresh spring scent of the out-of-doors. In front of the Oriental rug-covered staircase was a handmade, alder-wood shoe rack topped by another sign: "Please remove your shoes."

Our attention went to the room full of people beyond the large open double doors. Perhaps Nathaniel was more well known than I thought. The evening sun shone through white lace curtains and created a soft, settled springtime feeling in the room. People assembled on the padded wooden chairs that were arranged theater style. I looked for Nathaniel, but couldn't find him. Joseph was scrambling around in front of the group. He set a small table next to an armchair that was clearly for Nathaniel. Then he put a bottle of water and a lapel microphone on top of the table.

Ashley and I found some seats halfway back. After we got settled, I caught a glimpse of Nathaniel. He was standing in the kitchen talking with some of the guests. He was not wearing the traditional garb that Joseph described in his pre-film discourse. I was surprised to see him in a well-tailored, dark charcoal-gray suit. It tastefully fit the elegance of the occasion.

Joseph had already made a connection with the people in the front couple of rows, laughing and joking with them. When it was time for Nathaniel to speak, Joseph abruptly looked out over the crowd and began to loudly and deliberately clear his throat. As people quieted down, Joseph let out one of his big laughs and glanced at the people in the front row. He walked over to his seat and began fidgeting with the knobs of his audio equipment.

Nathaniel walked in from the kitchen, smiled at everyone, and welcomed them. "Joseph can always get people's attention." He chuckled as he put on his lapel mike and settled into his seat.

Nathaniel's demeanor was very sweet, even a bit shy at first. There was a soft sincerity to his tone that somehow was permeated with strength of conviction. He spoke very freely, apparently without any prescribed topic and appeared to be comfortable allowing the audience to determine the direction of the conversation.

Some people in front of Ashley and I appeared to be put off by that. Nathaniel appeared to sense their discomfort. He explained to the group that all things in life were interconnected. "We can talk about anything," he said, "and the knowledge of all life and existence will fall right into our hands. I'm not here so much to give you facts to memorize. Instead, I'm here to address your relationship with facts in general.

"Deep inside, you are eternally wise," he continued in a sweet, humble tone. "Today, many modern physicists believe everything is unified. Everything is one with everything else. Religions express it by saying that all things are one in God. But accepting that as a fact is of little value. Living it as a philosophy, religion, mood, or emotional attitude is also of little value. However, waking up to that aspect of your being that knows it as a direct experience is of *great* value. This I call the attainment of wisdom."

A woman in the audience interrupted. "Nathaniel, excuse me, but could you say that again?"

Nathaniel paused, smiled at her, and said, "I don't think I could."

A few people giggled.

"Well, could you say it another way?"

Nathaniel put his hands behind his back, slowly walked to a nearby window, and stared out pensively. "Accepting this knowledge as a philosophy, mood, attitude, or way of life is only a beginning step along the path towards wisdom. It's all too often mistaken for the attainment of wisdom. Wisdom is much more subtle and elusive than that."

As Nathaniel spoke, a feeling of timeless magic permeated the room. From any topic a person brought up, he would start with a simple premise and expand it out into profound and abstract understanding. All the while, he would weave in sublime emotions and practical experience. Simple common sense would then bring the conversation back to that same initial premise. He did this over and over again. Nathaniel's words exuded such simple wisdom. Life and existence all seemed so clear. Irresolvable paradoxes melted away.

Remembering his words from the night before, I began to see what he was doing. He was working with the consciousness of everyone in the group. He was using facts to bring people to a place within themselves that lay beyond the grasp of facts.

Sitting beside us that evening was a quiet man. He was short and a little heavyset, but with a very strong, healthy, and well-muscled frame. He had only nodded when we tried to speak with him before the talk. So when Nathaniel asked if anyone had any questions, I was a little surprised he put up his hand.

I leaned over to Ashley and whispered, "Finally, we'll get to hear what this guy's voice sounds like."

"My name is Henry," he said. "I'm in seminary. The church would probably not approve of me being here, but I'm interested in your comments. It is said that God has a thousand names. Could you please discuss this?"

It struck me as pretty courageous that in front of all these people, he would disclose that he, as a seminary student, was going against the wishes of the church. His speech was humble and sincere. His integrity was apparent. Not only was there purity to the tone of his voice, but his words were meticulously chosen. He showed notable respect towards Nathaniel.

"To really understand what that means requires a significant level of understanding of the mechanics of creation," Nathaniel replied.

I leaned over and whispered in Ashley's ear, "I know what it means." She gave me a gentle shove in response.

"I go into that in great detail in my classes," Nathaniel said.

"Sales pitch," I smugly whispered to Ashley. Her stern glance let me know that I had better stop the heckling. I instantly felt ashamed and was quiet, looking straight ahead.

Nathaniel continued. "It requires a series of lectures over several days. For now, suffice it to say that though the underlying basis of existence is one thing, that one thing is multifaceted. Each of those facets has a unique quality, or so to speak, a unique face, or a unique name. Some say that God, then, has many names or faces. That would be a monotheistic universe.

"Others say that each name and face or facet is a unique being. Therefore, it would be a polytheistic one. I say that what is important is that we understand the actual mechanics involved. We must understand what is actually going on—how the universe actually functions. The rest, then, is a matter of semantics."

Henry quietly stared at Nathaniel as he spoke. When Nathaniel finished, he remained silent for several moments and then said, "Thank you."

I was impressed. In only a few words, Nathaniel had resolved the split in religion that had lasted centuries.

Nathaniel looked at Henry, as if in anticipation of additional questions.

"I feel such commitment to my religion," Henry said. "It is something I honor and cherish. But somehow, the leaders of the church can't really answer all the questions that I have. I even feel uncomfortable asking them such questions. They judge me when I try to do so."

"The seed of religion contains all knowledge and wisdom of life," Nathaniel answered softly. "At the source of every great religion is an enlightened wise Master. But when the Master speaks, it immediately ceases to be what the Master said, and becomes what the listener heard." He paused. "Therein lies the birth of religion."

That statement grabbed me. I heard what Nathaniel was saying in a deeper way than I had understood it before.

"It's a double-edged sword," Nathaniel continued. "People are too quick to think they understand what their religion is all about. The knowledge is subtle and easily lost. To understand one's religion is a lifelong, elusive study. Humility is the key."

I leaned over to Ashley and kidded, "Yeah, and he's real humble." Her nudge in the ribs told me she didn't appreciate my humor.

"What lies at the basis of religion is a knowledge as subtle as life itself, because that is what religion is all about—life itself. All other fields of study—physics, biology, economics, and fine arts—are subsets of religion. Some people think religion is the easiest field of study to figure out. In actuality, it's the hardest. Almost everyone has a firm opinion about religion and those opinions usually contradict."

Didn't I know it.

"Opinions range from atheism to a plethora of fanaticisms. Yet at the core of all these divergent stances lies the same one truth. The problem with these perspectives on religion is they have lost their understanding of the subtle truth underlying them. As a result, over time, they have become distorted."

I wondered what that one truth was. And why didn't he tell us?

"Commonly, the truth underlying a profound spiritual teaching is referred to as a secret doctrine. What is meant by this is the true meaning of those doctrines remains a secret even to those who have read, memorized, and studied them for decades. That can be a curse or a blessing. It's a curse if someone too quickly assumes he or she understands the Master's secret doctrines."

That was a wake-up call. I guess I wanted Nathaniel to state the "one truth" as something I could quickly understand.

"It's a blessing if, like you Henry, that person humbly pursues the deepest truth in the Master's teachings. Unfortunately, that's rarely the case. In fact, to question the current understanding of a religion is usually considered blasphemy. This is the tragedy of religion."

Henry sighed. "I guess I'm feeling the pain of that tragedy."

Nathaniel spoke so sweetly to Henry. I was jealous. He was so hard on me. I wanted Nathaniel to treat me the same way he was treating Henry. Nathaniel looked at him with what I think might have been the softest, most compassionate look I'd ever seen. I died. His face looked as if it was made of water. The openness of the love that radiated from him touched my heart and probably everyone's in the room.

As he spoke, the gentleness of his voice held us. "But there's even a greater tragedy. It's that religion is a hollow shell left over from the time when the Master actually lived and taught Truth. Truth, you see, isn't contained in any religion; it's only contained in the awareness of the Master who was the source of that religion."

I looked over at Henry to see how he was digesting Nathaniel's debunking of all religion. I guessed being easy on him worked. He seemed fine.

"So, you see, we have a paradox. On the one hand, religion is the fountainhead of all the wisdom and knowledge passed down from generation to generation throughout the ages. On the other hand, it's like the old clothing of a being who was indeed great, but no longer exists. Henry, you have attained a great degree of purity through your religion. I can feel through you that many of the people you live and associate with through your church have done so also."

Could Nathaniel really see that? The look on Henry's face revealed that Henry thought he could. Maybe that was why he did not talk to me that way. I didn't have enough purity.

Nathaniel continued. "Yet, you long for a level of understanding they cannot provide you. Don't feel you must turn your back on them. All religions, in order to sustain themselves, must have new life breathed into them to renew their understanding of the truth that is their foundation. Through your pursuit of real knowledge, you'll be able to offer that to all those within your church. It's clear you love them deeply."

I could feel that Henry was holding back his tears. I, and probably everyone else in the room, was quite moved by Nathaniel's interaction with Henry.

When the talk ended, Ashley was in a hurry to leave. She grabbed my arm and whispered in my ear, "Let's go." We quickly put on our shoes and rushed out the door. Outside, Ashley took my arm again and with her head down, led me quickly, but silently to the car.

Hadn't she liked it? Had Nathaniel said something that offended her?

Crossing Summit Street, I pulled the keys out of my pocket and unlocked the car. After we got in and shut the doors, Ashley broke her silence with one word. "Wow!"

I waited to hear more.

"That guy is g-r-r-r-reat!" she continued. "Why didn't you tell me about him sooner?" Before I could respond she exclaimed, "I feel like I've been waiting to hear that talk my whole life!"

"So why did you rush us out of there?" I asked her.

"Are you kidding?" she exclaimed. "I was afraid I wouldn't be able to contain myself! I felt like jumping up and cheering right there in the room. I had to get out of there before I exploded! Who is he? I mean, really."

"I've been wondering that same thing my whole life," I half-whispered. My thoughts went back to the days of the golf course and the golden frog.

During the drive home, I thought of mentioning the film Joseph showed the night before, but decided to wait. I wanted to give Ashley plenty of time to form her own opinions about Nathaniel. We excitedly talked about the lecture. But when we tried to paraphrase

Nathaniel's words, to our amazement and disappointment, we both stumbled. During his talk, I'd felt I would be able to work with my clients in the same way he worked with Henry, but now I wasn't sure. Neither of us could remember what Nathaniel had even said!

Chapter 31

Chai

The next morning, Nathaniel was leaving for New York. But first, we all had breakfast at his parents' home.

Breakfast began with chai. Tara told us that she made chai in the same specific manner every morning. To learn the ritual, Ashley stood next to Tara and watched.

"Start by boiling water with a few pinches of cardamom," Tara explained as she performed the tasks. "Unground is better. Once it's boiling, add some organic tea. Green is best. Black is okay, especially if you're trying to wean yourself off of coffee. I have a great little diffuser at home, but here we're using tea bags."

She plopped the tea bags into the water.

"Then turn down the heat and after a moment or two, add some organic milk," she continued. "Right after the milk, add some fresh-sliced ginger." Having chopped it up earlier, she dumped it into the pan of chai. "Add some raw sugar to taste and, voila, it's ready."

"All this for tea?!" I joked.

Tara smiled.

Joseph got up from the table and held out his cup while Tara ladled the fresh brew. He took a symbolic sip, and loudly announced, "Man, that's g-o-o-o-od!" and let out his classic laugh.

Tara filled several cups with the chai and served it while we all settled into our seats around the table. It really was delicious.

"I make the chai according to precise Ayurvedic instructions that Nathaniel received in India," Tara said. "The order the ingredients are put in is important. Always put in the milk before the ginger."

"Why?" I asked.

"I'm not really sure."

Nathaniel smiled playfully. "That's how the subtle knowledge of life and existence is lost, as it's passed from one generation to the next."

"Yeah, Nathaniel, like your telephone game story," Joseph said.

True to form, Joseph was more than willing to share the story with everyone. I'd already heard the story, but played along as if I hadn't.

"When Nathaniel was little," Joseph began, "his mom took him to Sunday school. One day, his teacher had all the kids sit on the floor in a circle. Then she whispered into one student's ear, 'Davy Crockett was born on a mountain top.' She then told that child to whisper what she heard into the ear of the next child and so on until they got all the way around the circle. When they were finished, she asked the last child in the circle to repeat what she was told. The little girl said, 'Davy Crockett died at the Alamo with green tires.'"

Everyone laughed, but Joseph laughed the hardest.

"Where did the green tires come from?" Joseph roared. "That cracks me up every time."

"All the kids rolled around on the floor, laughing hysterically," Nathaniel chimed in. "It was a good lesson."

Ashley was smiling along with everybody. "Oh Nathaniel, that's such a cute story. But I've got to tell you, I'm stuck here. Why *is* the ginger always added after the milk?"

Another round of laughter.

Nathaniel, laughing every bit as hard as Joseph, blurted out, "I can't remember!"

We all roared and I wondered if he really couldn't remember or was just continuing to be playful.

"Oh, wait," Tara said. "I remember. Otherwise the milk might curdle."

Everybody broke up.

"Let's eat," Joseph said.

Everybody started laughing again. At that point, almost anything anybody said would've been funny.

The breakfast preparations continued when Joseph popped up from his seat, walked over to the stove, and started nosing around. Tara arose, filled a pan with some milk and oatmeal, and put it on the burner. Then she lifted the lid from a pan that had been slowly cooking on the rear burner. It was filled with a few prunes and figs, a large portion of cut-up pieces of apple, and a few cloves.

"According to Ayurveda, this is a great way to break the overnight fast," Tara announced while serving each of us our portion of the fruits.

It was delicious, I had to admit. We finished our breakfast with a generous portion of oatmeal Tara had flavored with a dash of cardamom and cinnamon, and followed that with a bit more chai. It made me wonder what else Ayurveda offered.

Joseph collected all the bowls, rinsed them off, and put them into the dishwasher. I wondered what I should be doing to help, but everything appeared to be handled. Tara, Nathaniel, and Ashley left the kitchen to get ready to leave. I was curious about Joseph, so I took the opportunity to talk to him by remaining in the kitchen and having a little more chai.

Chapter 32

Joseph

Leaning back in my kitchen chair, a cup of chai in hand, I felt myself shifting into psychotherapist mode. "So Joseph, tell me more about how you met Nathaniel."

He grabbed a towel and began wiping the counter. "Like I told you, I met him at Nancy's school. But the first time I attended one of his public lectures was in San Diego. I thought it would be a good place to meet girls." Joseph let out a thundering laugh.

"Why did you decide to travel with him?"

Joseph looked down and continued to clean the counter. "Well, my dad always used to say we should leave the world a little better off than we entered it. He and my mom used to protest nuclear power and almost everything else. That didn't work very well, so I decided to do this."

"Can I ask what you do for money?"

"Well, the way I see it, nature abhors a vacuum. So I spend money, create a vacuum, and nature always figures out how to fill it." He let out another loud laugh. "What I do is help out Nathaniel however I can. I figure anything less than saving the world is Mickey Mouse."

We both smiled.

"I'm going to go put the bags into the car," Joseph said. "Do you want some more tea?"

I got up from the table to rinse my cup. "No thanks, I've had plenty for now."

Joseph left to get the bags. I walked into the den to find Nathaniel sitting in the armchair.

Taking a seat on the couch, I continued my investigation. "Hey Nathaniel, I'd like to ask you about Joseph. I'm having a hard time understanding him." I think my tone of voice revealed that I felt Joseph was pretty weird. He and Nathaniel were *so* different. I was covertly asking Nathaniel to explain their friendship.

"Joseph has a very big heart," Nathaniel said slowly and warmly, as if savoring every syllable of his words. You know, Bruce, we're trained from childhood to access people based upon very superficial criterion. Assume for a minute that Joseph is enlightened. How would that affect you?"

"Well, I'd think enlightenment was something I didn't want."

Nathaniel laughed out loud. "Okay, okay, but what if you knew enlightenment was a good thing and you wanted it? How would that thought affect you then?"

"Are you trying to tell me that Joseph is enlightened?" Nathaniel had to be kidding.

"I'm not saying either way. But tell me. How would it affect you to learn he was?"

"Well," I said after some reflection, "I guess I'd have to reevaluate what enlightenment looks like."

Nathaniel chuckled and asked, "Would you have to reevaluate anything else?"

Clearly Nathaniel was leading to something. But what? After thinking for some time I said, "I guess I'd have to take a closer look at Joseph."

"Good," Nathaniel encouraged me. "And what would you have to reevaluate about yourself?"

"Um," I paused. "I guess I'd have to take a look at how I go about assessing people."

"That's the idea," Nathaniel nodded. "You see, if your world view is based upon a superficial belief system, your life will be superficial. Judging people based upon their personality is very superficial. Surya once said, 'If you don't like your personality, you had better change it now. Because after you are enlightened, you won't care.'"

That made me laugh, but I couldn't imagine not caring about my personality.

Nathaniel continued. "He also said, 'If you spend your life working on self-improvement, all you will have to show for it at the end of your life is an improved self.'"

"Wait a minute" I interrupted, "I got the first quote, but not the second one."

"He was saying," Nathaniel explained, "people look to their personality changes to ascertain their degree of self-improvement, but that's a waste of time. Evaluating Joseph based upon your notion of an ideal personality is equally a waste of time. By assuming, at least for a little while, that Joseph *is* enlightened, you might be able to see beyond your limited perspectives, and understand what human development really is."

Suddenly I felt embarrassed. I realized my assessment of Joseph was superficial. It seemed Nathaniel's relationship with people was based on something very deep. It transcended the value system we ordinary mortals often function from. But I didn't feel judged by Nathaniel. Apparently, he enjoyed the opportunity to rock my world.

Chapter 33

Identity's Backlash

I drove to the airport. Joseph sat next to me. Because of his large size, I thought it was better not to try to squeeze him in the back with two other adults.

"Nathaniel, that talk last night was great," Ashley said.

"Oh, thanks very much." Nathaniel sounded melancholy.

Joseph let out still another loud laugh.

"What's so funny?" I asked, irritated.

"Nathaniel gives great talks, but always manages to upset some people. Like the San Rafael film I showed you the other night," Joseph chuckled.

Nathaniel interrupted. "You showed Bruce that film?!"

Joseph said nothing, but had a good laugh.

"What film was that?" Ashley asked.

"Oh, Joseph showed it to me the night before last," I explained. "I didn't get a chance to tell you about it yet. I wanted to wait until after you'd heard Nathaniel for yourself. I didn't want to bias your opinion."

"Some of the people didn't respond very well," Nathaniel added.

Joseph laughed again. "All Nathaniel thinks about is the people he upsets." Joseph never missed an opportunity to tease Nathaniel.

Ashley looked dumbfounded. "How could anybody have been

upset about last night's talk? It was so beautiful. It was brilliant, and at the same time so kind and loving."

I piped in. "Yeah, I agree. How could anybody feel anything but inspired by that talk?"

"People's identities are very strong." Nathaniel looked sad, though he spoke compassionately.

"What do you mean?" Ashley asked.

"Humans function through conditioning," Nathaniel said. "Conditioning creates identity. We're conditioned from childhood to think and feel certain ways. We become very identified with those conditionings. We hang onto that identity for dear life. We seek out people who can reinforce our current identity and call them teachers. Our identity is how we define ourselves. We cling to it with all we've got. It defines everything for us: who we are, who other people are, who or what God is, what is true, and what is false. Though our identity is what limits us, we cannot and do not want to see past it. It's simply too scary, too threatening."

Nathaniel's perspective on identity was beginning to make sense. I started to see how it coincided with what I experienced as a therapist.

"Yet freedom from our identity is what true spiritual growth is all about. That's why it's called spiritual liberation. It's liberation from our conditioning. That's the next huge step in human evolution—for our species to learn to function from the place within us that lies beyond identity. When I make people feel like their identity is being threatened, they get angry with me. If you don't like the message, kill the messenger."

I began to understand why I'd become angry with Nathaniel. His letters threatened my identity. I thought I had spirituality and psychology figured out. When he put that into question, I felt threatened.

"Yeah, people have called Nathaniel arrogant, self-righteous, and condescending," Joseph said, enjoying himself thoroughly. "They really hate it when he tries to explain why popular spiritual teachers don't really understand spirituality," he teased. "He might as well be attacking God!" Joseph could hardly contain himself as he filled the car with his boisterous laughter. "Personally, I love it. The madder they get, the more I like it! Hey, Nathaniel, remember that lady in New Jersey who thought you were bashing Jesus?"

"I was merely saying that people would do well to try to better understand what Jesus was really saying." Nathaniel seemed a bit defensive.

"Yeah, we never saw her again!" Joseph, almost in tears with laughter, started mimicking some of the already classic criticisms Nathaniel had received. "'Why does he have to bash other teachers?' 'If he was really enlightened, I'd know it when I walked into the room.' 'I saw him drink a cup of coffee—he can't be enlightened.' 'If he's a spiritual teacher, then why is he charging for these classes?'"

I was actually enjoying Joseph's humor. That scared me.

Joseph continued. "'I already know all about unity. Tell me something I don't know.'"

"All right, Joseph, that's enough." Nathaniel forced a smile.

Joseph was encouraged. He was having an effect. "'He isn't spiritual, he even gets angry.'" He broke into huge belly laughs again.

Nathaniel shook his head and raised his eyebrows. Conceding he couldn't win, he joined in. "'How does he know he's right and other people aren't?' 'I've been to India too.' 'That might be his truth, but it's not mine.'"

I flinched at that last one, realizing I'd used it myself. I wondered if Nathaniel knew that or it was just a coincidence.

Joseph roared with laughter, but when Nathaniel joined in, it took some of the wind out of his sails.

The car became quiet for awhile until Ashley brought up another subject. "You know, the weirdest thing happened after your talk. Bruce and I tried to recollect the main points you made and we could not do it! During your talk we both understood what you were saying, but afterwards we couldn't recall what you said!"

Joseph let out another gigantic laugh.

"What's so funny now?" I hated this inside joke stuff.

But what Nathaniel said next consoled me. "Oh, we get that a lot. You see, deep inside, everyone is already wise. When you hear wisdom, it touches the place of wisdom within you and sort of wakes it up for a moment. But that place can quickly go back to sleep. Waking it up, over and over, in time, helps it to stay awake permanently. That's how people become wise. During the talk, wisdom began to more fully awaken within you both, but later it went back to sleep a little."

We were approaching the airport. A few moments later, we unloaded the bags and said goodbye. Ashley and I didn't realize it, but Nathaniel had lit an inner light within each of our hearts that would never go out.

Chapter 34

Home

Ashley and I spent the next Fourth of July with my parents at their home on Mulvern Street. It was a fantastic summer morning, reminding me of my childhood days. The air was fresh and clear. The plants were vibrant with life and saturated with nectar. The day was absolutely luscious.

On our way to their house, we stopped off at the post office to check the mail. We were captivated by a number of robins on the small lawn in front of the building. They were chirping and whistling in celebration of another beautiful summer morning. Ashley stayed in the car to enjoy the outdoor concert while I ran inside.

There was an unusually large stack in my mailbox. I impatiently tugged the bulky pile out of the small box, tucked it under my arm, and rushed outside. I tossed the stack in the back seat of the car, took in a deep breath of fresh summer air, and hopped in the car to drive down Cambridge Boulevard in the direction of my childhood stomping ground.

Before we got to the bottom of the hill, I asked Ashley if it would be all right if we took a short cruise around the neighborhood. My tone must have reflected my nostalgic mood, because Ashley's, "Of course, honey," was so very soft, compassionate, and endearing.

I slowly drove down Cambridge Boulevard to feel the presence of each house and the ambiance of the neighborhood that, to me, whispered, "Welcome, home." At the bottom of the hill, I turned right to go past the golf course. The fairways, greens, creeks, and ponds were almost surreal in their beauty and perfection. The smell of freshly cut grass and the warmth of the early morning sun intoxicated us.

While turning the car back toward my parents' home, I caught a glimpse of the creek into which Nathaniel and I fell so long ago. I was comforted that the scene had not changed over all those years. Though those childhood days were gone, they lived on, not only within my heart, but also in the landscape that lay before me.

Nearing my parents' home, we passed the house on the corner of Cambridge and Club where Mathew and Nathaniel grew up. Then we turned left, went over the bridge on Mulvern Street, the one that protected me from the shadowy creature that Halloween night, and passing my favorite buckeye tree, went on toward my parents' home.

As I drove, I told Ashley of how years ago, the neighborhood kids and I had collected shopping bags full of buckeyes to use for ammo. We would take a two-foot-long string, tie a nail to one end, and affix the other end to the tip of a stick. Then, we would cram the nail through a buckeye, take the far end of the stick to use as a handle, and fling the buckeye through the air for what seemed to be nearly a mile. We would go up and down Mulvern Street, flinging buckeyes at every conceivable target.

One day when a house was being built on Club Road, we were all playing, buckeye shooters in hand. A construction worker was carrying boards on his back in the attic of the newly framed structure. From a great distance away, one of the kids in our group flung a buckeye. Unbelievably, it struck the man! He let out a loud yell as the boards crashed through the attic, the second floor, the first floor, and all the way into the basement. Terrified, we immediately broke into a full-tilt run, sliding beneath hedges, leaping over gardens, and zigzagging between houses. It was our childhood introduction to the reckless use of power. But how had something so pure, simple, and harmless as an innocent buckeye become a weapon? One of my early glimpses of paradox.

Ashley and I pulled up my parents' driveway and got out of the car. I tucked the formidable stack of mail under my arm and we walked to the back door. Mom and Dad were there to greet us. After hugs and kisses we sat down at the kitchen table to have some coffee and talk. Dad, of course, was his typical stoic self. But Mom, as usual, made up for it with her loving and kind demeanor.

Ashley began to flip through my large stack of mail. "Junk mail, more junk mail, bill, bill, junk mail," she reported.

Then she picked up a letter, paused for a moment, and let out a squeal. "Oh, it's from Nathaniel."

At my prompting, she opened it and began to read. "It's a brochure for a course—no, a series of courses—that Nathaniel is offering this fall in the San Francisco Bay area! Bruce, we should go!"

Her excitement was contagious. I'd been thinking of studying with Nathaniel, but Ashley's enthusiasm sealed the deal. So, now it was certain we'd be there.

After a little while, Mom made an announcement. "You know," she began. "Your father and I have been talking and we've made a decision."

From the tone of her voice, I knew I wasn't expected to like it. Dad sat quietly, puffing his pipe and showing no emotion.

"These Ohio winters have been getting harder and harder for us," she continued. "So after visiting Florida over the past few years, we've decided to move there. Of course, that means we'll have to sell the house."

I froze. Sell the house? No way. "Now Mom, Dad, are you sure you want to do that? I mean, this has been home for you for so many years! Don't you think you'll miss this old place?"

From the look I got back from Mom, I could tell their decision was final.

I couldn't stand the idea of not coming back to my neighborhood. What came out of my mouth next, I think, surprised me more than anyone. "Mom, Dad, I think I'll buy it from you."

The rest of the day was filled with Fourth of July celebrations. We all went to the parade, where Ashley and I bumped into a number of my old high school friends. Ashley's lighthearted spirit prompted me to laugh and play like a child.

Later, we prepared a wonderful picnic feast in the backyard. Mom covered the picnic table with the old, red-and-white-checked plastic tablecloth I remembered so well from childhood. While Mom, Dad, and Ashley brought out the food, I couldn't resist but to try my hand at climbing the old maple tree.

Throughout my life, this wise old tree had soothed the backyard with summertime shade. When I was young, the lowest branch required my full extension and mightiest leap to ascend. Now it was at shoulder level, and I easily flung my body up and straddled the branch. It made me realize my love for that beautiful maple tree included precious memories undisturbed by time.

My reflections were interrupted when Ashley called me down to get ready for lunch. I smiled as I realized this day, too, would become an exquisite memory, with a feeling all its own. Memory is a funny thing. How it touches the heart means so much more than the actual occurrence of events.

I climbed down and we enjoyed a wonderful Fourth of July picnic, embraced by the comforting shade of the timeless maple tree.

Throughout the day, though, thoughts about buying the house and going to San Francisco to study with Nathaniel kept me a bit on edge. The feeling kept coming up that by going to San Francisco, I was giving in to Nathaniel. Though I had already accepted him as a teacher, it scared me to think I'd be giving control of my consciousness to another person. What might happen to me? Would I be giving up control of my own life? But then again, I'd known Nathaniel my whole life. He wasn't interested in controlling people.

Buying the house was a big step. Was I ready to make such a commitment? It seemed to assume I knew what direction my life was going in. Maybe I did. I knew I wanted to stay in this house and I knew I wanted to study with Nathaniel. Acknowledging that those decisions didn't spell out my entire life helped me rest more easily.

That night, my parents went to bed at their traditional early time. Ashley and I borrowed a blanket and drove to the large, well-manicured playing fields next to the Tremont swimming pool, where the annual Fourth of July fireworks display was to take place. We spread out our blanket and laid back to enjoy the display. I put my arm around her and she cuddled up next to me.

All of the excitement of the day melted into a warm feeling of love for each other. Any of my concerns about buying the house or studying with Nathaniel were completely overshadowed.

That year, the fireworks celebration seemed to be solely about us, our love for each other, and the decisions we made that day. Everything was so perfect. The explosion of each brilliant firework celebrated the happiness we felt within our hearts. That was the night of still one more beautiful decision. That was the night I decided to ask Ashley to marry me.

Chapter 35
Ice Diamonds

Before Ashley and I went to San Francisco in the fall, we were quietly married in a small ceremony at our local church. Neither of us cared for the pomp and hassle of a large wedding. After all, it was about our love, not a social event.

I remember when I gave Ashley the diamond engagement ring. I guess all couples have certain special moments. For us, that was one. She was so surprised and thrilled. We were very much in love. And she was delighted with the way the diamond sparkled in the light.

"It's like fiery ice," she said.

I told her it resembled the ice we used to snatch when I was a kid and the milkman came through our neighborhood to make deliveries. That was particularly fun on really boiling, hot summer days. When he was making a delivery to one of the homes, my friends and I would sneak into the back of his truck to get some ice. We would suck on the irregularly shaped, golf-ball-size chunks of frozen water. They glistened in the sun, crystal clear, with no white in the middle. I wondered how they were able to make them that way. They would melt quickly, the water dripping profusely down our arms as we used them to cool ourselves from the heat. When the milkman returned to his truck, he'd always chase us away. But we could tell he enjoyed allowing our brief adventure before performing the obligatory chase-out.

On those hot summer days, we knew another cooling treat was on its way when we heard the familiar music jingles of the ice-cream man. We would run into the house and plead with our moms to give us a dime or quarter and rush back outside to purchase a Popsicle or a Drumstick before he disappeared.

Somehow, though, it was the ice from the milkman's truck I really recalled as refreshing. I don't know if it was the way the crystal clear purity shimmered in the hot summer sun; the cool, clean, refreshing sensation; or the excitement associated with sneaking into his truck. Maybe it was all of those things. It was like my relationship with Ashley. I didn't know which aspect I cherished the most. I just knew I loved her and was grateful to have her in my life.

Part 3
The Process of Human Evolution

Chapter 36
School Begins

It was pouring rain. Nathaniel's class was being held in Tiburon, a beautiful area across the Golden Gate Bridge from San Francisco. Ashley and I splashed our way to the classroom at the Tiburon Lodge. When we walked into the building, we saw Tara sitting behind a table checking people in. It was good to see a familiar face.

Ashley and I walked up to the table as Tara greeted us.

"Boy, what weather!" I said.

Tara smiled. "In India when it rains, they say the gods are happy."

I don't know if it was what she said or how she said it, but I found a charming comfort in her words.

Ashley must have felt it, too. "You know, Tara, I've been a little nervous about this class. When Nathaniel spoke in Columbus, I really loved it, but afterwards neither of us could recall what he said. I guess I'll really have to take careful notes."

Tara's warm smile soothed us. "It's important to learn the principles Nathaniel teaches. But what's most important about Nathaniel's teachings can't be boiled down to a handful of facts or concepts. It's more about the effect those teachings have on you. He's fond of saying, 'Personal growth is not a curriculum you memorize or adhere to. It's a life you cultivate.' Nathaniel doesn't offer a step-by-step curriculum; he uses the curriculum to help us evolve."

"Yeah, that makes sense," Ashley said. "It's like artwork. Artists express themselves through the beauty of their painting. The techniques they use are only tools. In Nathaniel's case, his self-expression is the profound influence he has on people. Don't you think, Bruce?"

"He's not just painting by numbers," I chimed in.

"He sure isn't," Tara giggled. "So, don't worry too much about writing down all the facts. I think what's more important is to be open to Nathaniel and the unique manner in which he works. How he changes our lives is what really matters."

Ashley smiled and thanked Tara for her kind words. I realized then how much Nathaniel had already touched my life. It was in such a powerful, yet sublime way, that I almost hadn't noticed. We completed the check-in process and entered the classroom.

Ashley and I sat down and waited for class to start. It was a little before 9:00 a.m. and Nathaniel would soon begin his opening talk.

A lady in her fifties sat beside Ashley. She was a little heavyset with permed blonde hair, designer glasses, and a beige blouse with matching skirt.

She immediately struck up a conversation with Ashley. "Hi, my name is Rose. May I ask yours?" She had a Texas accent.

"I'm Ashley, and this is Bruce."

I smiled and said, "Hi, Rose."

"You know, I just have to talk with somebody. I am so nervous. I can't believe I'm even here. I was raised Baptist and if the people in my congregation knew I was here, they would just be sure I was going straight to hell."

I was a little surprised. It was an unusual way to start up a conversation.

But Rose's innocent, flamboyant charm made Ashley smile. "Oh, Rose, I don't think you have to worry about that."

Rose, somewhat soothed, chuckled. "Oh, really? Gee, I hope you're right. You know, I just moved here from Georgia and everything sure feels different around here. I hope I can get used to it. I grew up in Texas and have never lived in a big city before."

I tried to comfort her. "Oh, you'll love the Bay area. San

Francisco is a great city."

"Really? Gee, I hope you're right."

Nathaniel walked in and began his talk. It started out benignly enough. He welcomed everyone and did his best to make sure we were all comfortable. Then he began to speak about life, existence, the big bang theory, and human consciousness. It all seemed to fit together in a very natural way. He explained how humanity approached personal, psychological, and spiritual growth. In that context, there were clearly flaws in the approaches. He made those flaws painfully obvious. Then we had a 15-minute break. It felt like he gave us that time to think about what he had said.

When he walked out, Rose turned to us. "Oh my gosh, I think I'm going to vomit."

"You didn't like it?" Ashley asked.

"No, I loved it. I just think I'm going to vomit. You know, back in Georgia, I taught Bible class on Sundays. I had no idea!"

"No idea about what?"

"Oh, I don't know. I just think I'm going to get sick." Rose was clearly unsettled by what she had heard. It contradicted religious fundamentalism, but made complete sense.

After the break, Nathaniel asked if there were any questions. Rose put up her hand. Though I can't recall what she said, it was obvious to me she was trying to sidestep her discomfort with humor. Nathaniel interrupted her.

"Rose, Rose, wait a minute, hold on. Let's take a look at what's really going on here."

"What do you mean?"

"Well, you're saying one thing, but it feels to me that you're really meaning another."

"I a-a-am?" Her Southern accent was strong.

"Yes, I think so. You're saying that everything is fine and dandy, but what I sense is that you're trying to hide the fact you are shaken, by using humor and charm."

"Oh my gosh, my stomach is just turning upside-down. How did you know that?"

Like Rose, I wondered how he knew it. That was a pretty slick intervention, especially for someone who wasn't even a psychotherapist.

"It's obvious." Nathaniel smiled. "You know, people think they hide, but really, they don't. Everything about us is right there on the surface for everyone else to see, if only they would look."

Rose nervously giggled. "Oh, now I know I'm going to vomit."

The whole group laughed.

"And there you go again with that Scarlet O'Hara charm you use to cover up the uncomfortable emotions you feel inside." He smiled lovingly. "May I go on?"

Rose nodded.

"It relates to your mother. When you were little, things with her were very wrong."

"Oh, my God, how did you know that?"

The group laughed again, but I was offended. Who did he think he was, telling her that?

He smiled again. "It's what I do. It's not difficult. People try to make it out to be other-world-ish, psychic-type stuff, but really it's not. It's simply feeling people, being with people, seeing people. It's only common sense. I will teach you how to do it. It's not hard. What I find incomprehensible is not that I do it, but that other people don't do it. You have a great deal of wisdom, Rose, but it's hidden beneath the fear within you. Your aversion to that fear has prevented access to your wisdom. And do you know what else?"

"Oh God, tell me."

"The people you love know that. Maybe not clearly, but they do feel it and it makes them angry with you. They know you are withholding the best of yourself from them."

"You're talking about my daughter. She always does that."

"Not only your daughter, but also your husband, relatives, and friends."

"You're right. How do you know all that?"

Nathaniel walked over to Rose, and with her permission, put his hand over her stomach area.

"Oh, that makes me feel sick," Rose said.

At this point I didn't know what to think. As a therapist, I was strictly forbidden to touch my clients. He was breaking all of the rules. But at the same time, I was intrigued. How could he see so much so easily? I glanced over at Ashley, and from the astounded look on her face, I could see she was totally enthralled.

"This part of the body relates to, among other things, your connection with your mother. I'm flushing out the toxins and unraveling the obstructions. You may feel even a little feverish from this tonight, but it will be better soon." Nathaniel took his hand down after a few minutes.

"That felt so weird." She looked bewildered.

Everyone laughed again.

Nathaniel smiled. "Why don't we take another break?"

Ashley and I walked out into the hallway.

"Did you see that?" Ashley exclaimed. "This is unbelievable!"

Trying to keep my cool, I slowly nodded. "It is interesting." I wasn't quite sure what to do with it all. I needed to take my time and carefully review what had happened.

Chapter 37
The Kundalini Kid

The next morning, Nathaniel began class by asking, "How's everybody doing? Does anybody have any questions or comments they'd like to share?"

A beautiful woman with long brown hair and a sultry shape put up her hand and said, "My name is Sharon and I'm from L.A." Her clothes were stylish and her skirt was short. Her makeup was impeccable. "About seven years ago, I had a kundalini experience," she continued. "All this energy shot into my head and I saw all of these lights. It was absolutely incredible. I can't really explain it to any of you. It's really beyond description, but because of it, I understand things other people don't. For seven years now, I've been trying to have that same experience, but it hasn't happened. I was thinking maybe you, Nathaniel, could help me to have it again."

She looked to him for a response. I think she was hoping he would walk over and pop her on the head to make that experience return. Where did he get these people?

"You know," Nathaniel said, "every so often a person tells me about having had some such experience. I realize what an impact it has, but there is something very important to understand here. If, all of a sudden, you were to run 220 volts through a 110 volt line, the experience would be dramatic. You might see bright lights shooting from people's bodies or vivid images of angels and demons darting across the room. It could include a wide range of dramatic psychic experiences. But that's not a good thing. In fact, it's a state of confusion or even psychosis. For that reason, I'm fond of saying that the only thing better than a kundalini experience, is no kundalini experience."

"What do you mean?" she demanded.

Even Ashley smirked at that one. This Sharon lady was too full of herself. There were times when I was really rooting for Nathaniel. This was one of them.

"You see, when the physiology is obstructed, the electromagnetics of the body are diminished. When the physiology becomes healthy, more energy naturally flows, and the system gradually strengthens. That is what some esoteric literature refers to as the kundalini rising. Ideally, that process happens so naturally it goes unnoticed."

Sharon looked shocked. Nathaniel was subtle, but getting the job done.

"However, sometimes, it's like when a rubber band un-twangs. All of a sudden, a knot in the physiology unravels and a huge surge of energy releases. Though the experience can be dramatic, it's not really very healthy when 220 volts surge through a line only accustomed to running 110 volts. Ideally, the energy of the body gradually increases. That way the body tissues have the opportunity to grow along with it and accommodate the change in a healthy manner. Do you understand?"

That was good. I loved it. He had now called her unhealthy as well as unevolved.

Sharon held her ground. "Yes, but nobody appreciates how much more I know than everyone else. All these people in this room have no idea what I know. They'll never understand it."

She *wouldn't* give up.

"Eventually, everyone understands everything," Nathaniel said. "That is one thing that is guaranteed. In time, everyone returns to God. All of these people are here because they understand something about life. They simply didn't need to have the experience you did to realize it. May I ask you a question?"

"Sure, go ahead," Sharon growled.

"Would you tell us about your childhood? What was the relationship with your parents like?"

This had to be good. I could imagine her saying almost anything.

"When I was little, everyone thought I was stupid. They thought maybe I had a psychological deficiency or something." Sharon's voice quivered for a moment.

That was a definite possibility.

She regained her composure. "In elementary school, everybody thought the same thing. But when I grew up, I proved them all wrong. I started my own business and made a lot of money. I sell cosmetics and do some modeling."

From stupid to modeling to kudalini experiences. Quite a life!

"It must have been difficult to go through childhood with everyone thinking you were stupid."

"Yeah, but now I've done better than all of them," she said defiantly.

Yeah, right. I could feel my eyes rolling in my head.

"And spiritually, because of your kundalini experience, you have advanced beyond everyone else, too. Is that right?"

Sharon shrugged her shoulders. "Yeah, I guess so."

"Good. So I think we may talk more about this a little later on during the weekend."

I think everyone in the room could see where it was leading, but Sharon was becoming increasingly hostile. I was relieved Nathaniel didn't push it right then. Nathaniel was understanding and gentle...even with her.

Chapter 38

The Churning Process

We took a break. But even after class resumed, I was still stuck on my experience of Sharon. She continued throwing out comments about her kundalini experience. I couldn't believe it. She kept saying how no one in the room could comprehend what she knew. I think *she* was lacking a little comprehension. Maybe everyone from her childhood had been right.

In fact, I was getting a little bored with Nathaniel taking up so much class time working with the issues of all these different people. I was there to work on myself and didn't really care much about these other people. Finally, I decided to say something and put up my hand.

"Nathaniel, I don't really feel like I'm getting what I want here."

"Entertainers give people what they want. Teachers are more concerned about giving people what they need," he smiled back.

"Nathaniel, I understand that, but I'm a therapist and I've already done a lot of personal process work. Many people in this group are beginners. I want to progress and I wonder if a more advanced class might be more suited to my needs."

Nathaniel looked at me before responding. "What evolves us is the cultivation of our 'relationship with....' What is important is not the 'thing,' so much as it's our relationship with the thing. By exploring your 'relationship with' the group consciousness, you will evolve. Everyone in the group chips away at one another's identities. At the same time, the group creates a space that supports each and every individual in the group."

"But Nathaniel," I interrupted, "What about when people interrupt your talks to ask you things I already understand?"

"Then you can benefit in many different ways. For one, by watching how I work with them. You can also benefit by feeling into and exploring any impatience you may be feeling with others. It does not matter if you're in front of the boat or in back of the boat; that boat will take everyone to shore." He paused to look around the group.

I felt scolded. He did it nicely, though.

Nathaniel leaned back in his chair and stared out past the group. "To understand a person's behavior, you must see how it relates to that person's divine essence. Behavior is a superficial dance people do around that essence. Identity's limitations distort the behavioral expression of inner divinity."

Nathaniel's gaze was cast beyond the limits of the room as he spoke. "Distortions, limitations, identities: three different words for the same one thing. As you become free from them, you naturally rest into your divine essence and realize it's the one essence shared by everyone. To understand another…is to see that person's divine essence…is to love that person. When you can do that, no one is boring to you."

Nathaniel reached for his bottle of water and took a drink. "And it's not something you can decide you are going to do. It's not an attitude. It's a physiological state you must culture within yourself."

I felt self-conscious and a little embarrassed. I tried to save myself by asking a more positive question. "So how can I speed up my evolution?"

"The tide comes in and goes out again. The sun rises and sets. Everything cycles. An ancient legend tells of the tug-of-war in the ocean of existence between the gods and the demons. As they pulled back and forth, the ocean churned. Out of that churning process emerged the nectar of divinity.

"Your own inner churning process evolves you. We tend to freeze the process by trying to hold fast to one side, the side we are identified with. Freeing that up is called healing."

"Nathaniel, is that why you drive me so crazy sometimes?"

People laughed.

"No really," I persisted, "sometimes it feels like you are jerking me around."

More laughter.

Nathaniel lit up like a little boy. "Yes, exactly. It's like stretching exercises. You simply invite your body to move in its resistances. We evolve through that churning process. We churn the complexities and distortions within us until they melt away."

"Is that why sometimes it feels like you give something and then take it away?"

"Nature gives and takes away, Bruce. Try to grab onto anything and hold on tight. Sooner or later, nature takes it away. In so doing, you are, in time, freed from your identities. Speeding up your evolution means cultivating a healthy relationship with that process, the churning process."

I was tired of feeling beaten up by what Nathaniel was calling the churning process. I wondered if there was a back door. The look on my face must have given me away.

"There is no escaping it, Bruce. But you can speed up the process by actively working with identity. Meditation waters the root, but responsible inner exploration tills the soil."

Ashley smiled and looked at me with too big a glimmer in her eye. This class was even harder with loved ones around.

Chapter 39

Conviction

That afternoon, the classroom discussion took a religious turn.

"Like Karl Marx used to say, 'Religion is the opiate of the masses,'" Steven said.

This was one intense person. He was a physician and his pager was always going off. Steven wore slick suits and talked fast. He had dark curly hair and a stocky build. He called himself a recovering Catholic.

"I have very little patience with such irrationality. Nathaniel, I would like to know what you think about all of this. Who was Christ anyway?"

I liked this. I, too, had a real problem with religious fanatics and wanted to hear how Nathaniel would handle this one. I noticed Karen squirming in her seat. She was a thin lady with short, curly brown hair. It made me uncomfortable to be around her. Her eyes were tense, her movements jerky and nervous. Her husband, Mark, who sat beside her was the opposite—a very peaceful, easygoing, and reserved man. I felt sorry for him.

Nathaniel remained silent for a moment. He looked down at the floor and then looked up at Steven and out over the group. It seemed to me he was waiting for the room to settle down a bit. Steven's emotional tirade had stirred people up.

"Well, Steven, we have to begin by understanding Christ was

great. The problem is not with Christ. The problem is with what people have done with his teachings."

Karen leaned back and smiled. She was a devout Catholic woman and a happily married mother of four. Ashley thought she was friendly, but I thought she was neurotic.

Steven shot back. "Christians make me sick. Look what they have done. Look at the crusades. Thousands of innocent people slaughtered in the name of Christ!"

Rose, who was sitting next to Ashley, got really uncomfortable. She shifted around in her seat, and I noticed her glancing up to the ceiling for a second. I wondered if she was expecting a thunderbolt from heaven to, at any second, strike Steven down.

Karen started to get up, but Mark put his arm around her shoulders and whispered something to her. I was kind of hoping she would leave. I was having fun. It felt to me like Nathaniel was in a real awkward position here and I wanted to see if he would start to squirm.

Nathaniel smiled, nodded, and looked down at the floor again. "Yes, what you say about the crusades is true, but that's not about Christ. That's about some people many years ago who misunderstood him."

"But it's just as ridiculous today." Steven was practically shouting. "I was brought up Catholic. The priests, the altar boys, and all of them would dress up in these silly outfits and perform ridiculous rituals. Those garments were not even around when Christ was on the earth. All those rituals are from Celtic and Druid traditions. If the Christians looked at history, they'd realize that. Even Christmas was originally a pagan holiday that the Christians made their own. That's a historical fact. Plus, the Bible has been written and rewritten, translated and retranslated, edited by King James and all these other people. It has practically nothing to do with what Christ originally taught. And then these people line up and light their little candles and get down on their knees. It's pure superstition, isn't it Nathaniel?"

This I liked. Nathaniel was really painted into a corner. How was he going to get out of this one?

Karen stood up, picked up her purse, and left. Mark looked sad and a little shaken, but he stayed in his seat. Rose's eyes bulged and I wondered if she was going to follow Karen out the door. I think she was hyperventilating.

Nathaniel glanced at the class and then looked to Steven. "At the depth of every individual lies a field of unity, the transcendental level of life. That is simply modern physics. We could say it's the scientific understanding of the One. In religion, the candle, the cross, a statue, or scripture represents that One. The One is something very exquisite you can feel in the heart of your being. It's the source of your love and sincerity of intent—even the sincerity of intent you brought here today that inspired you to speak.

"People associate, even equate, their religion with the One. If they hear you knocking their religion like that, they feel you are knocking what lies at the depth of their soul."

That was an example of identity! I must have outwardly shown my excitement because Nathaniel, without breaking stride, glanced over at me and nodded.

"Steve, you and I know that isn't your intention. You and I both know religion is about their longing and pursuit of what dwells hidden in the depth of their being. But in their minds, they equate their religion with that which is most sacred and holy, that which dwells in the depth of their being, God, the One."

"So," Steven said, "you are saying religion is like the dance people do around God, but it's not God, even though they mistakenly believe it is. And if you point that out to them, they get mad. Is that right?"

"That's pretty much it," Nathaniel acknowledged.

Rose flared up in her most dramatic Scarlet O'Hara demeanor. "Oh, if my minister could hear us now, he would say we were all going straight to hell."

We all broke into laughter. Finally, a little tension release.

Nathaniel chuckled and nodded. "Yes, we all tend to convict one another with our convictions."

That was deep. It was amazing how he could do that. We were all still laughing as several people nodded in agreement.

"The thing that scares me is that I agree with Steven," Rose said when the noise died down. "All these different religions are talking about God. Each one thinks it is God, and says the other ones are the devil. I finally think I understand what's going on here. Oh-h-h my Lor-r-rd."

Nathaniel smiled as the group broke out again in hysterical laughter. When the room quieted down, he continued. "What is needed here is a clear understanding of the entire dynamic of religion. Once we have that, then all of this sorts itself out and becomes fine. Steven, your anger is not really at religion. It's more about your history with religion. We live in an intellectual age. We demand things make sense. The way religion was presented to you didn't really make sense, but it was forced upon you anyway. That's why you're angry. Now is the time when we can make sense of it. For you, this will be experienced as a great healing balm. It will be a source of peace and fulfillment for your heart and mind that have become quite troubled on this matter. But for now, I think this has given you enough to think about. We'll talk more about it later."

Steven calmed down. He seemed satisfied.

That interaction made me appreciate the intense passion of divergent religious beliefs and the sensitivity around it. What a powder keg! I gained a new level of respect for Nathaniel. Even while dealing with their passionate convictions, he could still help people find a place of deeper understanding within themselves.

Nathaniel understood people beyond what I had ever seen. I wondered if he was able to feel one with them somehow, the way he had experienced being one with the tree on the Oval. I envied that level of understanding. It would really help me in my counseling practice. I wondered if I could ever really be at one with anything.

The Golden Frog

Chapter 40
Spiritual Knights, Bishops, and Guides

Nathaniel began the third day of class with a talk about true spirituality vs. emotionalism. "Emotions and thoughts are fine, but the best of who and what we are lies deeper than our thoughts and our emotions."

"But wait a minute. What else is there?" Cynthia asked. She was a heavyset woman, wearing a flowery dress and pink plastic glasses. "I mean, what are we other than our thoughts and our emotions and, I guess, our physical bodies?"

Nathaniel put his hands behind his back, walked to a window and cast his gaze outside.

"What lies beyond thought and emotion," he said and paused, "is the depth and breadth of the source of all existence…the kingdom of heaven…the true final frontier of every human soul throughout eternity. It cannot be touched. It cannot be felt, for it lies beyond the senses. Yet, just as the sun in the sky cannot be touched, it can be known by experiencing its influence. The sun is warm. It gives light. It gives life. It's central to our very existence."

That was interesting. I asked Nathaniel that same question at his parents' home. Maybe I'd been too upset to fully hear the answer. This felt so much more complete.

"It's called by many names," Nathaniel continued. "Some call it the transcendent. Some call it the kingdom of heaven. Some call it

God. A physicist would call it the unified field. Call it the Soul, if you'd like. It wells up through our being. We can feel our soul within us. Though we can think about it, it's not a thought. Though we can get emotional over it, it's not an emotion."

Nathaniel looked away from the window and over to Cynthia. "See?" he asked.

She nodded.

Nathaniel continued talking about that which lies deeper than thought and emotion. As usual, he gave us plenty to think about.

When we broke for lunch, I approached Nathaniel in the hall and asked him about Karen. "It's too bad she didn't stick around."

"She's very delicate around her religion," Nathaniel replied. "She equates it with her soul. She feels like any change in her relationship with it would rock her very foundation. Her religious identity is her source of stability, but it also prevents her from more deeply understanding the true greatness of what is the basis of her religion. For now, it's enough she heard what I said. She must move slowly, at her own pace. As the saying goes, 'You can't take heaven by storm.' She will in her own way, in her own time, reflect on these things. That's simply physics. Just as a leaf falls from the tree and blows in the wind until it finally comes to the earth. Like that, in time she will inevitably find her way."

At lunch, our class sat together at one end of The New Morning Cafe. Rose, Cynthia, Ashley, and I sat at the same table.

"Oh Cynthia, wasn't that beautiful how Nathaniel answered your question? I mean, I just couldn't believe it," Rose said.

Cynthia forced a smile and politely agreed.

"I swear if the people back at my church could hear me now," Rose continued, "they'd be sure I was going straight to hell. I mean, you have no idea."

"Why?" I asked. I felt my body and jaw tighten. What did she mean I had no idea? I was familiar with fundamentalism.

"Well, Bruce, you have to understand that where I come from, we aren't really allowed to think about these things. They would say it's a sin. I taught Bible class for twenty years and I never..." Rose rolled her eyes and let out a nervous giggle.

I held back my response, knowing that Ashley was quite fond of Rose.

"Well, I'm here because my guides told me to come," Cynthia said. "When my guides tell me to do something, I just do it. They always know best."

Rose's jaw dropped. She blurted out, "Your guides? Well, that's fantastic! Do you speak to guides? Can you talk to my guides too? How about angels? Can you talk to them?" Rose was wide-eyed and at the edge of her seat.

Cynthia was nonchalant. "Oh yes, my guides tell me what to do and help me in many different ways."

Rose was flabbergasted. "Well, I never. I've heard of people who can do that, but in all my life, I never thought I'd meet someone who could. Would you talk to my guides for me sometime?"

"Sure, I'd be happy to."

I started to get the idea Cynthia found a great deal of self-esteem in her ability to channel her guides. It seemed to make her feel rather special. I started to dislike her. Maybe tomorrow Ashley and I would eat lunch alone.

Finally we finished our lunch, did a little window shopping in Tiburon, and returned to class. When we walked into the classroom, Joseph had rearranged the chairs in a horseshoe-shaped, single row, with Nathaniel's chair in front.

"Oh, my gosh. Does this mean I have to sit in the front row?" Rose giggled with trepidation.

Rose sat down with Cynthia on one side and Ashley on the other. I sat next to Ashley.

After everyone took their seats, Nathaniel looked around at all of us. "How is everyone doing?"

No one spoke.

"Is everybody doing well?"

Spiritual Knights, Bishops, and Guides   203

Still no response.

"Are there any questions about what we discussed this morning?"

Nobody said anything.

Nathaniel smiled.

Then Rose spoke up. "You know, at lunch some of us were talking about channeling guides. Are you going to teach us how to do that?"

Nathaniel smiled. "To do that is very simple. I could teach anyone to do it in an afternoon, but I think we'd do well to ask why you would want to learn it. Motivation is an important concept. It's good to look at the motivations behind what we do. Why, Rose, would you want to learn to channel?"

"Well, I just think it would be really neat. I mean, if I had a question about anything, I could just ask my guides. I think that would be just great!"

"Rose, have you ever heard of the word 'codependency'?"

This was clearly a setup.

"Yes." Her voice stuttered with reluctance.

"Would you like to tell everyone what it is?" Nathaniel asked.

I could tell he was preparing his move. Chess anyone?

"I would rather you do it."

"Well, basically, codependence is when people have psychological issues that work off of one another. For example, Rose, what would you say if Cynthia told you that every time she wanted to do something, she asked her husband first? Whatever he said, she would do. If he said they should have spaghetti for dinner, they would have spaghetti. If he said they should watch football on television, they watched football. When he said it was time to go to sleep, they slept."

How or even if Nathaniel knew Rose was referring to Cynthia's channeling, I couldn't really say. But I had no idea how he possibly would have known. I decided he picked Cynthia only because she was sitting next to Rose.

Rose looked at Cynthia and let out her typical nervous giggle. "I would think it was really sick."

Cynthia shook her head. "I would never do that."

"I know that, Cynthia. Of course you wouldn't," Nathaniel said. "You see, Rose, that would be an example of a codependent relationship. The husband would be controlling, and the wife would passively go along with it."

Cynthia nodded in agreement while Rose said, "Icky. That's disgusting."

The group broke out in laughter.

Nathaniel, his eyes and voice soft and gentle, looked at the group. "You see, we need to be a little careful here. What we might do with our spouse and call codependence, some do with a spirit and call it guidance."

Knight to bishop six. Check. That was a good move.

Nathaniel continued. "'My guide says this, and my guide says that.' Isn't that an example of codependency?"

Another nice move.

Everyone in the circle nodded, but two seats away, I could feel Cynthia tighten up. She abruptly shifted in her seat.

Nathaniel picked up on her response and turned his head her way. "Cynthia, are you okay?"

"Well, I channel, but I don't do that," Cynthia snapped.

Nathaniel stayed with her. "Oh, well, good. But could you tell me why you're upset?"

"Well, I feel like you're knocking my guides."

I certainly hoped so, and her relationship with them too!

"Cynthia, I wouldn't do that. But I would like to work with you. And maybe explore your relationship with guides. Would that be all right?"

Come on, Nathaniel, I thought. Time to bring your queen into play.

Cynthia settled down a bit, but was still defensive. "Sure."

Nathaniel got up from his chair, walked over to Cynthia, and said to the group, "If you look at Cynthia, what part of her body catches your attention?"

Cynthia mumbled something about being overweight. Someone called out, "Her head."

"That's right," Nathaniel responded. "Can you see the look in her eye that shows her love and longing for spiritual connection? It's almost like a faraway sort of look, or an ethereal look that reaches to the heavens above."

Several students nodded.

I was having a hard time at this point. I felt like the faraway look in her eye was her being in la-la-land. I wanted the chess match to resume.

"Is this all right Cynthia? May I continue?" Nathaniel asked.

"Please," she urged, clearly wanting to hear what Nathaniel had to say.

"And now, look into Cynthia's eyes. Compare her right eye to her left. Cynthia, please look around to the group. Can you tell me how her eyes look different from one another?"

Someone spoke up. "The right one looks sort of empty, like she's not there as much."

"Very good. Some ancient forms of medicine say the right side of the body is male, yang, father, and husband, and the left side is female, yin, mother, and wife. You see, what happens in a person's psyche is reflected in the body. So, can anyone say what sort of a psychodynamic we have going on with Cynthia?"

At this point Cynthia appeared fascinated and very curious about where Nathaniel was going with this. I had to admit, I was too. All chess masters have a brilliant plan. But what was Nathaniel's?

"Cynthia, would you like to tell us?" he asked.

She was speechless.

"Well, Cynthia," Nathaniel prompted, "would you mind telling us about your father?"

She began to cry. Rose handed her a tissue. "I was the apple of my father's eye. He loved me more than anything. He made me feel so special. Then when I was five years old, he left my mother. I never saw him again after that. My whole world had revolved around him and then he left."

Cynthia softly wept and Rose put her arm around her.

I started to feel for Cynthia.

Nathaniel began to speak. He was so gentle and loving. "You see, Cynthia's father leaving like that created a void in her heart. She felt abandoned. Her sense of self-worth was shaken. She looked for something to fill that fatherly void. She looked to food and she looked to heaven, to Father Heaven. She looked to guides to fill the void and restore her sense of self-esteem and specialness. She allowed her world to revolve around them, just as it revolved around her father when she was a little girl."

I felt moved by the tone of his voice and deeply touched by what Cynthia endured in her life.

"Now, Cynthia." Nathaniel's voice was still gentle and kind. "Are you married?"

It was clear to me by this time that he already knew the answer to many of his questions.

"Yes," she replied.

"And may I ask how that relationship is?"

"Well," she said. "I love him and all, but we really can't talk. He's into his business and work. He doesn't think much of my interests. He comes home, I cook and we eat, watch TV, and then go to bed. I know he loves me and all, but…" She stopped.

"Cynthia was hurt by her father," Nathaniel explained. "After that, she didn't feel safe to let another male come in close to her heart. So she married someone who would accommodate that. She tried to fill that void in her heart with her guides." Nathaniel peered into Cynthia's eyes. "Do you understand?"

Cynthia nodded. "Thank you."

Check and checkmate. Beautifully placed. No one lost, but Cynthia certainly won.

Chapter 41
The Whale

By the end of the day, I felt like I needed a break. Class was getting pretty intense. The next morning, I put on my sneakers and jogging clothes, and took off out the door. I didn't really enjoy jogging. What lengths I'd go to if it meant escaping that intensity!

Tiburon Boulevard was quiet that early in the morning. The air was brisk and refreshing. I paused for a moment, intrigued by the array of houses perched on the hillside, illuminated by the morning sun. Their windows glistened like a matrix of sparkling diamonds. I started running down Tiburon Boulevard and passed the New Morning Café where Ashley and I were planning to meet Joseph for breakfast. By the time I got to Shoreline Park, I was breathing hard. The view helped. The long narrow park hugged the coast. I could see San Francisco across the bay. Angel Island was to my left and The Golden Gate Bridge was off to my right. The park was empty except for an occasional jogger. I enjoyed the privacy. Finally, the distant end of the park, my turnaround point, was in sight. When I was halfway across the park, I noticed someone in a wet suit, dragging a kayak off of his van.

At last I arrived at the end of the park and turned around. On the way back, I spotted the kayaker entering the water. After passing him, the park was once again all mine. I was panting loud now, only suppressing the sound if another jogger ran by. Suddenly, a bizarre noise shook the morning stillness. The resonant, deep swooshing, thrill sound vibrated the earth. I held my breath. What was it? Not wanting to look like a foolish tourist, I kept running. Then it happened again. My whole body, my chest, flesh, my core, vibrated with the sound. Then, it appeared—slingshot range from the shore—a whale with water shooting out its spout. Fantastic! What a sight! So primal, so free, so natural. Somehow it fed me. The vibration resonated in my soul.

Awestruck by the image, I stopped and watched, motionless. A whale rolling through the water. A pivotal moment, independent of time. Its course paralleled the shore. As it surfaced occasionally to shoot out more water, its presence permeated everything. The kayaker paddled in pursuit of the whale, but it moved away too quickly. It was like a dream. Mysteriously, the kayaker was a perfect part of that dream. I stood and watched transfixed as the whale gradually disappeared from view.

I remained still, reflecting on what just happened. I remembered a book on dream analysis. The first half explained that the feeling of every object in a dream determines its meaning. How something felt was the gateway to understanding its meaning. The second half stated: "All of life is a dream. Now interpret that dream." I liked that. I could never really accept there was some guy named God sitting on a cloud somewhere sending me subliminal messages. But it *did* make sense that experiences like the whale were poignant because they resonated within the psyche.

The whale, I realized, represented nature. My nature, as well as Mother Nature. It represented the one primal force underlying all of nature. My ego resisted as I understood that Nathaniel, like the whale, represented the one primal force. Nathaniel *was* the whale. Yet, *my* core resonated with the whale. I, too, was one with the whale. And the kayaker, pursuing the whale, longing to merge with it, who was he? How did he feel to me? He embodied longing, my longing to embrace essence. But he was more. He was Nathaniel pursuing me, to awaken me to my essence. I was the pursuer and the pursued, and so was Nathaniel. In that moment, the complexity of life's paradoxes overwhelmed me. I realized I wasn't glimpsing a higher state of consciousness, but simply having an emotional and intellectual experience. Yet in that moment, I gained a greater insight into life's unity.

When I arrived at the restaurant, Joseph and Ashley were sitting at a table sipping coffee. When I sat down, I went right into the story about the whale. I hoped I didn't sound too much like a tourist to Joseph who had lived in the Bay area for years.

Joseph immediately bounced up off his chair and plowed his way to the door, calling back, "Sorry guys, but I've gotta go find that whale."

Dumbfounded, Ashley and I looked at each other.

"So much for looking like a tourist," I chuckled.

Completely confused, Ashley cocked her head, wrinkled her eyebrows, and looked into my eyes.

Chapter 42

Bruce's Day Dream

When we got to class, I went over to Joseph. "Hey Joseph, did you see the whale?"

Seated at his audio station, he didn't even look up, but only pouted and grumbled. "Naw, I went way down the coast, but could not find it anywhere."

His boyish manner cracked me up. Feeling silly and playful, I couldn't resist teasing him. "Well," I grinned, "I guess the gods just didn't find you deserving."

Joseph looked up at me with a confused and goofy look on his face. "What?"

Giddy, I broke out into foolish laughter, turned around, and toddled away.

Once we all took our seats and quieted down, Nathaniel offered to work with Rose again.

"Oh God, I think I'm going to get sick. Well, okay."

Everyone laughed.

Nathaniel smiled and addressed the group. "I'm sure you remember I worked with Rose and her Scarlet O'Hara syndrome."

Everyone smiled fondly and nodded.

"If you notice, that hasn't really gone away."

More laughs and nods.

"But if you notice, at the same time, Rose is more connected to what's going on inside her. Her wisdom is more available to other people now, as is her humanity in general."

He was right, I thought. Although on the surface Rose hadn't changed at all, she was somehow more connected to herself. I had noticed this yesterday after class.

Nathaniel continued. "This is an important lesson. Personal development is not about trying to turn an apple into an orange. It's more subtle than that. All too often in the fields of self-help and spiritual growth, people try to change themselves into what they think they're supposed to be. That's a mistake. True personal development is about resting into your true nature. No gardener would ever peel back the petals of a rose to turn it into a blossom. That would only make a mess of it. The wise gardener facilitates the natural blossoming of the rose in accord with its own true nature."

As he was talking, I felt Ashley tense up. I resented how he continually put down the field of psychology. It sounded to me like he was doing it again. We were always doing it wrong....But he did get results we didn't get....

"Rose's nature is what it is," Nathaniel went on. "It doesn't need to change. That's why I like to say I do not know what you'll be like as you develop spiritually, I only know it'll be grand. You are what you are. It doesn't really need to change. It simply blossoms."

This was fascinating. I helped many people change. My greatest successes were, I thought, the ones who changed the most. Had I really helped them? I could hear the wisdom in his words. He had a very good point. And the little I knew of Rose, I could see something was working. The shift in her was really remarkable, yet intangible. She *had* changed, but he wasn't trying to change her!

"Nathaniel," I said. "As a psychotherapist, I must say I'm impressed at how profoundly Rose has changed in such a short time. Yet it's subtle. It appears to be a genuine change, not a new act she's putting on. But I'm wondering how such a thing could occur so quickly. Are you sure it wasn't your intention to push her in a certain direction?"

Nathaniel nodded. "If we try to change people to become what we think they should be, it can go against who it is they really are. That's like trying to swim upstream. It's difficult and goes very slowly. If we help people to rest into who they truly are, it's like swimming downstream and can happen very quickly."

I nodded back and looked away. His words were so simple, yet so profound. This was so different from how I'd been working, but it made such obvious sense. It was so much more effective. I was humbled.

That afternoon, Nathaniel worked with person after person. By the third person, I was bored. Though I didn't mean to be rude, I gazed out the window and let a big yawn overtake my body. I gave up trying to focus on what Nathaniel was saying to the person he was working with. I slouched in my chair, feeling disgruntled that he was wasting my time. Suddenly, I heard Nathaniel say my name.

"Bruce, how are you doing?" Nathaniel asked.

I snapped out of my daydream. "Oh, I'm fine. I just spaced out for a little bit."

Nathaniel looked into my eyes with a compassion and understanding that made me feel I should give him a more honest response.

"Well, Nathaniel, I guess I lost interest. The truth of the matter is I got bored again with other people's stories. I was just waiting for it to be my turn."

A gentle smile came across Nathaniel's face as he looked to the floor and nodded.

"I know, I know. I'm supposed to be looking for people's divinity," I acknowledged as I sat up in my seat.

"Bruce, it's not about doing something because you're supposed to. Personal unfolding is a process. It's not something you just do. As we continue to work together, you'll discover from within *yourself* there is nothing more wondrous than people. Everything they do— every emotion, every thought, every feeling, every aspect of their humanity weaves its way to the depth of their soul. It's all a dance around their inner divinity. If you can't see that in other people, it's because you haven't yet seen it in yourself."

He looked into my eyes and away again.

"Boredom is a lack of awareness. As you start to see the universal humanity in others, you awaken to it within yourself. As you awaken to your humanity, you become more able to see it in others. It works both ways. Bruce, when I am working with other people, use it as an opportunity to awaken that ability within yourself."

That was easy for him to say, but I wondered how to do it. Where should I start?

"I don't work with people's distortions," Nathaniel went on. "I work with people's divinity. In doing so, divinity comes forth and permeates their life, their humanity, their humanness. If you listen to what I'm doing in that context, you will find it anything but boring."

"I *understand* that Nathaniel!" I countered. "But it's not that easy. How do I actually *do* it?"

Nathaniel's response was heartfelt. "What's happening right now is the 'doing.' This work tills the soil that facilitates the self-correcting mechanism. I say again, *this is the 'doing.'*

"All human beings share the same one humanity. By that, I mean all facets of the psyche are shared by everyone. You may think a quirk or idiosyncrasy is unique to you. You may think someone else has an aspect to their psyche that you don't. It's not so. We all have within us the full range of humanity. Certainly for some, one quality may be more dominant or hidden than another, but within every single person, all the same facets of humanity do exist. At first, this may be frightening, but in time you'll understand it's liberating. You really have nothing to hide. There are no secrets."

"Oh-h-h my God," Rose interrupted. "Nathaniel, you do have a way of shakin' my world. I just don't know if I can sit here thinkin' you can see all of my little secrets." Rose giggled nervously.

Everybody laughed, but I was annoyed. Nathaniel was on a roll and I really wanted to hear what he had to say.

Nathaniel smiled at Rose and then continued. "We're not separate. We're all one. What dwells within you also dwells within me. We share the same one universal humanity *and* the same one universal divinity. But we each dance with it in our own unique way. In other words, we each have our own *relationship with* the same one universal humanity and the same one universal divinity. Saying it still another way, there is one, big, huge, cosmic psyche that resides deep within us all and we each have our own unique relationship with it."

Steven put up his hand. "Nathaniel, the idea of a big, huge, cosmic psyche is pretty far out there. Could you say it in a way that makes more sense to me?"

"Well, Steven, let me see," Nathaniel responded. "You're a doctor, right?"

Steven nodded.

"It's like a fundamental genetic code inherent to the human species. The nature of the human psyche is structured right in the DNA. It's common to everyone. Does that work for you?"

Steven nodded. "Yes, it does."

"The reason I said it the other way is because it addresses the greatness of what it means to be human. Our psyche has developed to a level that reflects the unbounded intricacy of the Unified Field itself. The way it's said in the Bible is that we were created in God's image."

Steven smiled and said, "Man, that's pretty cool. I'm going to have to think about this for awhile."

"Yes you are," Nathaniel responded. "I must say I've been thinking about it my whole life. Do you get my point? You have to think about this stuff. There's a lot more to it than just learning a bunch of facts."

Nathaniel looked out over the group and continued to speak. "Healing is all about exploring your inner being. This tills the soil that frees you up so you can rest into your true nature. It awakens you to the divinity *and* the humanity we all share. This occurs for both the client and the healer."

This time I got it. He was saying the client *and* the healer awaken to universal humanity *and* universal divinity during the healing.

"You see, this tilling of the soil will also occur for you when you watch me work with other people in the group. That will till the soil of *your own* inner landscape, bringing about *your* healing." Nathaniel looked out the window.

"What really reflects your level of development as a human being isn't what inventions you come up with or how much money you make. It has more to do with how you touch the souls of others. What I'm offering are the tools to assist you in touching them profoundly. As you do so, your own soul will learn to sing. You will cease to be bored with other people. You will find them wondrous, exquisite, and truly divine. This is a royal road for your own personal evolution. It's not a technique you learn. It's an awakening that happens…to the divinity *and* the humanity within you and within others."

Nathaniel focused his attention fully upon me and said, "Bruce, I can see from the expression on your face you have received these words on a very deep level."

I looked up at Nathaniel and there was that look in his eyes. The one I had seen that day on the golf course, in the restaurant in Florida, and the time I met his plane. He saw me and he loved me. I felt a lump in my throat and became choked up. Somehow he knew it was time to give me space.

He turned to the group and said, "Let's take a break."

"So, how are you doing?" Ashley asked as we walked outside.

"I-I'm fine," I stammered. "I don't know what all happened in there." But I did know Nathaniel uncovered a very vulnerable facet of my psyche.

Ashley tried to console me. "Nathaniel can really be intense sometimes. I don't think you're expected to know all that happened."

Frustrated, I snapped back. "Well, it would be nice if I did. He was talking about what makes people tick and I'm a therapist. I'm beginning to think all of my years studying psychology were a self-indulgent, self-perpetuating, ego trip."

"How's that?" Ashley asked supportively.

"I was looking to fill myself up. It was *all* for my own self," I exclaimed with disdain. "Nathaniel made me realize that."

Ashley, now in psychotherapist mode, offered, "I'm surprised you're not angry with him."

"Why would I be angry?" I fired back.

"Well," Ashley calmly replied. "You get angry when someone suggests what you're doing is off."

"No I don't." I barked. "Not necessarily."

"What about your dad?" she coolly inquired.

"Who are *you*, asking *me* these questions? Nathaniel?" I yelled. "Lighten up! I just got off the hot seat!" I was out of control.

"Look." Ashley stared me down. "You're angry. Why don't you admit it?"

"I am now that you are asking me these inane questions," I hollered. I knew I was out of line, but couldn't hold back. "And making these absurd statements! I wasn't angry when *Nathaniel* was talking to me. He saw *me* for who I really am and he loved *me*. My whole life I've been angry at other people for not recognizing me, for not seeing the divinity that's there within *my humanity*. Now Nathaniel made me realize it was because I refused to see it in *them*. How do you think I feel?" I huffed.

Ashley raised her eyebrow. "Phew, that's big."

"Yeah," I sighed, regaining my composure.

"So how is that going to change how you relate to people?"

"I don't know. I can't just throw a switch and begin to do what Nathaniel does." I felt drained and exasperated. "I can't all of a sudden start seeing the divinity and humanity within everyone."

"That's good," Ashley consoled. "Give yourself some time. This is a lot."

"Yeah, but Nathaniel's words were a wake-up call," I groaned.

"Then I'm glad for you," Ashley said, still in therapist mode. "But tell me, why did you listen to him this time?"

"I *always* listen," I objected.

"But last time you got defensive," she offered neutrally, but it sparked my anger again.

"Oh stop! I'm trying to tell you something!" I shouted.

"Oh, okay," Ashley wisely backed off. "Go ahead."

"I didn't like what Nathaniel had to say." I forced out the words. "When I looked at myself in that light, I hated it. But at the same time, something inside me said he was right. Now I have no choice but to face this and work through it. Part of me wishes he never called it to my attention."

"But part of *me* was relieved this came out." Ashley's tone was reflective.

"Yeah, me, too." My own words surprised me. "Do you know what else I realized?"

"What?" Ashley asked.

"You know how my father issues keep coming up?" I too was becoming reflective.

"Yeah."

"Well," my voice quivered. "I think that relates to this. I think when my father never finished his interactions with me, I felt like he didn't see or acknowledge me as a person." Choked up, I continued. "When Nathaniel looked deeply inside me, I felt understood. I did not feel angry or diminished. I felt loved."

"That's really beautiful." She smiled affectionately, her hand reaching out to touch mine. "He gave you something your father couldn't."

"And by doing that," I said, feeling more at peace with my vulnerability, "Nathaniel enabled me to see the divinity within him."

"I guess the next step is to see the divinity in your father," Ashley suggested.

"You're always pushing!" I started to boil again. "I tell you about my realizations and you want more!"

"It just came to me," Ashley pleaded. "Sweetheart, I didn't mean to push."

"Yeah, I know." Catching myself, I gave her a weak smile. The storm was over.

She rubbed my back reassuringly as I moaned.

Sometimes I didn't like having Ashley in class with me. It would be nice to have a little space during such vulnerable moments. Yet, she did help me clarify my realizations. But it was such a volatile process. Nathaniel called it a churning process, but I felt more like I was in a washing machine. Brutal. I had a lot to think about and a lot of feelings to deal with. I planned to apologize to Ashley tomorrow, after I calmed down. But right then, I just couldn't.

As we returned to class, I realized Nathaniel hadn't forced me to change or imposed a new belief. But I felt different and I was having insight after insight. It was uncanny. Yet, it was subtle.

Chapter 43

Ashley's Secret

Before class started the next morning, I was with Joseph when he told Nathaniel about Sharon. "She left last night. She told Rose you couldn't help her reawaken her kundalini, so she was wasting her time."

"It was good she came," Nathaniel said. "She heard what she needed to hear. She will need to sit with it for some time. These things must be measured in her time, not in our time. I think we helped her all we could for now. In the depth of our being, everyone already understands everything. In time, what she already knows deep inside of herself will surface. Everything will sort itself out eventually. If not during her lifetime, then later."

I was struck by the profundity of his words, but also sensed his sadness. It seemed he would have liked to help her more, but understood she wouldn't allow it.

"In the classroom, I don't have the power," Nathaniel added. "Each individual student has the power. They have the power to receive what I offer or not. Anything can be justified with the intellect. If a person wants to, that person can justify anything he or she does."

Later that morning, Nathaniel's extraordinary intuitive radar zeroed in on Ashley. Nathaniel was sitting back in his chair, resting one elbow on the table next to him. He had finished discussing free will vs. predetermination, and paused as if to switch gears and move in another direction.

Nathaniel's pauses were always powerful. They were clearly deliberate. After some time, he spoke. "Silence is not merely the absence of noise. It's a thing. You would do well to make it your friend. It's a powerful tool. It gives us time to rest with the ideas we bring forth. As we rest with ideas, we digest them. They sink more deeply into our being and touch the place of wisdom within. Many people fear silence. They don't know what to do with it. They feel like they must fill it with talk or music, or some sort of noise. So make silence your friend, learn to use it, learn to work with it."

He looked out to the group and then straight at Ashley. "Would anyone like to work?"

The hint of a smile came across Ashley's face as she raised her eyebrows and sweetly put up a hand.

"Yes, Ashley, how may I help you?"

"Well," she began, "I tire easily and often have headaches. But I don't get them all the time, only sometimes. I wonder if maybe they're related to—"

"May I ask you some questions about your life?"

"Sure," she responded with her usual enthusiasm.

"Tell me about your father, Ashley."

Once again, Nathaniel had set something in someone's lap, seemingly from out of nowhere.

Her face went blank and uncharacteristically lifeless. "How do you know about that?"

I thought I knew where Nathaniel was going, but hoped he was not. This was a very personal thing. I was afraid Ashley wouldn't be comfortable talking about it in front of the group.

Ashley started biting her lip and shifted in her seat.

"You know Ashley," Nathaniel said. "You remind me of the water bugs on the creeks back in Ohio. They were impossible to catch as they darted about on the surface of still water."

He had just compared her to a water bug. I hardly knew how to react. Since when did you compare a person to a bug in therapy, especially to their face? Not only did he do this at the beginning of working with Ashley, a *quality* way of establishing rapport, but he even did it in front of the group! I didn't know whether to laugh at the absurdity of the situation or blast Nathaniel for insulting my wife. The funny thing was, he was right. She did move very fast and was always active or talking. If I was this rattled, I wondered how Ashley was doing.

Ashley was shifting around in her chair, true to form. Her eyes were moving even faster and now she looked downright fidgety. She was picking at her fingernails and swinging her foot. Nathaniel had really thrown her.

It was all I could do not to say something. Where was Nathaniel going to go next? How do you follow a water bug intervention?

"We all think we hide, but really we don't."

Even though he'd compared her to a bug, Nathaniel's compassion for Ashley was clearly evident. How did one deeply feel for someone and still confront that person so completely? How could he feel the depth and comment on the surface at the same time?

"Everything about a person is right there for everyone else to see, if only people would look. It's just obvious. It's not a psychic gift only a few have. Many spiritual seekers contort their awareness to become what they call psychic, but that's unnatural and unhealthy. It's a shortcut that in the long run costs them dearly."

I was glad he was talking about something other than Ashley. It soothed things. Ashley became less agitated. I felt like reaching over and holding her hand, but I knew better than to interfere with her process.

"As you grow spiritually, you will naturally see more. It will be through the eyes of love and understanding. And note the word is not '*over*-standing,' it's '*under*-standing.' In other words, it's not arrogantly standing over, but humbly standing under. Humility is built right into the word.

"So Ashley, are you ready to tell me about your father?"

Ashley squirmed in her seat. Back to the water bug thing.

"My relationship with my father wasn't normal. We always had problems. Well, maybe not always. When I was real little, I loved him and felt safe with him. But then he molested me and that changed everything."

Nathaniel's voice was so tender it was almost beyond description. "I'm sorry to hear that." But it was clear to me he already knew it. His love went on forever.

I felt relieved because I wanted Ashley to feel loved and safe.

"You have already been working with this issue in therapy a lot. Yes?"

"Yes."

"And you have headaches, get tired, and have backaches..."

"That's right. I get backaches too!" she interjected.

I noticed her voice came from somewhere up in her head. You started to notice everything in these classes.

"...because you physically and emotionally tightened up your body in response to that trauma with your father. That tightening of your body has become a habit. The trauma created such pain in your heart that you withdrew from it, and tightened up all the muscles around it in your upper back and chest for protection. This prevents the energy from moving through. That obstructed energy backs up in different parts of your body, creating headaches, indigestion at times..."

"Right! Amazing!" she exclaimed. "I get indigestion a lot!"

"...and tires out your back muscles, making them sore, and depleting your entire system, making you tired. At this point, the best way to deal with it is to free up the muscles and help the energy to move naturally. Would you like to do that?"

"Absolutely!"

You had to love her enthusiasm. Who else would be wild about working out their childhood abuse issues on a table in front of a group?

"So let's get a massage table up here. Come on up Ashley."

Joseph sprang up from his audio equipment station in the back of the room, grabbed a massage table, and set it up in front of the class.

She kicked off her shoes and stretched out on the table.

"What we'll do here is open the channels of energetic circulation. To talk about this, it's more convenient to speak in terms of what I call the psychophysiological centers."

"What are psychophysiological centers?" Rose asked.

"Classic literature refers to them as chakras. But I find there is so much mystical hype about chakras and what they're supposed to be, that it's often better to avoid the word 'chakra' altogether."

Cynthia probably thought she was an expert on chakras. But I sure knew I wasn't. I felt overwhelmed with the thought I was being introduced to working with people's chakras.

"You see, when Ashley tightened up the area around her heart, it pulled the solar plexus region—often called the third chakra—up against her diaphragm. So, the first thing to do is peel it off of there."

Nathaniel's fingers disappeared into her upper abdomen. It looked like he was being gentle, but boy did he go deep. Ashley's face changed completely. For that matter, so did everyone's. What he was doing looked sort of like massage or some kind of bodywork, but I'd never seen anything quite like it.

"Good. Now we need to open up the main channel that goes up through her body from the sacrum to the head. It's obstructed in her chest. The best way to get to it is through the back." Nathaniel put his hands behind her back and gently lifted up.

"Wow. That's incredible. I can feel a warmth moving up my spine," Ashley said.

That *was* incredible. She was half-lifted off the table, looking more like a marionette than a real person.

Nathaniel lowered her and moved his hands onto her neck. "Now we need to open it up in the area of her neck. We can move a little energy through that area while we free up those muscles a bit."

I waited for her neck to get longer, but it didn't happen.

He worked there for a few minutes. "Ashley, you center your being up in your head because you want to stay away from the emotional upset in your heart. This is why your voice is sort of high pitched and doesn't resonate in your chest. Does that make sense?"

Ashley responded with a forced melodic, "Yes," from deep inside her chest.

Everyone chuckled at her response. She was such a ham.

Nathaniel finished his work. "Okay Ashley, that should do it."

She got off the table. "Thank you."

Joseph removed the massage table and Nathaniel took his seat in front of the group.

I was relieved. She was off the table and out of the spotlight. Her body wasn't going to contort in any more strange ways and I did not have to feel anxious about what Nathaniel was going to say next.

"I can't believe how different I feel," Ashley told everyone. "It's like, for the first time, I can feel inside my chest and move my back and neck. I didn't realize how locked up I was."

She was wiggling around like a rubber band, showing off her new flexibility.

As the room settled down a bit, I looked around at everyone's face. It was quite a sight. I guess they were all as astonished as I was by what had happened.

"This stuff is all very simple to do. It may seem remarkable, but that's because we live in a world that hasn't understood this sort of thing. Even more, when people start working with energy, they usually get caught up in spiritual hype and drama. I'll show you how to develop a mature relationship with energy and hands-on healing."

He said simple, but it hadn't looked simple to me. I'd seen that *something* was happening, but I couldn't really describe what I was seeing. This was very different. I wondered how I was going to develop *any* relationship with energy and hands-on work, much less a mature one.

"What comes out of your hands is very easy to learn. What comes out of your mouth is more challenging. By that, I mean the hands-on work is easy, while choosing the proper words when counseling someone is the more intricate art."

Finally psychology was getting some respect. I felt validated. However, I clearly couldn't do what Nathaniel did and wouldn't even try to do most of it. There was definite wisdom involved in his work because he so artfully cut to the quick of things and his results were amazing. But how could he say the hands-on work was easy? What he was doing was mind-boggling. How easy was that?

Cynthia put up her hand. "Nathaniel, you only briefly touched upon Ashley's abuse and then worked with something else."

"No, no," Nathaniel responded. "This is all related to the abuse. We can work with things from different angles. Sometimes it's of value to feel the emotional pain of a trauma we have experienced in the past, but not always. Sometimes it's of value to analyze it, but not always. We can affect the psyche by working with the energy and oftentimes that's a more effective way to heal a psychological trauma. If we had to relive every single psychological trauma we ever had before we could get enlightened, no one would ever get enlightened. The trick is in understanding what we need to revisit, for how long, and when it's not necessary or even counterproductive to do so."

Steven put up his hand. "Nathaniel, you've told us that like healing a cut finger, the self-correcting mechanism is what heals in counseling and hands-on work. But it looked to me like you were in there healing and fixing Ashley. What's the deal?"

"Yes, the self-correcting mechanism heals, but sometimes it needs a little assistance. The energy in people's bodies can get stuck. All we do is free it up so the physiology can self-correct. The process is sometimes called self-referral. The body refers to its own inner intelligence to heal. Like the waiter in a restaurant, the healer is only a humble assistant."

That evening after dinner, Ashley and I went back to our room. "So how was it working with Nathaniel today?" I asked. Now that we were alone, I could finally talk to her about it.

"It was amazing," Ashley whispered with breathless enthusiasm. "I still feel more flexible and have more energy moving all through me. Did you see how deeply he went into my stomach?"

"Yes, I did. Did it hurt?" I had forgotten about the stomach work and was now starting to feel a little queasy.

"It was unreal! It felt like he was reaching way into my insides, but it didn't really hurt. There was a moment there when I wondered how I was going to breathe. He really digs in. But I could tell he knew exactly what he was doing. And he was so in tune with me that I wasn't scared."

"Well, I was. You looked like a marionette at one point."

Ashley laughed.

"So did you get any new insights about your issues with your dad?"

"At the time, not really. But now I feel so much happening to me on all different levels. I have so many feelings and sensations. I think I'll have to give it some time before I know where I'm at with my dad. I feel really vulnerable right now. I'm not sure I'll even be able to deal with class tomorrow."

"You wouldn't think that little bit of work could've had such a huge effect. Can I get you anything?"

"No. I feel like all this just needs to settle down."

"Yeah, I can imagine that's true. After a good night's sleep, I bet you'll feel better."

"I guess I will."

We climbed into bed and Ashley dozed right off. I stayed awake, watching her sleep and wondering how healing really worked. It was beyond my comprehension. Then I had the terrifying thought that all this time, I'd been going down the wrong path with my clients.

I caught myself frantically searching for a way to override that thought. I felt bewildered. In only a few days, I was completely questioning the very premise of my life's work. What a class! I rolled over in bed and decided to let it go and think about it tomorrow.

Chapter 44

Trees

"Well I don't know." Beth blurted out, interrupting Nathaniel's lecture the next morning on what was the final day of class.

Where did that come from? It had nothing whatsoever to do with what Nathaniel was talking about. She had been interrupting his talks all week. Sometimes he had stopped her, but most of the time he responded. I was so annoyed. Where was her divinity? Did I even want to find it? This could take me the rest of my life.

Beth's face was set in a permanent scowl. I'd heard she lived in a house in Alaska she built with her own hands. She wore white ankle socks and had short, straight, jet-black hair pulled a bit forward to cover her face. The buttons of her blouse were buttoned all the way up.

"My sister studied meditation in the past and they really messed her up and she doesn't meditate at all anymore," she continued.

Nathaniel handled it effortlessly.

"Oh really? Do you know what kind of meditation she practiced?" His voice was calm and friendly. He just left what he was talking about and completely went with her lead. It didn't throw him off a beat. All of his attention was on Beth and her comment. I wondered why.

"Well," she stammered as if surprised by the kindness of his tone. "I'm not really sure. I just know it messed her up and so..."

Nathaniel looked down at the floor and then began to speak to Beth as if she was the only person in the room. "There are many forms of meditation. Some try to focus and control the mind. Some try to still the mind and force out thoughts. Some impose a trance-like state. Others involve pondering or allowing the mind to wander within one's imagination, thoughts, and emotions. Different meditations have different values. Still again, some meditations program the mind so that undesirable traits may, on the surface of a person's life, appear to be under control. For example, they may stop smoking. But deeper within, they can impose a block or freezing of certain parts of the brain which can actually not be healthy at all."

"Yeah, I think that's what my sister did."

I wondered what he was doing. He was direct and indirect at the same time.

Nathaniel nodded. "The meditation we teach here allows the mind to rest. If it is simply allowed to rest, it's given the opportunity to naturally heal itself, to self-correct."

Beth sunk her head down and didn't say anything. She was heavyset, but the way she held her shoulders slumped forward, her face down, and jaw locked, made her appear even heavier. After a moment, she pulled a large cloth bag to her lap, stuck her face in it, and shuffled around looking for something.

It seemed to me like she was going to need a lot of self-correction. I wondered if that was even possible.

"The mother principle is a quality that is generally carried by your birth mother," Nathaniel went on. "In your particular case, Beth, that influence was somewhat lacking. This creates abandonment issues. As an infant and small child, you really didn't feel held, nurtured, or supported by your mother. As a result, you didn't feel lovable. That dynamic carried through into your adult life. That's why the world feels to you like a very cruel and unsupportive place."

Beth's eyes began to tear.

"If you felt held and nurtured, the tissues in your body would have learned how to more fully relax. As we continue to work together, you'll find that will change. And as it does, you will feel less emotionally guarded. You know what I'm talking about, don't you?"

Beth nodded.

"You might say you will learn how to rest within your own self," Nathaniel continued. "When that happens, you'll feel supported and nurtured by all of life." Nathaniel was quiet. Presently, he asked, "Are you okay with that?"

"Yes…that's good. Thank you." she muttered as her chin quivered.

Nathaniel didn't return to what he was talking about before she had interrupted him. He sat back in his armchair in front of the room, crossed his legs, and silently stared out the side window of the classroom. Something very strange seemed to be happening. A calm silence took over the room. I felt like I was going deeper into myself and could access places in my consciousness I never could before.

When he began to speak, his tone was philosophical, even poetic. Though he continued to look out the window, and though he was speaking to all of us, somehow it seemed he was still speaking to Beth. But it was more than that. It was as if he was talking to her soul, telling her what she longed to hear. It was only for her, but at the same time, it was for us all.

"What could be more beautiful than a tree? On a gorgeous summer day, it reaches to the sky with joy and celebration. The life-giving sap saturates its every cell, oozing in places through the bark, offered as ambrosia to any of God's creatures who may pass by or crawl upon the branches."

Nathaniel paused. The room was silent. I found his reference to trees fascinating. It was like poetry, yet more than mere words. I could feel it, but for the life of me, I didn't know what it was.

"What could be more comforting than a soft breeze moving beneath the branches on a hot summer day, freely offering refuge and peace to anyone? The shade cools our planet. The leaves nourish and purify our air. The seeds serve as food, and the flowers from trees grace our landscapes. Trees ask for nothing in return. It is simply their nature to do such things."

Nathaniel continued to look out the window. His words were heartfelt, maternal somehow. Beth's face had softened. Tension washed from her body. It seemed he was providing her with the motherly love for which she so longed. Was he giving her a healing? I felt a little uncomfortable with that. It was too bizarre to entertain, even as a possibility.

"During a cold winter storm, the branches toss about and bend, sometimes even to the ground. If the roots are strong, no storm, however great, ever uproots the tree. In fact, during the storm, there is exquisite beauty in the movement of the branches. Leaves fly from the tree as the branches rhythmically twist one way and then another. The entire trunk can bend in one direction as every fiber of its flesh vibrates to the frantic rhythm of the fierce winds.

"A person is like a tree. The soul is like the roots. All their emotions, thoughts, and actions in life are like the branches. If one's soul is firmly rooted in the soil of Mother Nature, that is to say, in one's own true nature, then one can endure the greatest storm. Everyone has turbulence in their life from time to time. Living in harmony does not mean evading this reality. To understand the nature of harmony, we need only to look to the trees."

On one level, it was just words. On another level, something profound was happening. I could feel it. I felt like crying when I realized Nathaniel was, indeed, healing Beth. The actual words he was speaking became secondary. I didn't know if I believed in miracles, but what was going on in the room certainly felt like one to me. There were tears in Ashley's eyes.

"Firm roots bring infinite stability to the entire tree. Yet, the branches are infinitely flexible. Our emotions, like the branches, may toss about in a storm, but if the roots are solid, a fierce but harmonious dance ensues."

Nathaniel lovingly looked out over us all, then to Beth. I felt very moved, but at the same time, a little nervous. Nathaniel was rational and straightforward, but this talk was flowery and mystical.

"We find harmony in life by becoming established in our being. Then, sunny day or storm, it doesn't matter; life is lived in harmony every single moment of every single day. We may at times feel anger. Doesn't matter. We may at times feel sad. It's okay. When we leap with joy, we can leap even higher and not lose our balance. The full range of human emotions is still there, yet we live in total harmony with all of nature. We do this by living in harmony with our own true nature.

"Sometimes, people try to live in harmony by keeping all the branches of their lives rigid and firm. They try always to wear a smile, radiate inner peace, and nurture others. They may try never to show anger. They avoid all negative emotions and judge themselves as good or bad, evolved or unevolved, based upon their success in that endeavor. To them I say, look to the trees. Trees do not hold firm and rigid in the wind. If they did, their branches would snap in the storm."

Beth's eyes hadn't left Nathaniel's face. She was still and appeared to be taking it all in. Someone in the group began to sob. To save her from embarrassment, I tried not to look. When I glanced at Ashley, she was wiping tears from her face. I felt heaviness in my chest and pain in my heart.

"Sometimes, people try to make every day of their lives a sunny summer day. They think if they can only create the perfect life situation, then every day will be sunny. They may think getting a lot of money will provide that. Perhaps the answer is a perfect spouse. Perhaps it's a little cabin nestled in the woods away from the hustle and bustle of life. To all of them also, I say, look to the trees. Over time, you will see them endure all sorts of weather. In summer, trees joyously reach out to the sky with their branches. In autumn, the leaves are a dazzling display of color as they wither in anticipation of the frigid cold that is to come. In winter, they become bare and desolate—an austere beauty—in sharp contrast to the abundance of summer. In spring, they burst forth—alive, vibrant, fragrant, exploding with color. Sometimes the spring branches rattle frantically in a thunderstorm. Yet notice also, there is a harmony to their motion, always. It is always a beautiful dance. The storm shows the beauty of the tree even more so than if the winds never blew and the snow and ice never burdened its branches."

I thought of the old maple tree in our backyard.

"Notice also the tree never has to try to live in harmony with all of nature and all of God's creatures. It does so naturally, spontaneously, effortlessly, and without question. To be healthy, it does not avoid or attempt to control life. That is not its nature. To be healthy and live in harmony, it only needs to be firmly rooted in the soil of Mother Nature. For us to be healthy and live in harmony with one another and the whole planet, we only need to become established in the depth of our soul, the depth of our being. There is no other way. Ancient sages referred to this as the state of enlightenment. I invite you to ponder…"

Nathaniel never finished that last sentence. Instead, he was silent.

Then he turned his head towards us. "Let's take a brief break, and then we will come back together and talk some more."

Everyone remained still in their seat. I was overcome with the whole experience. I didn't want to go anywhere or talk to anyone. I just wanted to be in this place. I knew I was changed forever.

Chapter 45

Real World Healing

When class resumed after the break, I raised my hand. "Nathaniel, when you were talking about trees, were you giving Beth a healing?"

"Every moment of every day is a healing for all of creation," he responded. "Sometimes people think they have moved backwards in their evolution. At those times, it's important to understand karma has been delivered and by moving through it, they evolve. Everything continually evolves moment by moment. As I'm fond of saying, the latter is always a more evolved state. Giving a healing is simply helping people move through their karma more quickly and easily." Then he changed the subject.

I think he was responding to my tone more than my question. As I reflected on his response, I could see I was trying to make his interaction with Beth out to be some sort of supernatural event. Nathaniel had very little patience for that sort of thing. He thought it only muddied the waters. Instead, he encouraged us to stay in the real world with our healing work.

The last afternoon, Nathaniel announced he was going to demo a healing and asked for a massage table. Joseph immediately charged to the front dragging a massage table, and began to unfold it. Nathaniel continued talking as he helped Joseph flip the table upright.

"There's really nothing to hands-on healing work," he said. "People try to make it out to be almost magic, but that's ridiculous. It's completely natural and simple.

"Imagine, for example, it's the end of a rough day. Your spouse comes home and flops down on the couch exhausted and tense. You just naturally put a comforting hand on their shoulder."

Cynthia interrupted. "Nathaniel, what does this have to do with healing work?"

Not Cynthia again, I thought.

"It *is* healing work," Nathaniel continued. "A sensitive touch is a healing touch. You don't have to stop and think about the color or frequency of your touch—whether you should run pink or green energy! It's really much easier than that."

Cynthia spoke up again. "Nathaniel, I've gone to a lot of energy healing schools and I consider myself to be an advanced student. I learned to run different colors and I don't think it's easy at all."

I wished she'd stop hassling Nathaniel and just listen.

Nathaniel looked down, nodded, and said, "Well, you know, a gentle caress can be thought of as pink, and a sense of spirituality can be thought of as gold. But the feeling is what counts more than the color."

I couldn't believe how patient Nathaniel was. Hadn't she been listening?

Nathaniel continued in a very gentle and respectful tone. "Trying to do it by color is all upside down. That approach takes something inherently easy and twists it up in a knot."

Cynthia crossed her arms in a huff. What Nathaniel said made perfect sense to *me*. She had an ego problem.

Nathaniel went on. "You *feel* a person when you interact with him or her—whether you look at that person, touch that person, talk with that person—whatever. Feeling is the gateway to healing. It's just that simple."

Nathaniel looked directly at Cynthia. "If you understand the fundamental principles of anything, it becomes simple. Without the fundamentals, the whole thing becomes very complex—fantasy and reality can even get blurred together."

Cynthia bristled. "Are you telling me all the advanced healing work I did was a waste of time?"

There it was. Cynthia was compensating for a poor self-image by considering herself an advanced healer. If she was an advanced healer, then turtles had wings!

"Cynthia, this is why I talk about identity, 'relationship with...,' and all those other concepts before we do any healing work. If you're identified with the idea you're an advanced healer, it's difficult to move forward and learn. You'll take whatever anybody says, stick it in a box, and define it in terms of your identity."

Oh man, that felt good. Yet, the kindness with which he did it humbled me.

"It's one thing to learn a concept like identity," Nathaniel continued. "It's another thing to apply it to yourself."

I almost jumped up and cheered. Yeah. Go Nathaniel! Go! The look in Cynthia's eyes confirmed Nathaniel had gotten through. I was impressed. He actually pulled it off.

Nathaniel smiled warmly at her and she smiled back.

Then Nathaniel looked to the group and said, "Hey! Who wants a healing?"

Somebody jumped up on the table and Nathaniel started to demo a healing.

As he worked, he explained what he was doing. I'd always thought energy work was flaky, but I could follow along! It even made sense! How weird was that?

Nathaniel had us divide into pairs, set up massage tables, and practice on each other. I paired up with Steven, figuring he was probably as anti-touchy-feely as I was. We did the energy healing work as Nathaniel talked us through it. Who would have thought I'd be doing this?

Nathaniel gave us a break after we finished the table work. I went out to the hall to get a drink of water.

"Oh my gosh, I can't believe we're doing energy work!" Rose said. "If the people in my church ever got wind of this, I'd be receivin' prayers for the rest of my life."

"Yeah, it isn't in my comfort zone either," I said. "I could lose my license if I tried this on clients without proper liability procedures in place. It's really a big leap for me to even touch people."

Rose went on. "It felt so creepy. I don't think I was doin' it right."

"I was really surprised I could feel anything," I confessed. "Weren't you?"

"Well, I don't think I was feeling what I was supposed to be feelin'," she nervously giggled. "It just felt weird."

Steven walked up, stretching. "That felt *so* good. I think I fell asleep."

"Really?" I asked. "You mean something worked?"

"Yeah, that was great. Bruce, I'll be your partner anytime."

"Well this is really terrific." Rose's eyes were wide open.

I was delighted. "So something happened that was good?"

"What did you feel, Steven?" Rose asked.

"I felt warmth and opening where he was working. Then it spread through my whole body. It seemed like there was a river flowing in me."

"A river?" Rose locked her gaze on Steven. "Well, I never. I wonder if my partner felt a river...or even anything."

Joseph came out and rounded us up. The course was about to end. I was glad I didn't have to deal with all this anymore. At that point, I was just too tender.

When we came back from the break, Nathaniel had left to catch a plane. I felt jolted. How rude for him not to even say good-bye to us. It felt like an intentional slap in the face. The agitation I felt in the room told me everybody else felt the same way. Joseph walked up to the front of the class and began to read a message from Nathaniel:

When I lived in the ashram, people would come and go. Through the years, we became like brothers. But when someone left, there were no good-byes, no hugs, and no well wishes. At first, it was very odd to me. In time, I understood.

Our connection is much deeper than emotion. It transcends space and time. The opposite is affirmed by an emotional display of good-byes. Close your eyes and feel me now. I am not gone. When you return home, you will find me there. Just as you are with me now. Our connection is in the eternal. It is not transient. We need never suffer the pangs of separation.

Remember:

- These teachings, if converted into a set of facts and concepts, become a hollow echo of what they are.

- The group dynamic will carry you along much faster than you could progress alone. I work not only with your individual consciousness, but also with the consciousness of the group as a whole.

- I caution you, habits reinforce identities. For that reason, it's easy when returning home, to lose what you gained in class. Work with these teachings. Keep them fresh in your life.

- These teachings are not the gold. They are the shovels and the tools you use to uncover the gold that dwells at the depth of your being.

- Meditation is the most powerful tool you have.

- We all share the same one humanity.

- Everything about everyone traces back to their divinity.

I look forward to seeing you all again,
Nathaniel

• • • ◈ • • •

Chapter 46
Ashley's Upheaval

After we returned home, Ashley and I tried hard to incorporate the idea of working with people's divinity into our practice. It was quite a stretch. At first, I tried to do it by finding the positives in each client. That was superficial, although more upbeat than focusing on the problems all the time. But it was also a lot of work.

Then I tried to make divinity the theme of the session. I had the client feel into his or her divinity and make a list of words to describe it. More hard work. A painful struggle actually. I kept hearing Nathaniel's words, "One's divinity is right there." That only added to my frustration and sense of failure.

But over time as we continued to study with Nathaniel, the process became easier. I became more relaxed and natural with it. I began to notice people touched my heart more deeply and more fully. As my clients and I explored their motivations, I became enthralled to see how all their motivations traced back to their divinity. The connection was sometimes quite twisted and distorted, but it was always there. Eventually, I couldn't help *but* see their divinity.

Our personal lives blossomed into something quite divine as well. Ashley and I had a little girl named Suzanne who brought us unbounded delight. The love I felt for her from the day she was born was something that is, to this day, indescribable. Watching the bond between her and her mother filled me with a fullness and sense of contentment that was beyond the greatest joy I'd ever known. We lived happily in our home on Mulvern Street as Ashley and I juggled our time between our counseling practices and family.

One summer Sunday, we organized a picnic with a group of friends. In the morning, we prepared many of the typical picnic delights—potato salad, baked beans, apple pie, and assorted sandwich fixings. Everyone had agreed to bring additional treats and meet at our favorite spot along the Scioto River. We had a wonderful day hiking and skipping rocks by the side of the river. The hilariously rambunctious game of softball right before lunch was unforgettable. The rules weighed in as less important than everyone's desire to run around the bases, grab something else to drink, and congregate anywhere they wanted on the playing field. Two people running the bases together seemed to be more fun than one person doing it alone. Fortunately, Ashley's photographic genius created a plethora of Kodak moments.

Later in the afternoon, Ashley and I decided to take a walk down to the boat docks. I strapped Suzanne to my chest in her halter carrier. She was ten months old at the time and the joy of our life. Ashley took my arm, as we proceeded down the grassy hill. We took the path that ran along the river toward the boat docks. It was one of those classic, ideal summer days in Ohio.

Ashley pointed out a white puffy cloud. "Look Bruce, it looks like an angel."

Sure enough, there it was: wings, gown, flowing hair, and all. Suzanne was having a great time, looking around and kicking her little feet.

"She'll sleep well tonight," Ashley smiled with love radiating from her eyes.

"Look," I said, pointing in another direction. "That one looks like a giant bird flying through the air."

Ashley said nothing, but her soft sigh confirmed my sighting. We proceeded on quietly.

We walked around on the docks looking at the assortment of boats. The wood decking beneath our feet rolled smoothly from side to side, supported by barrels bobbing in the gentle waters below.

After a short time, we hopped back to shore and peacefully ambled along the path to our picnic site.

"Oh my God," Ashley whispered.

From her tone, I thought she had some sort of frightening realization.

"What is it?" I whispered back.

She could only say it again. "Oh my God."

I waited, quietly giving her whatever space she needed.

After what felt like an eternity, I whispered again, "What?"

"I don't know how to describe it," she mumbled. "This is so strange. It's…It's like none of this is real. It's so…beautiful."

"Ashley, are you all right? What's happening?"

"I have no idea. This is strange."

"Ashley, you're reminding me of Nathaniel when he had his first enlightenment experiences. Maybe you're witnessing. Do you think?"

"No, no way. We've both experienced witnessing before, and I can tell you this is completely different."

"Well, what about unity…?" I was grasping at straws for an explanation. "Ashley, do you think you might be having a unity experience?"

"No, Bruce, we've heard Nathaniel talk plenty of times about unity and this isn't it."

"Okay, okay. Well, don't worry. We'll figure it out."

Ashley stopped walking and watched her arm as she slowly raised and lowered it several times. "This is wild," she whispered, "It's like nothing is really happening and I can see out to the edges of the universe." Her arm reached out into empty space as she tried to steady herself.

Struggling not to show my fear, I took hold of her hand, offering what support I could. Would Ashley be all right? I put my arm around her, and helped her walk forward.

"Are you okay?" I asked.

"I'm…I'm not sure. I think so." Her voice trembled.

A flurry of thoughts rushed through my mind: If it's not witnessing or unity, what could it be? Psychotic break? Brain tumor? Should we go to the hospital? What about Suzanne?

"Really, I think I'll be fine. Things just got a little weird for a second there, that's all," Ashley said.

I bent forward a little, so I could look straight into her eyes. "What do you want me to do?"

"No, really, I'm okay. Just give me a second."

She did appear to be getting better. As we started walking along, I tried to follow her lead and not show any alarm. I could tell she was still overwhelmed by what she was experiencing. Our life together was so great right now. I hoped something wasn't happening that was going to ruin it. I felt guilty for having such a pathetically selfish thought, but couldn't help it. Keeping my fears to myself, I watched her carefully. She seemed to be experiencing an odd combination of delight, awe, and fear.

By the time we returned to our friends, Ashley reported she was completely fine. I tried to tell myself she had a little fainting spell, perhaps from overexposure to the sun. She always overdid it with the sun. But somehow I could tell the ordeal was still on her mind. She needed to know what had happened.

Over the next couple of weeks, Ashley kept returning to the experience she'd had that Sunday at the river. We talked to a colleague of ours who had more experience with dissociative states than either of us. Ashley went early for her annual physical. I flipped through my old psychology textbooks trying to come up with some ideas of what might have happened. I kept coming back to the notion she was having a unity experience. But when I first brought it up, she excluded it as a possibility.

Three weeks to the day after Ashley had that experience, we were sitting under the maple tree in the backyard while Suzanne was taking her nap. Over the years, we came to cherish the tranquil sanctuary created by the shade of that old tree. We were both catching up on the week's reading, going through an assortment of magazines, mail, and the like. I was thinking about Nathaniel and what he might say about what had happened to Ashley.

"Ashley," I started. "I know I already mentioned this once, but I really wonder if you were glimpsing a level of enlightenment. Do you think that's possible?"

"Well, to tell you the truth, I thought about that later, but I really don't think that was it. I even looked over some of my old notes from Nathaniel's talks and things didn't really line up."

"Like what?" I asked.

"Well," she said, "Nathaniel said it's a blissful state, but I was afraid."

"Yeah, but Ashley, think about it. If your mind didn't kick in with doubts, would you have found the experience to be blissful?" I felt certain I was onto something.

Ashley hesitated. "Well, I guess so. I know everything isn't all of a sudden perfect when you first experience higher states of consciousness. But…it's still hard to let that idea go. If it *was* a little glimpse of enlightenment, you'd think it would have been fun or enjoyable or at least not so upsetting."

"Oh, come on, Ashley," I tried to convince her. "Nathaniel's told us plenty of times about 'the Hollywood version' of enlightenment. And do you remember when he said no words can prepare you for the experience? Why don't we get him on the phone and see what he thinks?"

She agreed.

I went into the house to get the phone and Nathaniel's number. Coming back outside, I straddled the picnic bench and dialed his number.

"Hello." It was Nathaniel!

"Hi, Nathaniel, this is Bruce."

"Bru-u-uce."

It was always great to hear that traditional greeting.

After the obligatory small talk, I came to the point. "Nathaniel, Ashley had a strange experience the other day, and we were wondering if you might have some ideas about it."

"Well, I'll do my best."

I mouthed the words to Ashley, "Do you want to talk?"

She nodded and I said, "Hang on, here she is."

Ashley took the phone. "Hi, Nathaniel, how are you? Oh that's great....Well, hang on Nathaniel, I'm going to have Bruce get on the other phone."

I obediently jumped up and ran into the house to pick up the extension. Ashley proceeded to tell Nathaniel all the details of her experience.

He listened to her lengthy description. "That's it. You were experiencing a higher level of consciousness." His confidence was comforting.

Ashley needed to hear it again. "But it was so different from what I thought it would be, even after hearing you talk about it so many times."

"Right. That's the way it is. That's why the knowledge is so delicate and easily lost. No amount of description will do. You have to experience it to understand. I refer to this frequently as the difference between 'knowing about' and 'becoming.'"

The phone was quiet. I hoped he'd say more.

"You'll have this experience from time to time," he continued. "As you do, you'll become more and more comfortable with it. It will, in time, become second nature. But then one day, it will stabilize. And when it does, it will again be a whole new experience. There's a big difference between the glimpse of a higher state of consciousness and living it as a permanent state." Nathaniel paused.

"But Ashley," I interjected, "tell Nathaniel what you said about seeing out to the edges of the universe."

"Well, yeah," Ashley said as she struggled for words. "I don't really know how to say it but, for a time, I sort of felt like I could see the shape of the universe."

"What shape was it, Ashley?" Nathaniel sounded interested.

"That's the thing, Nathaniel. I remember you saying the universe was shaped like a flower, but to me it was more like an oblong ball."

Nathaniel laughed with a delight that seemed to come from the depth of his soul. "Ashley, that's great. The manifest universe is flower shaped but it is contained in an egg-shaped ball that includes what physicists call dark matter. You were seeing the whole thing. You were experiencing a level of enlightenment beyond simple unity. You were experiencing many wholeness values simultaneously, including the wholeness of the entire universe."

"But Nathaniel, how could that be? I don't even witness very often."

"You see, Ashley, everything oscillates, vibrates. Electrons have a pulse, the sun rises and sets, and our experiences do also. It's like a pendulum swinging. You experienced a very high level of consciousness for a brief period of time and then the pendulum swung back to a state more natural for you right now.

"This is a tangential thought, but I think it merits repeating: after the early stages of enlightenment, witnessing eventually goes away. It's also possible to move through that stage very quickly. It's ironic there are large groups of people who try to force themselves to witness. Hey Bruce, remember Carol? And how I tried to get her to witness?"

"Yeah, I remember," I chuckled.

"It doesn't work," Nathaniel laughed.

"No, it certainly doesn't," I agreed. "But Nathaniel, I think I'm starting to feel a little jealous here. When do you think I'll start having experiences like Ashley's?"

"Some people have glimpses of higher states for a long time and others for a short time before they stabilize enlightenment. The most important thing is to do your meditation regularly. There are many forms of meditation. They all have their own values. The most powerful type for cultivation of enlightenment is the Surya Meditation—with it you regularly transcend relativity and rest into the deepest part of your being. Do your meditation regularly and enlightenment will come for both of you."

"In this lifetime?" I asked.

"That's up to you, but it's certainly within your grasp. After all, it's your birthright. It's everyone's birthright. The path of attaining enlightenment is as subtle as traversing the razor's edge. But the knowledge you have affords you every opportunity for success."

Ashley was comforted by what Nathaniel said. It would've been tough to go through that without talking to someone who knew about it. In fact, Nathaniel later told us about a woman who was subjected to shock therapy in an attempt to "cure" her early enlightenment experiences. What a bizarre world.

Chapter 47

Life's Images

As the years passed, we continued to study with Nathaniel. Even while our personal lives became extremely busy, we managed to attend one of Nathaniel's courses at least once a year. Ashley and I had two more children, Peter and John. Our daily life was very happy and revolved largely around raising our three kids. How could I convey what all my years with Ashley had meant to me? Perhaps through the images I recalled, pictures held in my heart....

Ashley's hair bands on the bathroom doorknob. Her face, as she lay asleep in bed with the kids cuddled up beside her. The wrinkled-up little face of Suzanne the moment she was born. And that night of her birth, when Ashley sent me home from the hospital to get some sleep. I wanted to stay with her that night, sit in the chair beside her bed. But she insisted I go. On the way home, I stopped for dinner. How extraordinary that the image in my mind is like a photograph taken from across the room. A scene in a restaurant, alone at a small table, in silent celebration of love for my wife and newborn child. A cherished image, a timeless moment, impressed upon my mind and held within my heart.

Images. So many images. The time when John played hooky from school. The timid look on his face and the meek way he held his body when I picked him up at the principal's office. How it was all I could do to keep from smiling. The day Peter won the spelling bee. The night Suzanne went out on her first date. The image of our driveway, dimly lit by the outside lantern as I secretly stared out, awaiting her return. The Christmas tree in the front window. Graduations.

Images held in my heart are what I really remembered, more than the story or accounting of events. Those images appeared in my mind like blossoms in the intangibility of memory. That was, it seemed, the most honest, pure way to convey my life with Ashley. Mental photographs seated in my heart's memory.

And so many images of our times with Nathaniel. Images of moments in the classroom:

Nathaniel pacing in front of the chalkboard—intellectually focused, yet expanded. His eyes bright. Brain busy. Gestures alive and dynamic.

My water bottle beside me on the floor in the lecture hall. I'm thirsty, but can't move. The moment, too deeply captivating—rich, unbounded, timeless…utterly pristine.

Nathaniel staring out the window—thinking, reflecting, somewhere else, somewhere unimaginable. Silence suspended.

So much held in each moment. So many images of so many moments. Memories—impressions upon my mind.

The Golden Frog

Chapter 48
Tara

Time—doesn't it flash by in a moment? One night, Ashley and I tucked Suzanne into her little bed. Now, suddenly, we were wondering what college she would attend.

It had been fifteen years since that first class in Tiburon. Nathaniel continued to be an important part of our lives. He wrote less frequently, opting to phone instead.

It was late in August and Tara had come to visit us. On a quiet Sunday morning, she and Ashley took the boys for a walk along the Scioto River. Suzanne was away on a camping trip with a girlfriend and her family. I enjoyed having the house to myself. As I sat at the kitchen table, looking through the morning paper, I could hear a robin sing. After finishing the paper, I grabbed a sweater, refilled my cup with chai, and stepped outside. The sky was blue. The air was sweet. The sun was quickly heating up what was the summer's coolest night so far. In a few more hours, it would be hot.

Several months had gone by since I got the news my father had passed away. Dad had been ill for some time. I had always hoped that someday he would open up to me—share his inner thoughts and feelings, and strive to understand me more fully. Now with his death, it was painfully clear—that would never happen. I was left wondering about the fleeting nature of life. Everything comes and goes. At some point, the world will continue as normal, but without you. My father's death and my mother's old and frail appearance at the funeral confronted me with the notion of my own mortality. It was as if I suddenly became older.

I walked around to the backyard and sat at the picnic table by the old maple tree. I don't know how long I sat there, but I do remember how my body felt—peaceful, settled. Satisfied somehow, but independent of any circumstance. I felt wise. Actually, my body felt wise. In that moment, I understood that wisdom is a state of rest in the physiology, not a philosophy of life. I understood things because I could rest with them, within my own body.

My thoughts were interrupted by the car pulling up in the driveway. I heard the door slam as Peter and John called out, "Hi Dad!" and ran into the house.

Ashley poked her head around the corner, "Tara and I will come out and join you in a minute, okay?"

I smiled, waved, and nodded yes.

Sunlight filled the backyard now. I moved under the shade of the maple tree as Tara and Ashley joined me.

Tara sat in the shade. "I've gotten enough sun for one day already," she smiled.

Ashley sat in the sun, declaring, "Oh, not me. I love it so much!"

"How was your walk?" I asked.

"It was nice. The boys entertained themselves by skipping rocks on the water, so Tara and I had a chance to catch up. What did you do while we were gone?"

"I had a nice time. The house was quiet and it gave me a chance to do some reading. I was just now thinking about one of my clients. She was asking me what meditation was like and I had a hard time explaining it. How would you describe it, Tara?"

"You know," Tara responded, "when people ask me what meditation is like, I don't even know where to begin. Sometimes I feel so enraptured with pure ecstasy. I feel so full, so expanded, yet so solid. I told that to someone once and they said that's how they felt when they smoked pot. Talk about missing the point!"

Ashley wrinkled her brow and shrugged her shoulders. "How do you convey that experience?"

For awhile, we all searched for words.

Then I made my attempt to describe meditation. "Sometimes in meditation, I feel rock solid, like I am a perfectly coherent package." I struggled with how to say it. "Sometimes it feels like I am over-taken by a fullness that's the source of the entire universe, like I have merged with God." I leaned back and looked at the blue sky through the branches of the maple tree. "Then there are all the times I just sit there with thoughts, thoughts, and more thoughts."

We all chuckled.

"I can totally relate to that." Ashley added.

"Yeah, I can go there," Tara confessed. "But as Nathaniel says, the meditation is still working."

"Have you ever noticed," Ashley changed the subject, "how Nathaniel can say something off-the-cuff in a completely casual way, and then later it's absolutely perfect? I remember the morning I had my first experience of unity. I was sitting at the kitchen table and the sunlight was hitting a vase on the windowsill. For awhile, I could see that I *was* the vase. Then I recalled a talk Nathaniel once gave about the experience of unity. He briefly mentioned that when it first hap-pens, it's completely overwhelming. That little comment was so important to me. I'd felt overwhelmed before, but never like that. In that instant, his words meant everything—it crystallized the moment."

"Sort of like a mini-mahavakya?" I asked.

Ashley looked at me puzzled. "What's that?"

"Honestly, I'm not exactly sure. I read about it once. Something like when a teacher says something and it hits you just right and gives you an experience of a higher level of consciousness."

"That's it! It was exactly like that!" Ashley exclaimed.

I got excited. "You know, this reminds me of when Nathaniel used to share his experiences with me. Something happened when he did that. I changed. It was like, for awhile, I merged with him. My consciousness shifted. Then after some time, he would do it again, over and over through the years. Gradually, I came to understand him."

I paused in reflection until Tara interjected. "You know, I've heard that's how gurus in India teach. The same divinity that dwells deep within everyone radiates from the guru. So, by attuning to him, students attune to their own divinity through him. That's why they say it is so good to live around enlightened people."

Energized and inspired, I popped up and began to pace around the yard, leaving Tara and Ashley to talk. I needed to think about what Tara had said. It sorted things out for me. Tara's words somehow crystallized my changes over the years. It was like Tara gave *me* a mini-mahavakya!

I walked around the house thinking and then returned to share another thought with Ashley and Tara who were now standing by the back door. "For years," I said, "I kept getting infuriated with Nathaniel, but never really understood why until now. I think he was blasting all the impurities out of me! They just came out as anger. What do you think?"

Tara smiled, "Well, when you're around the sun..."

Ashley looked at me, raised her eyebrows, tilted her head, and playfully sang the words, "...you can't help but to get a tan."

"Yeah," I added, "I guess I got burnt quite a few times."

They both giggled and we all walked back into the house.

That evening after dinner, the kids settled in to watch TV, and the three of us went for a walk down Mulvern Street. We stopped at the bridge by the old buckeye tree, and sat on the stone wall. The grass and trees were lush, and the creek was filled with rushing water. We reflected over the early years of our friendship. Ashley asked Tara about her relationship with Nathaniel back then, a subject of considerable speculation over the years.

"Nathaniel and I loved each other very much. We still do, of course, but back then, I thought maybe...Well, I thought maybe we would end up together. But Nathaniel seemed to know the direction his life was going and it didn't include marriage and kids. He even said it wouldn't be fair for him to get married. He wouldn't be around enough. It was a strange feeling when he told me that."

"Yeah," I said, "disappointing."

"Well, yes. But that isn't what I mean. There was something strange about it."

"Like what?" My curiosity was aroused.

"I don't know, really. Maybe he just knew he was going to be traveling a lot with his work."

"It sounds to me like a typical male not willing to commit," Ashley moaned.

Tara pushed a little twig off the stone wall and into the rushing water below. Watching it float down the creek and away, she sighed. "If only life were that simple."

Chapter 49

Time and Timelessness

Through the years, Nathaniel remained dear friends with Tara, but they never married. His life was his work with people. She eventually married a very nice man, named Charles, and they both actively attended Nathaniel's classes. Nathaniel loved them both dearly. Tara and Charles started a family shortly after they were married and had twins, two beautiful girls.

Children are perhaps the best barometer of the passage of time. Years are just numbers on a page, but the growth of a child is a vivid reminder of the true chronology. Suzanne is grown up now. How could that be? It seems like she is still my little baby girl. Yet she has a boyfriend and is planning to marry. Our sons are both in their twenties. The kids have moved out of the house and are on their own. Thirty years had passed since that first class Ashley and I took with Nathaniel in Tiburon. It all happened so fast.

It was a cold wintry Saturday afternoon in January. I put on my boots, coat, and hat, and leaned into the cold wind as I ventured outside. It was so cold that I soon decided to turn back. But first, I checked the mail. There was a thick stack of letters. I tucked them under my arm and with the wind now at my back, rushed back inside. In the stack of mail was a letter from Nathaniel. The sight of it warmed my heart. Nathaniel's letters from India had arrived in that same mailbox so many years ago. I sat in the armchair by the living room fireplace, and began to read:

•••◈•••

Dear Bruce and Ashley,

I've been teaching for over thirty years now. It's been quite a journey. As you know, I've been spending more and more time in the mountains of western North Carolina. I find it to be peaceful here. As I get older, I feel a longing to go inward. I plan to spend more time in meditation and writing. I want to reflect on how I can reach more people. I need to let them know that all questions have a common answer. If only they could rest into the depth of their being, they would find the one answer to all questions.

I want to do for my students what my teachers did for me. That is, I want to create an environment where people can evolve as quickly as possible. So I've found a lovely piece of property not far from Asheville and am going to start a spiritual community there. There are plenty of spiritual communities in the world, but generally they fall prey to dogma or even fanaticism. I want to create a place where people can grow spiritually that is free of such influences. There are a lot of people around now who want to help me create this.

We have a retreat coming up in North Carolina this summer. I would love to see you both there.

Fondly,

Nathaniel

•••◈•••

That evening after Ashley had gone to bed, I put one last log in the fireplace. Sitting in my armchair, I looked out through the picture window. It was a classic Ohio blizzard. Outside, the spotlights lit up the falling snow. Wrapped in a quilt, I sipped some tea and pondered.

I thought about Nathaniel's letter and his reference to getting older. I wondered what life would be like without the aging process and the eternal threat of death. Wouldn't that be odd? Somehow, life's transient nature made it exquisite. The sublime flow from generation to generation. The sun rose and set as did the existence of our physical bodies. Without that process, things would lose dimension. The drama would become sterile. The poetry of life would no longer sing so sweetly.

I had become increasingly reflective as the years passed. There was a time when intellectual understanding seemed so important to me. Now, savoring the subtle nature of things was more important. The elusiveness of life gave it meaning. When I was young, I would look at a mountain and wonder what was on the other side. Now, I looked out my window and relished the unsolvable mystery of what lay right before me. I understood that to know something was to embrace its unfathomable nature.

And so was my vision of life—memory's images were framed in the unfathomable context of life's flow. The future could be felt, but never known. I had a sense of my future—my purpose. But it was not something I could put into words. It was only something I could feel abstractly. And in that moment, looking out on the snowy scene of Mulvern Street, I liked the way it felt…very much.

Chapter 50
Retreat

As the years rolled on, the groups that assembled to see Nathaniel had gotten larger and larger. But the numbers mushroomed at that summer retreat held in the Blue Ridge Mountains. It was odd to see so many strangers bustling about in the assembly hall. We stood in one of several lines to check in and were happy when we saw a familiar face, particularly fellow "old-timers" from our first class. In fact, it seemed like they all made it to this retreat, stopping to chat when they spotted us in line.

Cynthia, wearing her characteristic flowery dress and plastic glasses, stopped to give us both a big hug. She received a big boost when her husband, several years ago, had begun to attend Nathaniel's classes. She had become a dear friend. As Ashley began to tell her about our daughter's wedding plans, I recalled how, years ago, Cynthia lacked her current self-assurance.

She turned around to look for her husband. "James is around here somewhere. When I find him, I'll bring him over to see you."

I spotted Steven and Henry in deep conversation. They were both gray now and Henry was heavyset. Who would have thought those two would become friends? There they were—Henry, still dedicated to his religion and Steven, a self-proclaimed recovering Catholic—the best of friends.

I had a great respect for Henry. Some religious people had

walked out of Nathaniel's introductory talks the moment he started speaking about religion. Henry wasn't like that. He was always willing to reflect and refine his beliefs.

Steven and Henry came up to greet us. Steven was still intense. When I noticed the cell phone in his hand, I grinned. We all hugged before I had a chance to comment.

A little later, Beth came by. As she told Ashley about her difficulty getting to the retreat, I continued to reflect on how we'd all changed over the years. The dark shadow that enshrouded Beth at that first class had disappeared. Her thick black hair, now streaked with gray, glistened. Her face was soft with love and compassion. The scowl had transformed into what was now an insightful snicker.

Nathaniel always said spiritual evolution was not about personality modification. It was about the depth of one's own divinity welling up and radiating through the personality, whatever one's personality might be. Beth was a superb example. She really hadn't changed at all, yet she'd become completely different. How offensive she had seemed to me in that first class. Now she was endearing to everyone.

Through the crowd we could see Joseph. He was behind the row of check-in tables, rustling through some boxes. Evidently he was trying to find some missing papers or equipment. Through all of the years, Joseph had continued to help Nathaniel. Though he had clearly aged, he still enjoyed vibrant health and robust vitality. I'd grown fond of Joseph, appreciating his big heart and how his rough demeanor was a charming aspect of his personality.

"Joseph!" I called.

He looked up and peered through the crowd. When he looked our way, we waved. Suddenly his eyes lit up and he walked around the tables and through the people to greet us.

It was good to see him again. "Joseph, what's going on? This group is huge. There are so many people here we don't know."

"Yeah," he replied. His belly shook as he laughed. "I'm loving it. This is fun! That's one thing I'll say about Nathaniel—he always keeps things hopping! You know Tara is coming. I can't wait to see her again!"

We were delighted with the news and looked forward to spending some time with her. We chatted a bit longer with Joseph until we reached the front of the line, where we recognized the polite and friendly young lady sitting across the table. Rebekah had been assisting at retreats and classes for the past few years.

"Hi, Bruce. Hi, Ashley. It's great to see you. How are you doing?"

"We're fine," Ashley said." It's great to see you, too."

Rebekah checked our names on her list and then paused. "Did you know Rose Barker included you in her book?"

Now I put it together. I'd known Rose was writing a book about her class experiences with Nathaniel and the effect he'd had on her life. But I didn't realize it was already out. We had no idea we'd be in it. I imagined that might be why the group was so large. Rose had put Nathaniel on the map.

I wasn't surprised. Rose had become a mentor to many people as they went through Nathaniel's program. She was still the bubbly, vivacious Scarlet O'Hara she had always been, but her wisdom was readily accessible.

"Oh, there's a note for you here in your folder." Rebekah handed me a sealed envelope. "Well, here are your badges and keys to your room. I hope you enjoy the retreat."

We thanked her, collected our bags, and found our room. I sat down on the edge of the bed and began to open the envelope. Inside, I found a handwritten note. "It's from Nathaniel," I announced. "He's asking to meet with us after the retreat."

Those retreats were always very powerful. The focus was on deep rest and meditation. "If your physiology is just allowed to rest," Nathaniel often said, "all of your distortions will simply let go. But it's important to realize 'letting go' is not an attitude or mood. It's a physiological state. So, holding onto the idea of letting go doesn't work."

The retreat was a time of restful rejuvenation. We enjoyed walks, mealtimes with our friends, and Nathaniel's wonderful talks.

Though we had listened to him speak for many years now, his knowledge still seemed to be without limits. He always had new insights to share.

Nathaniel's last lecture at the retreat was particularly powerful, even for him. His words were very passionate, yet his movements were slow and graceful. "Spiritual growth is a physiological process. It's an evolutionary process, very much in a psychological, Darwinian, and anthropological sense."

Nathaniel leaned forward in his chair. "Our species has arrived at the threshold of its next great evolutionary step. It's now within our potential to embody all wisdom and knowledge. This is the time of a great phase transition. This transition can be compared to the tuning of a fine instrument; a subtle adjustment here and there, and suddenly sweet, sweet music. Prior to those adjustments, there's great discord: senseless wars and suffering on global as well as individual levels. That shift is not a shift in philosophy, attitude, or understanding. It's a shift in physiology that *transforms* philosophy, attitude, and understanding. That shift subtly, but profoundly, transforms *all* aspects of human life."

He stopped and took a sip of water. I noticed that the lighting in the room made him look almost transparent. "That is what, all of these years, we've been working to bring about. I don't offer new thoughts; I offer a new way of thinking. I don't tell people how to think; I assist them in finding within themselves the place of inner wisdom and intelligence from which they naturally think and act wisely."

Nathaniel was deliberate and reflective in his speech. It seemed he was reviewing his life—his purpose, his mission. He was passionate, yet somehow detached.

"Throughout the ages, we mistakenly believed that proper thoughts, philosophies, rules, laws, or attitudes would lead us to a wise world. The truth is we need to evolve our species to a level of wisdom that lies beyond the grasp of thoughts, philosophies, rules, laws, and attitudes. Attaining that level of life is our purpose here."

Nathaniel's heartfelt longing touched everyone in the room. "If only people could understand it's their conditioned thoughts and emotions that enslave them. If only they would practice the subtle and elusive art of allowing their physiologies to rest into that source of wisdom within them. Then, and only then, will we have peace and fulfillment on the earth."

He paused again. The hall was still. Everyone was deeply moved by Nathaniel's words. It felt like he had reached each person's soul.

"Throughout the ages," he continued, "great teachers have given out this knowledge. But over time, human mentality changes. The knowledge is eternal, but must be expressed in new ways to match the mentality of each new era. What is unique about our era, this scientific age, is the world consciousness has intellectually developed to the point where many people can begin to comprehend the message. The intellect, when used properly, can be a powerful catalyst for spiritual growth."

His next words seemed to be more of a proclamation than a statement. "We are exceedingly fortunate in that we happen to find ourselves at that critical point in human history, at just the right time, at just the right place, and with just the right knowledge. With this profound understanding of life, we have the ability to bring about a great phase transition in human consciousness. An opportunity like this only comes once every few million years."

Nathaniel's words were a synopsis of his entire life. He was pouring out his heart, but somehow I felt he was unable to say it all. I'd never seen him like this before. In that moment, it was so apparent. The wisdom of life.... His dedication to it.... That's what Nathaniel was about.

Chapter 51

Chaitanya Avarta

Throughout the retreat, Ashley and I wondered why Nathaniel wanted to speak with us afterwards. Did he have something in particular he wanted to tell us? Or, did he simply want to visit?

The retreat ended with lunch on the last day. Joseph joined us at one of the large round tables in the dining hall. There was still enthusiasm in his step. His jovial zest for life and dedication to humanity hadn't faded a bit. Everyone at the table shared in his laughter and joy. We were all inspired by our experiences at the retreat, but were now excited to return to our daily routines at home.

Towards the end of our meal, Joseph said, "Hey, Bruce, Nathaniel asked me to take you to where he's staying. I thought you could follow me over, and then I've got some errands to run."

"Sounds good. Do you know what Nathaniel wants to talk to us about?"

"Oh, who knows. Over these past few years, it's been hard to keep track of everything Nathaniel's up to. He has a million different projects going. If you aren't involved in one of those projects, you don't see him much. He's entirely focused on his work."

"Maybe he has a project he wants to talk with us about," Ashley said.

"Yeah, maybe so." Joseph nodded and reached for his tea.

We finished our meal, said our good-byes, and followed Joseph to the house where Nathaniel was staying. Large trees lined the street and thick vegetation crowded the well-cared-for lawns. The shade from trees protected the house from the hot summer sun. It was a nice old house in a beautiful neighborhood, reminding me of streets off campus around Ohio State.

Ashley and I parked on the street and began to walk up the steps to the house. We were all still feeling quite emotional from Nathaniel's final talk. As Joseph drove off, we both stopped and watched as his car moved away. He didn't look back, but extended his hand out the window and waved good-bye. He couldn't have known for sure we were watching. But we understood that to him, it really didn't matter. It was his way of feeling his love for us—Joseph always had such a very big heart. Ashley wiped a tear from her eye. We turned and quietly proceeded up the steps to the front porch.

I peered in through the screened door. "Nathaniel, are you there?"

Only a soft breeze moved through the screen.

"Nathaniel? Anybody home?" I called again.

"Bru-u-uce." The old familiar greeting came from the back of the house. "Come on in."

Ashley and I entered, and walked through the kitchen to a large back porch. The exterior three walls were lined with open screened windows, the source of the gentle breeze that filled the home. The backyard was gorgeous, manicured to perfection, and filled with flowers, trees, and bushes. Robins played in the old stone birdbath that served as the yard's centerpiece.

Nathaniel was seated on a wicker couch against the far wall. "Ashley, Bruce, how are you? Did you enjoy the retreat?"

"Oh, it was great." I smiled as we approached and each sat on one of the wicker chairs next to Nathaniel. "Everyone was so moved by your last talk. It was so powerful and inspiring."

"How have you been, Nathaniel?" Ashley's love radiated through her words.

"I'm good," he responded.

Nathaniel's face was so soft, it almost appeared edgeless.

Nathaniel reached for the pitcher of water. "Would you like something to drink?"

We nodded. Nathaniel reached for a glass.

"Let me do that for you, Nathaniel." Ashley took the pitcher from his delicate hand and poured the water.

Nathaniel's presence was odd. He was delicate and strong at the same time. His skin glowed like a baby's. There was life in his eyes and power in his presence. Yet, it almost seemed like he wasn't really there. His body seemed somehow to be light, almost ethereal; his skin, translucent. It made me think of that day so long ago when I rescued him from the creek. I remembered how he felt—weightless. Where had the years gone?

I looked over at Ashley. How beautiful she looked. Three friends, together through the years, and now, sitting on a porch one lovely summer day. We sat together in a communion that transcended time and space—I felt so very lucky. I wanted to savor that moment forever, that feeling with our friend and teacher.

"Nathaniel, can we help you with anything?" I asked.

"Your presence here is a *great* help to me. Thanks for coming. How are the kids doing?"

"Oh," Ashley smiled. "They're all doing great. As you know, Suzanne's getting married soon. Peter recently opened his own accounting office and John is working on his dissertation on autism."

Nathaniel smiled at the news. "That's wonderful. And how's the old neighborhood?"

I understood from his tone that Nathaniel was feeling sentimental and followed his lead. "It's great! And living in that house with Ashley and the kids is fantastic. That maple tree in the backyard is huge now. And a very nice young couple bought your old house on Cambridge Boulevard. They have three children. We see them outside, playing with the other neighborhood kids. It's so beautiful to watch them all, scurrying about, just like we did so many years ago."

Nathaniel smiled.

A voice called from the front door. "Hello. Anybody home?" It was Tara.

Ashley sprang up from her seat to let Tara in. Tara's husband, Charles, was busy with work, so he had been unable to make the retreat. The four of us sat and chatted a bit. Then Tara announced she had some errands to run, and asked Ashley if she would like to join her.

Ashley was delighted to spend some more time with her friend, but first asked, "Nathaniel, was there something you wanted to speak with us about?"

Nathaniel said, "No, no. I just wanted to spend a little time with you. Why don't the two of you go ahead?"

"Don't worry about Ashley, Bruce, we'll meet you back at the center when we finish," Tara said as they left.

I sensed that Nathaniel was pleased to have this opportunity to talk with me. So, as we settled back in our seats, I waited for him to speak first.

"Bruce, we have really accomplished a great deal. I've put out the knowledge I wanted to convey. I think I've given an understanding of spirituality that can be heard by the people of this age. As I said yesterday, the knowledge is eternal, but people change, times change, civilizations change. That's why the expression of the knowledge must change from generation to generation. Otherwise, what remains is a hollow shell of what it was for another people, at another time. I think we have done well. The knowledge is there, lively, for those who are willing to hear it."

I could tell Nathaniel was setting something up. There was something he wanted to tell me, but in his own unique way. It reminded me of when he introduced me to his teachings in the den of his parents' home, so many years ago.

"I remember when I first felt, deep within me, my commitment to the teachings. It started to consume me when I was living in India at Surya's ashram. I had to go back to the United States and teach. I felt so full of knowledge. I could do nothing else but teach.

"You know, there is a stage of enlightenment call Chaitanya Avarta. It's a brief period in a person's life. Imagine you are with a group of people looking for a passageway. Everyone is searching and searching. Finally, you find it. You begin to run to the passageway in your excitement. Well, it is, of course, only natural to turn around as you run and call over your shoulder to your friends, 'Come on, it's this way! I found it!' You may come back to show them the passageway for a time, but, at some point, it's time for you to go through yourself. That stage, Chaitanya Avarta—when you feel compelled to show others the passageway—is, in the greater scheme of things, a brief moment in time. It's a time when you are compelled to do everything you can to free others of their identities. What else could be as important? You have found the passageway. You must let everyone know. Whatever obstacle, whatever judgment, whatever resistance you experience is a small price to pay. Your message is simple: 'Hey, come on! This way. There's no reason to suffer, struggle, or fight. I've found the passageway to enlightenment. It's right here.'"

I waited as Nathaniel paused. I sensed he was talking about himself, but wondered where he was going.

Nathaniel's tone became more reflective, almost philosophical, as he continued. "The winds blow in the direction they do. The leaves have little choice but to move in that direction. As the cosmic winds blow, they carry the consciousness of all of God's creatures with them. Some call that karma. Whole cultures, whole civilizations, and all the individuals within them are directed by those cosmic winds. People think they have free will, and they do, but they underestimate the power of those cosmic winds. What they consider to be their free will and their independent thought is, more often than not, simply the direction the cosmic winds have blown them. It determines their religion, their ethics, their science, and their law. A spiritual teacher assists them in learning to navigate those cosmic winds. This enables them to see beyond the limitations of their conditioning. They become free. They can then find the passageway and move through it.

"But now, in my life, I'm beginning to see something more important than showing others the passageway. I'm realizing it's actually possible to change the directions of the cosmic winds. Sometimes, the wind blows people to the mountain peaks and sometimes it blows them into the gutter. I see now that I can help the whole universe more by healing the direction those winds blow, than by helping the individuals, one at a time, fight the way the wind is blowing them. By helping individuals, I can help a handful. By helping the wind, I can help millions."

As Nathaniel spoke, I tried to grasp exactly what it was he was trying to tell me. At the same time, I knew him well enough to know he was not trying to convey facts. It was the feeling underneath the facts he cared about. I felt him working with my consciousness, expanding my awareness, so I could see life in a broader and broader light. I didn't know where he was going with this, but that really did not matter. He was waking me up to feeling, experiencing directly, the order and scheme of the universe. That's what was important.

"This is new for me," Nathaniel continued. "It's the passageway that lies beyond the one through which I previously passed. But just as I was compelled to show others that earlier passageway, I'm now compelled to move through the new one that lies before me."

This was a lot to take in. It sounded like he might stop teaching. Did this mean he was going to start working in another way? But how could that be? Maybe he was just giving me the big picture.

"This is the way it has been throughout eternity. It's the way of things. Teachers teach, and then they move on to what is next. I'm feeling the need to move on with my work. At the same time, I wonder in awe. How can I leave anyone behind? How can I not reach out my hand to all the others? But I'm understanding now, that is not the way of things. Everything evolves in nature. It's only natural that we all move on to greater and greater ways of being."

Nathaniel finished speaking and sat back, melting into the couch. He gazed off into the backyard. I looked out with him and saw the robins bathing in the cool waters, fluttering their wings as they danced in the birdbath. To me, in that moment, all of life was expressed in that simple scene of birds doing whatever it is they do. That was the way of all things. Wasn't it?

I could tell Nathaniel was tired. I was tired too. I could also tell he'd said what he wanted to say. It was time for me to leave.

Chapter 52
Golden

Ashley and I woke up the next morning, just in time to rush to the airport and catch our flight home. The next couple of weeks were filled with activity as we both worked hard getting back into the swing with our practices.

It was on a Tuesday evening. Ashley wasn't home yet when the telephone rang. It was Tara. She was crying.

"Tara," I said, "what's the matter?"

"Bruce, it's Nathaniel." Tara stammered and hesitated. "He...he's dead."

I froze. My body was numb. "What...? What...? How could that be?"

Silence.

"How did it happen?"

"He just went to sleep—at least that's what Joseph said. Supposedly he was fine, maybe a little more quiet than usual over the past week. Then one afternoon, he went to take a nap and never woke up." She began to cry softly again.

What could I say about the loss of such a presence in my life? My world, my direction, was based upon what Nathaniel taught. What would I do now? How could he be gone?

I walked into the living room, sat in the armchair, and stared out the front window. The house was quiet. I could hear the refrigerator running in the kitchen. The sound held time in suspension as I reflected about my dear teacher and friend.

I remembered the dream I had about him long ago. I was trying to find my way through the jungle and took a turn down a path that was strewn with dead and withering human bodies. Daylight flickered as Nathaniel moved away from me further down the path.

I understood it now so clearly. Nathaniel led people out of the jungle. That was his life. The dead bodies along the path were the deaths of the identities they left behind, strewn along the side of the path that led to the passageway—their enlightenment.

And then I remembered the golden frog. I had reflected for years over how that frog appeared golden. At times I nearly believed it was actually made of gold. I often wondered if the golden frog represented Nathaniel: the frog aspect was his humanity, his personality; the golden aspect was his deeper essence, the divine part of him that lives on throughout eternity.

But now I began to understand I was the golden frog. Nathaniel sought me out when I was but a frog, vaguely aware of my deeper self. And through his wisdom, introduced me to my essence, the part of me that was golden, the part of me that was divine and eternal.

He showed so many people that they were the golden frog—divine, yet so very, very human. I remembered when Nathaniel worked with people in the classroom as I stared out the window almost bored. Now, it was clear he was teaching us to perceive the gold that dwells at the depth of every human being. Through the years, the ability to see that had gradually awoken within me. The beauty of his artistry—how masterfully he introduced us all to our deeper selves. It seemed only now after his death, did I yearn to thank him for that most precious of all gifts. Now I saw so naturally, so obviously, that all creatures, in fact all things, in their essence are golden. It wasn't a philosophy I had learned. It was simply the ability to truly see whatever it was that lay right before me.

Looking out through the picture window, I could clearly see that everything was the golden frog. So real and so physical, yet so ethereal, so elusive, so radiant with divinity—that same divinity I experienced as the source of my own being. Everything I looked at was me. Just an everyday scene on Mulvern Street, yet one with all that is.

All of life's secrets were revealed, simple, innocent as a frog. To truly see that scene was to see its connection, its oneness with all that was. To truly perceive anything was to perceive everything within it. Yet so uncomplicated, so pure, so self-evident, so self-revealing. Like a little frog leaping through the bushes on a hot summer morning, simple, uncomplicated, even mundane on the surface, yet profound and sublime at its depth.

The golden frog, like the transcendent, was elusive. It couldn't be captured. The only place it lived was within. It couldn't be named. It couldn't be grasped by the hand, the mind, or even the heart. It could only be lived. It was eternally unfettered by thoughts, emotions, pleasure, or pain.

Ashley and I held each other and cried. Later that evening, we went for a walk down Mulvern Street to the corner of Cambridge and Club. As we passed by my favorite old buckeye tree, I snatched up a few in my hand, and peeled off their spiky coating. Fiddling with the buckeyes, I forced a smile, and whispered to Ashley, "Ammo."

We crossed the bridge and walked by Nathaniel's old home. As we stood under the streetlight at the corner, I choked back my tears. Memories. Sweet impressions on the soul that touched and transformed my life.

Ashley comforted me. I looked at Nathaniel's old home illuminated by the streetlight, glowing in gold, pregnant with knowledge of all life and existence—all past, present, and future—full, unbounded, and eternal.

Then like a whisper in the evening darkness, it came to me. I felt from deep within my soul that there was but one thing for me to do. It was time for me to teach. In that moment, my entire memory of all my years with Nathaniel shifted. It became so clear to me. I, like Nathaniel, had been very thoroughly trained. This was his intention all along—I was to teach and spread those teachings through the written word. Relying upon what Nathaniel had awakened within me and this new understanding—this shift in memory—I would do my best to give to others what he had given to me. This book is my first attempt to do so. I believe Nathaniel would be pleased.

—Columbus, Ohio, February 5, 2004.